TREE OF
REDEMPTION

BY JIM DAVIDSON

First publication 2022

ISBN 979-8-9870756-0-9

This is a work of fiction. Names, places, characters, and incidents are the product of the author's imagination and are fictitious. Any resemblance to actual persons, living or dead, events or establishments is solely coincidental.

For Mandy—

The most kindhearted person I've ever known, and the best muse a man could have.

Contents

Prologue 1

Chapter 1 3

Chapter 2 23

Chapter 3 40

Chapter 4 53

Chapter 5 66

Chapter 6 81

Chapter 7 95

Chapter 8 109

Chapter 9 128

Chapter 10 147

Chapter 11 160

Chapter 12 181

Chapter 13 193

Chapter 14 216

Chapter 15 229

Chapter 16 247

Epilogue 260

Prologue

This book is a work of fiction. However, some of the events within are true. I forget which ones.

Chapter 1

"God Damn, it's hot,"

Chris said as he exited the plane. Not the sweltering heat that he was used to in Virginia, but a searing heat that reminded him of the hot dogs he had seen as a child being cooked on rotisserie grills at the State Fair. And it was loud. Like someone had busted open a piñata of sound with all the commotion swirling around him as if they were different colors. A cacophony of noise that contrasted with the monotonous droning of the prop plane's engines.

His mint-green linen shirt was becoming even more drenched, that by the time he was at the bottom of the plane's stairs, most of it was soaked and displayed sort of a shade of turquoise.

Walking through the airport, he dodged a maelstrom of porters, tourists, trinket barkers, food hawkers, and various nefarious loiterers. He also felt that the baseball cap he wore, with "Pirates" boldly written in gold letters on a black background, was to many he passed a neon sign that said, "Stupid Tourist," a type of translation so many in the crowd were adept at picking out.

Outside, bilingual shouts of "Welcome to Laredo" were as insincere as the tourist guides trying to lasso a dozen overweight sightseers into an old bus.

Chris knew to bypass all the cabbies at the front of the pack and go to the ones near the back that were not on the take. At the end of the line was a dark-skinned Mexican who seemed more interested in finishing his cigarette than working that day.

"Hablas inglés?" Chris shouted.

"Un poco," the driver said.

"111 Flowering Cactus Drive," Chris said, hoping he would not have to translate.

"Sí!" The driver enthusiastically responded by dropping his cigarette as if he knew a big tip was coming his way. Chris tossed his bag into the back seat and climbed in.

Somehow, it was hotter in the car than outside. And it smelled. Too much spilled tequila and beer, prodigious amounts of sweat, and only God knew what else. Chris wondered why he chose this cabbie. Was it the fact he was driving an old Studebaker, similar to one he used to have, or was it the artistry of the hand-painted Mexican flags that adorned the now faded maroon paint?

4

Feeling the urge to practice his Spanish, Chris asked, "Por qué el Studebaker?"

"It was my father's," the driver responded in perfect English.

"You speak more than un poco English," Chris said.

"It's a trick we use on tourists. We get better tips if we act like dumb Mexicans."

"Don't I look like a tourist?"

"Yes, very much, but you know the Guerras, yes?"

Chris felt this was an oddly phrased question. It seemed more like a test, and how did he know?

Cautious with his response, Chris said, "Yes, I knew one of them well."

"Which one?"

Another testing question.

"Chico."

The driver stared at him in the rearview mirror for several seconds. His gaze made Chris feel like some young kid caught in a lie.

"There was no Chico."

The driver was terse in his speech, making Chris somehow feel even hotter.

"I'm sorry, his name was Armando. I knew him as Chico."

The driver continued his stare. However, it was less glaring, as if Chris had said a magic word to open a door.

"When did you know him?"

There was still skepticism in his voice.

"I knew him in Virginia for a long time until he moved back down to Laredo for his health a couple of years ago."

"Then you know what happened to him?"

There was a sense of relief in the driver's voice.

Chris stared out the window for just a moment before answering, "Yes, I'm aware."

"Then why are you here?" asked the driver.

Perhaps the driver had asked one too many questions, or it was just the heat. Chris exploded, "Hey, what the fuck, man? I'm here to visit his sisters and pay my respects. Why do you give two pesos why I'm here?"

Taking the opportunity of stopping at a red light, the driver slowly turned and, in a very calm voice, said, "Because my father knew them well. They are some of the 'Old Ones.' They are very much loved in this community.

"Their family goes back centuries, so there is much respect for them. They have been through a lot, and only Rosa and Isabella are left. Now, we watch out for them just as their family used to watch over us."

The light changed and the driver began to drive, giving Chris a few moments to digest what he had said. Chris sensed the need for qualification after such an impassioned speech from him.

It took a few seconds, then Chris said, "Armando was an extraordinary man. He was a friend and mentor to me."

The driver looked at Chris in the rearview mirror for a moment before saying, "Then I'm sure his sisters will be happy to see you."

Chris felt like he had just run some kind of welcoming committee gauntlet and was trying to understand what he had stepped into.

"Why do you call them the 'Old Ones'?" he asked.

The driver spoke in a different tone, more relaxed. "The Guerras come from a family that goes back before the Spanish landed. Some say to the Aztecs, but that may just be a myth," he explained to his passenger.

"They have lived in this area for centuries and are considered by the locals to be aristocracy. They were the lawgivers for many years around here. When there were disputes, they settled them, and no one argued over the outcome. They arranged marriages between families to keep the peace, helped the poor, and taught the uneducated. My grandfather knew Armando's grandfather, and my father knew his father. They both worked for them and considered it an honor."

As the old Studebaker turned onto Flowering Cactus Drive, it was as if they had driven through a time portal. Just blocks away from fast food restaurants, dirty bookstores, muffler shops, and strip malls was a place of serenity. There were only about a dozen houses on the street, which stretched a mile or so, each one built in the lavish Spanish architectural style that dated back hundreds of years. Chris noticed an absence of cars parked in front of the houses and thought that it gave the neighborhood a sense of elegance and old-world charm. He imagined it probably looked the same as it would have a hundred years ago.

As they drove past the houses, Chris wondered which one he was visiting today and how it would compare to the others. Reaching the end of the cul-de-sac, he got his answer. They turned into a beautifully paved lane of multicolored tile work. It went on for about a hundred yards before circling a giant fountain nearly fifteen feet high, its water tumbling and splashing loudly. Chris felt the cooling effects of the water just by looking at it. On the right was a wide staircase made of the same material, leading past various desert plants that looked like they had been planted before the Spanish arrived. Some were tall and majestic; some were dying. The stairs led past iron gates that showed the skill of old-world craftsmanship that was becoming a lost art.

Chris sat in the taxi and admired the setting. The cab driver had come to a stop and been silent for almost a minute, allowing Chris to take in all that he saw. Was the driver being polite, or was he showing reverence for the home, as if to pay homage?

Stepping out of the cab, Chris set his leather overnight bag on the beautiful tiles. He saw some of them were cracked and chipped. Walking around to the driver's door, he asked, "How much do I owe you?"

"Twelve dollars."

Chris handed him a twenty and said, "Keep it."

"Perhaps I'll change my dumb Mexican act to being obnoxious. It pays better." He smiled as he spoke, and Chris noticed how white his teeth were against his dark skin.

Chris returned his smile and said, "I appreciate all your information. Thank you. By the way, what is your name?"

The cab driver reached into the glove box and handed him a card, at the same time saying, "Juan."

"Thank you, Juan."

"Señor," the cabbie now spoke with a more friendly tone, "if you need a ride, you can call me anytime. Any friend of the Guerras is a friend of mine."

"Thanks, I appreciate it. That's very kind."

"It's not out of kindness, Señor. It's out of respect for my father. Adios."

Chris picked up his bag and started up the stairs. When he reached the top, he saw a large hanging bell with an old rope attached to the clapper. He grabbed the rope and rang the bell several times. He was amazed at the sound it made, like a cross between a gong and a bell tower's chimes; low yet penetrating, it spoke of the quality of the metal.

He waited for a minute but heard or saw no one. Wasn't he expected? He hesitated to try the beautifully ornate gates but was spurred on by the lack of response. Perhaps this was not the actual front entrance. He pushed open the giant iron gate, and it protested with squealing and moaning from the weight of the iron. He stepped into the courtyard and paused for a moment. It was much more substantial than it appeared from the circular driveway. Chris guessed about a hundred feet square. The walls were two stories tall on all sides, with a walkway around the entire second level. The courtyard was barren of plants, save for the occasional potted ones scattered about for decoration. Another fountain stood in its center, not as large as the one in the driveway but more ornate. Its bottom section was decorated with handmade tiles that were wide enough to form a bench-style seat.

The courtyard's floor was made of very light-colored tile, almost pink in hue. The walls were a traditional stucco painted a brilliant white. It hurt Chris's eyes to look at it for long; however, he did notice more than a few cracks. Surrounding all the windows were more handmade tiles, and the roof seemed to be made of thicker-than-normal terra cotta. It was magnificent.

Chris wondered how such a space was used. Dances? Weddings? Family reunions?

"Señor Hamilton!" A rich, warm voice echoed off the walls as though coming over a loudspeaker.

Chris turned to see a man walking toward him, his hand extended and smile as white as the stucco walls.

"Welcome, welcome," he said while shaking Chris's hand. "I apologize for my delay in meeting you, I was upstairs when I saw you arrive. I am Eduardo."

His tone and affable demeanor made Chris feel like he was a visiting foreign dignitary. Chris assumed this skill had been honed by years of practice.

"The señoras are having tea at this moment in the garden and would like you to join them."

Chris was struck by the ebullience of Eduardo's nature and how handsome he was. He was sure he was the kind of man who had used his personality and good looks throughout his life and was well aware of his charm.

Eduardo gestured toward the large double front doors he had just exited through, and Chris dutifully followed. Walking into the first floor of the house, Chris felt the air was much cooler, although there were no signs of air conditioning. The large and heavy pieces of furniture scattered throughout the room were old, and some of the upholstery was threadbare. The room looked as if it was seldom used now, the wear and tear a sign of entertaining long past. The floor was dark, and the ceilings were low and made of heavy timbers, which added to the cooling effect. Eduardo's steps across the floor were quick and light, representative of a much younger man.

Exiting onto the patio, Chris stopped for just a moment to adjust his eyes to the sudden brightness and to admire the way the light was filtering through the pergola. Beams of the sun's rays darted through a wisteria-like plant that all but covered the giant structure. It reminded him of the lighting in some film noir movies, where there's just enough illumination to make out shadowy characters' chiseled features. The perimeter was draped with Spanish moss, which enhanced the shade.

Stepping underneath the pergola, it somehow seemed as cool as the inside of the house. How was that possible? Perhaps it was the colors of pinks, purples, and yellows that emanated from all the plants, above and surrounding, or the small and charming fountain in the center that was more gurgling than flowing. In the farthest and darkest corner was a black wrought iron table and chairs. Sitting at the table with their backs to Chris were two black shawls that appeared to be moving, barely sticking out above the chairs.

As Eduardo approached them, he spoke, "Señoras, our guest Chris Hamilton is here." He motioned to one of the empty chairs across from the two ladies. As he pulled it out, he smiled. Chris noticed his smile illuminated even the darkest corner of the patio.

"Welcome, Mr. Hamilton. I am Rosa, and this is my younger sister, Isabella."

Isabella nodded. Chris sensed a certain formality to their speech.

"Good morning. Thank you for seeing me." Chris observed how small and frail they were, even while sitting. He calculated he weighed more than both of them combined.

"Our brother spoke of you often. You were very dear to him," said Rosa.

"That's very kind of you to say that. I have been trying to come visit him since he left Virginia."

"You have poor timing." Isabella's first words were cutting.

"Isabella is still mourning the loss of her brother. They were very close." As she spoke, Rosa looked at her sister with a combination of envy and sadness.

"I am also mourning, Isabella," Chris replied. "Armando was more than a mentor to me, more than a friend."

"And he was more than a brother to us," Isabella shot back.

Before Chris could respond, Rosa defused her statement. "Please, these are family matters of which my sister speaks. But you have more important questions?"

Adroitly handled, Chris decided to deliver the question he had flown halfway across the country to ask.

"I received your note, thank you, but it was quite short on details. Can you elaborate on what happened?"

Before anyone could respond, Eduardo interjected, "Señor Hamilton, may I get you something? Coffee? Something to eat?"

"No, thank you, Eduardo," Chris said, then, realizing there would be no response to his question, continued, "Perhaps this

14

would be a good time for me to pay my respects to Armando. Could you—"

Before Chris could finish his sentence, Rosa said "Come" and started to rise from her chair. Chris was a little surprised at the sudden action but did not find himself able to object. He followed the ladies, walking a few feet behind. Rosa and Isabella moved very slowly. They stepped out from under the protection of the arbor back into the sun. Chris had forgotten how hot it was. They walked beside very old hedges that towered over them on one side; after a while they were on both sides acting as a guide to their inevitable destination. Laced among the hedges were bougainvillea plants, like the ones draped over the pergola. They appeared as though they had been growing there for decades, to the point where they cascaded down the fifteen-foot-tall structure like little waterfalls of varying colors—orange, white, pink, and magenta. They smelled like the honeysuckle plants back in Virginia, but with a more subtle, delicate fragrance, like a woman wearing just the right perfume. Chris appreciated the skills and dedication it took for such landscape artistry.

The walkway became shaded again, and Chris noticed that the señoras had pulled their black shawls over their heads, making them hard to see in the shadows. The path turned at right angles several times as he wondered, *Where the hell are we going?*

After a final turn, the walkway stopped at an iron gate with the hedges now growing into an arch over it. Embedded in the arch was a white cross that looked to be made of marble yet seemed to float among the hedges. Isabella and Rosa pushed open the gate, its heavy iron bars requiring their combined effort. As they stepped through the opening, Chris could see past them.

My God, he thought, *they have their own cemetery.*

He noticed the space was similar in size to the magnificent courtyard he had just seen that morning. The hedges around the cemetery were much denser, as if having intertwined over centuries. It seemed more like a fortress, with no way of getting anything more than the size of a coffin inside. He assumed all the graves had been dug by hand. The hedges were tall enough to cast a shadow over more than half of the cemetery. Butterflies darted in and out of the darkness to become brightly illuminated when the sun's rays hit them. It was an odd spectacle for such a place, as if children were playing tag in a church. Isabella and Rosa had continued walking to one of the graves in the far corner, its shiny gray headstone radiating in the light. It was freshly dug. As they approached, both sisters made the sign of the cross. They turned to

16

Chris, who had stopped, to beckon him toward the gravesite. Chris approached silently and cautiously, not knowing what to do or say.

Isabella broke the silence. "Armando would be very happy to know you have come. He said you were like a son to him."

Even if he could have thought of something to say, before Chris could respond, the señoras turned and walked away silently, as if floating across the grass. Chris turned back to look at the headstone:

Armando Chico Guerra

1925-1995

"Querido Hermano"

Chris stared at the headstone. Now what? When you plan something—a goal, an objective, a trip—then you finally arrive, what do you do? What is there to say when you are speaking to yourself?

He started to reminisce about the last time he saw Chico in person. The crisp fall afternoon when Chico's dogs, Mouse and Seal, chased the blowing leaves across the front yard. Chris had helped him pack his meager belongings into his Pajero with a small U-Haul attached to the back. He remembered wondering how such an amazing man could have so few worldly possessions at this stage in his life. His architectural books, music sheets, clothing, a few paintings from friends, one chair, food for himself, and his dogs. That was it. How could someone who has come from such grandiosity, such beauty, live so humbly, almost like a vagabond.

Chris thought of when, after everything had been packed, he and Chico sat on the front porch for half an hour or so petting the dogs and talking about Chris's future life, as if Chico was giving him some last words of wisdom before his departure. He had wondered if Chico had planned this parting conversation but dismissed such thoughts, since Chico was not prone to such superficial gestures. He was sure it was spontaneous and heartfelt, as if Chico was as reticent in his leaving as Chris was.

As Chico was walking to his car, he'd turned to Chris, hugged him, and said, "I love you, my boy."

Chico sometimes referred to Chris as "my boy" and often told him how much he loved him; however, that was the only time he had said them together. Did it have more meaning phrased together, or was it the moment that made it carry more weight?

He could visualize Chico driving down Ellwood Avenue, turning onto Sherwood Street toward the interstate, and how he thought it might be the last time he would see him. He had quickly dismissed the idea as maudlin and promised himself he'd visit Chico within the year. And yet, as he stared at the shiny new headstone, he realized his gut feelings had been right, and his self-made promise never came to fruition.

As Chris stared deep in thought, he sensed, as people often do, that he was not alone. He tried to look around without being obvious, either out of cautiousness or to avoid offending an intruder during such an intimate time.

Out of the corner of his eye, he could see a person standing at the gated entrance. With a slight adjustment, a movement so small as to not be detected by the onlooker, Chris could make out the figure: Eduardo. How long had he been standing there? A minute? Ten? He thought that one of Eduardo's well-learned duties must have been the art of waiting. Chris started to walk away as if done with his payment of respect and took a few steps before he looked up to acknowledge Eduardo.

As Chris approached him, he noticed how Eduardo was standing, hands clasped behind his back, almost as if he was a matador waiting for the bull to arrive. He thought Eduardo would

19

have made a terrific matador: tall, with elegant posture. All the señoritas would have swooned.

"I hope I have not disturbed you in such a private moment, Señor," Eduardo politely said.

"No, Eduardo, thank you. I had finished my goodbyes."

"Señor, I have been asked to inquire how long you will be staying here in Laredo?"

"My plane leaves at noon, day after tomorrow. Why do you ask?"

"The señoras have invited you to stay with us until you leave."

"Thank you, Eduardo, that is very kind of them, but I don't know if I would feel comfortable staying in the house. Besides, I have a hotel reservation."

"The house? No, Señor, that would not be permitted. The house is only for family. We have several casitas on the property. I have prepared one for you. This gesture is out of respect for their brother, Armando. He would have insisted you stay with us. It would be considered an insult to decline."

Chris knew that in many older cultures throughout the world, it would be undignified not to accept such a gracious offer. He appreciated Eduardo so delicately pointing this out.

"Thank you, Eduardo, I would be honored to stay."

"Excellent," Eduardo said with a smile. "I have taken the liberty of putting your bag in one of the casitas. If you would follow me."

As they walked, Eduardo took the time to tell Chris about some of the plants on the estate. He also gave a brief history of the house and some of the honored guests: Benito Juarez, Santa Anna, Presidents Teddy Roosevelt and Woodrow Wilson, King Gustav of Sweden, and many other names that Chris did not know, but Eduardo named each with such pride. He said his family had started service at "Casa de la Guerra" when his grandfather's grandfather worked as a horse trainer, and they had been there for over one hundred and fifty years.

Chris wondered how often Eduardo had entertained presidents, celebrities, and honored guests with such stories. Even though he was sure this presentation had been done dozens and dozens of times, it was the charm and enthusiasm with which Eduardo told it that made it even more entertaining. He seemed genuinely proud of this place where he had lived all his life.

As Chris and Eduardo passed the garden where tea had been served earlier, they turned down a side of the house that led into another, smaller garden. At the back were two cottages that faced each other at an angle, each one with the front door leading into the garden. It was a picturesque setting. In the center was a Royal

Poinciana tree with small flowering leaves that looked as if they were on fire; they lit up the garden even in the afternoon sun. Scattered about the intertwining walkways were various small flowering plants and cacti, each displaying a variety of colors from yellows to purples. Eduardo led Chris to the casita on the left. The front door was open, with a screen door keeping the plentiful bugs out. Eduardo pulled open the door and allowed Chris to walk through first, then he followed, the door softly closing behind them.

"The señoras have an important obligation in town this evening and will not be able to join you for dinner. I will bring you dinner here around 7, if that is what you wish."

"Yes, Eduardo, that would be great, thank you."

"Now," Eduardo said as he pushed open the door to leave, "it is time for a siesta."

Chris thought that was a great idea, and just as Eduardo was closing the door, he laid down on the bed.

He awoke around six. The siesta had been just what he needed after the plane flight, the heat, and the emotional energy spent from seeing Chico's grave. While lying on the bed, he appreciated the cooling effect of the ceiling fan that was driven by a motor and a leather strap. It seemed like it had been days since he had enjoyed the wonders of air conditioning.

There were long shadows now being cast by the flaming tree outside, its crimson buds seemed to glow even brighter in the sun's last gasp of the day. He looked around the room, observing it for the first time. There was a desk with writing paper and pens, and a small table sat just inside the doorway, flanked by two chairs that looked out onto the garden. On the other side of the room was a small hallway leading to a closet and a bathroom that appeared newer, Chris calculated 1930s. Comparing the quality of its craftsmanship to the rest of the casita, it seemed oddly out of place. It was the first thing he had seen that did not fit the grandiose nature of Casa de la Guerra.

Chris decided to shower before dinner. He felt that was the appropriate thing to do and regretted not having packed better clothing for the occasion. The shower was lukewarm at best, but considering the heat of the day, it was refreshing.

At 7:00 exactly, there was a knock on the door. Chris opened the door to see an older Mexican lady standing there, her hands holding something wrapped in a kitchen towel.

"Señor, Eduardo has been delayed in town. He asked me to serve you dinner in the garden. He said he will see you in the morning."

With that, she directed Chris to a small table for two in the center under the burning tree. The garden was lit by oil lamps around its perimeter. The sun was all but gone now, allowing the light of the oil lamps to illuminate the tree and plants with the warmth of their flickering light. Chris thought how unfortunate such a romantic setting was only for himself.

The food was delicious and presented on beautiful Mexican-style plates with ornate silverware. *Real silverware*, Chris thought. He had not realized how hungry he was, but it had been almost twelve hours since he had eaten. After finishing his meal, Chris sat quietly for a while, enjoying the pleasant setting of the garden and thinking about the people he had met that day and his visit to the gravesite.

When was the last time he had talked to Chico? A month ago? Two? Their phone conversations were infrequent but lengthy, always discussing Chris's building projects and his daughter. Chico always said he missed her, adding his endearing chuckle to the comment. He did not have a phone in his room. The only ones in the house were in the upper and lower hallways; however, he never complained about having to sit in the chair next to it while they talked.

Chris then thought of the letter, which was the reason he was here. He remembered going to his mailbox that day, wondering what annoying little bills were insidiously waiting for him inside. After removing the mail, he noticed a handsome, handwritten envelope, quite strange amongst all the computer-generated letters he usually received. It was addressed to:

Mr. Chris Hamilton

601 Red Maple Drive

Manakin, Va. 23103

The return address was:

Casa de la Guerra - Laredo, Texas

Chris had thought this odd; Chico had never written to him. He opened the letter, which read:

"Dear Friend,

This letter is to inform you that Armando Guerra died on August 15, 1995.

Rosa and Isabella Guerra"

He recalled staring at the letter while standing there in the street. For how long, he couldn't say. He contacted a couple of other people Chico had known in Richmond, Lewis Whitt and Jim Payette. They had known nothing about his passing, which had left Chris to deliver the sad news.

Phone calls to Casa de la Guerra rang endlessly until eventually, Chris's call was answered by a maid, who passed his message on to "the señoras." A couple more days passed before Chris received a return phone call from Eduardo and was granted permission to visit them and pay his respects to his friend.

But it was still unclear to him what had happened. Chico was not in the best health, and he was 70, but having come back to Texas because of nerve damage to his legs, he had said the heat was making his legs better. Chris was unaware of any heart conditions or other health issues. So what happened?

One thing he did know, Rosa and Isabella were not going to be the ones to answer his questions. Chris rose from the table, thinking for a moment about whether he should do something with his plates or turn off the oil lamps, but he was sure these services would be taken care of soon.

He went back to the casita and sat at the desk for a minute, again asking himself the questions of why the details of Chico's death seemed to be so clouded. It was as if it wasn't just the simple passing of an older gentleman.

People's actions had made something that appeared so simple on the surface make him question their behavior. Even the cab driver, although Chris could not define how or why, seemed to act in a peculiar way.

He reached for a piece of the fine writing paper on the desk to make some notes on what he might be able to ask of the señoras. He paused and reflected for a moment as to how many important people, maybe even presidents, had sat at this desk and written letters. He then noticed that the stationery was the same as that of the letter he had received announcing Chico's death.

There was a knock on the door. It was almost 10 p.m., and Chris thought this was an odd occurrence. After all, how many people knew he was here? With mild trepidation, Chris opened the door. It was the friendly image of Eduardo.

"Señor, please pardon the interruption," he said. "I apologize. I had to accompany the señoras to a very important meeting in the city."

"No apology is necessary, Eduardo. I understand. I very much enjoyed the evening and my dinner." Chris hoped this placated Eduardo, who seemed less the confident tour guide he had been just a few hours ago. Perhaps, Chris thought, this was the demeanor he had learned for when a "mea culpa" was to be performed.

Eduardo then said something that, although very simple in its statement, took Chris by surprise. "May I come in, Chris?"

He wondered if he was more taken aback by Eduardo addressing him as "Chris" or the fact that he asked to come in, and the two combined seemed to have an ominous tone. As Eduardo entered, Chris noticed he was carrying what looked like a jug of milk and two glasses.

"Have you ever tasted 'The Drink of the Gods'?" As Eduardo posed this question, he lifted the jug of milk as if presenting a truly rare commodity.

"No, what is it?" Chris asked.

"Pulque! It has been in Mexico for centuries. It was drunk by the Aztecs! It is made from the sap of the maguey. I know a local that brings me some from time to time."

Eduardo set the jug and glasses on the small table. They were oddly shaped and tinted green, with the base and rim being a shade darker. They appeared lopsided, like some failed attempt in a pottery class, and they were thicker than any glass Chris had seen.

"Please, sit." Eduardo gestured at the chairs and table.

Eduardo sat in the chair closest to the window. The oil lamps could still be seen flickering outside, and this provided a foreboding backdrop. As he poured the milky-looking drink, Eduardo started speaking without prompting, as if he was more an old friend now than a recent acquaintance. His personality seemed less performative and more open. Chris thought that this was probably more like the real Eduardo than the one that represented Casa de la Guerra.

"You must try to understand the señoras. It is their way," Eduardo said. "They do not dislike you. Armando was very dear to them, especially Isabella, because they were so near in age. When he left so many years ago, there was much sadness."

Chris sipped from the oddly shaped glass. The drink tasted bittersweet, like beer mixed with yogurt. *An acquired taste*, he thought.

Eduardo continued but in a different tone. "I grew up here at Casa de la Guerra. I've spent my whole life here. When I was a little boy, this place was like its own village. Dozens of workers from town would come every day—carpenters, maids, cooks, gardeners—and we had dozens of our own staff. It was a magical place for a boy to grow up in." Eduardo used his hands in a very descriptive manner as he spoke.

"My father was always busy with important matters, so I was often left on my own. Armando...he was not like his two older brothers, Victor and Salvador. He was not interested in matters of state, or business, or money. He was more of a free-spirited man, more intellectual. He loved to travel and would often take me with him when I was not in school, and I learned more from spending time with him than any school could teach.

"We would go to Mexico City and visit the countless museums. We spent a month in Peru once when I was 14 and climbed to the top of Machu Picchu. He even took me and several of my friends to New York City when we graduated from high school. It was like going to the moon."

Eduardo's eyes grew wide as he talked about his visits, like he was a young boy reliving them all over again. "When I was 16, the señoritas started to behave differently around me. I didn't understand what was happening. Armando explained to me how I was becoming a man, and the chicas were flirting with me. Armando was quite the ladies' man. Beautiful women were always coming to visit him. He taught me much about how to be with a woman, and it has served me well for many years."

His tone then changed again. "When Armando's father died, there was much fighting between his two brothers. Money, property, horses. It was a terrible time, 'Cuando los buitres circulan.' Armando's sisters tried to keep peace in the family, but there was so much greed.

"Soon, there was property being sold. All the horses were gone, and many of the staff, some whose families had worked here for generations, were fired. It was during this time with all the fighting that Armando left. Perhaps he was not concerned with such matters, or perhaps he wanted to pursue interests beyond these walls. There were even rumors of a scandal with a woman. I was very young, so I cannot say for sure.

"Then…" His eyes fell to the glass in his hands, as though examining the many imperfections in its making. "My father died a couple of years after Armando left. The brothers, they had looted what they could save for the money left to their sisters and departed from Casa de la Guerra. For many years, the señoras, myself, and the few staff that had stayed were all that was left…"

There was a pause in his monologue, almost as if he needed to gather himself before taking on the next topic.

"Then Armando came back home," Chris said, encouraging Eduardo toward the story's conclusion.

"Yes," Eduardo spoke, his eyes still on the lopsided glass. "Armando came back home, and there was much happiness, for a while."

Eduardo now looked up at Chris and made a wry smile, gesturing broadly with one arm. "Armando and I spoke often about his friend in Virginia, the one that was the baseball player. He said he thought of you as a son, much like he thought of me as a son many years ago. So"—Eduardo held up the remaining contents of his glass to offer a toast while smiling— "we are like brothers, you and I."

Chris tapped his glass with Eduardo's, feeling both a sense of honor and surprise. "Thank you, Eduardo."

They drank from their glasses and set them down almost simultaneously. Eduardo then leaned back in his chair, his face now showing signs of resignation and sorrow.

"So, as my brother, I feel there is something important you should know." Eduardo's eyes now seemed to grow even darker.

"Armando was murdered."

Chapter 2

Spinning.

That's what Chris thought about his head when he opened his eyes the next morning. Whether it was from the pulque, the events of yesterday, or his late-night discovery of his friend's demise, his head was indeed spinning. It was also pounding; that he was sure was from the "Drink of the Gods." *Perhaps that's why they are Gods,* Chris thought.

He stared up at the swirled stucco ceiling, analyzing last night's discussion with his newly found brother. Armando was the kindest, gentlest, most giving person Chris had ever known. Who would possibly want to kill him; and moreover, why? Theft? Chico had very little in the way of belongings and rarely carried money on him. A fight? Impossible! Not him, not that gentle soul. He was a pacifist in every sense of the word. He had only been in Laredo for a year or so since he moved back. What could have happened?

33

Although Eduardo informed him that Armando had been murdered, he did not give Chris any details.

Was that intentional? Lack of knowledge? Was there something he was hiding? Did the señoras know?

The señoras.

Chris also remembered Eduardo had sworn him to secrecy regarding Armando's sisters. Was this some kind of vague clue? Was Eduardo shielding them? Were they aware of Armando's murder but didn't want outsiders to know? Certainly, the police had informed them as Armando's next of kin.

And what about the police? What do they know?

Ah, shit!

Chris knew there was no way he could leave without some answers, with all that Chico had meant to him. His mentoring of life, teaching of music and architecture, the hundreds of hours spent discussing everything from engineering to women, from baseball to Bach...but most of all, his paternal spirit. Growing up without a father, Chris had never known the valuable benefits of such a male guiding force until Chico befriended him.

How can a son, even a surrogate one, walk away from such a responsibility? Isn't this one of the times when a man is morally obligated? Wouldn't this qualify as a son's duty?

Ah, shit!

Chris then remembered he was supposed to leave the next afternoon. What could he possibly accomplish in a day? He didn't know anything, anyone, or even when or where Chico had died. He then thought of something Chico used to say to him when he had a major task to accomplish: "Every journey begins with a first step."

After showering and dressing, Chris packed all his belongings into his travel bag. As he was leaving the casita, he noticed the empty pitcher and two empty lopsided glasses on the table. "Oh, God!" he said.

Walking onto the patio, he saw a man working in the garden. As he approached him, Chris asked, "Pardoneme, habla usted inglés?"

The man looked up from bending over some plants, as if he had been waiting for Chris to emerge. "Yes," he responded.

"Where is Eduardo?" Chris asked.

"He is away on business this morning. My name is Luis. May I help you?"

"I would like to find a place to rent a car."

"Eduardo said if you would like to go into town, you may take one of the cars we have in the garage."

Chris said, "Eduardo thinks of everything, thank you. Could you show me the way?"

Luis silently led Chris through a labyrinth of hedges, buildings, and gardens until they finally emerged at what had once been the horse stables. The building seemed to be older than the house or the casitas and less well maintained. It had been converted years ago from the housing of horses to its present-day role of housing cars. Chris thought to himself that this building had not seen horses for probably 30 years, yet it still had a strong stench of horse manure. There were several doors that slid sideways like traditional barn doors. Chris was sure that it contained many cars, and he wondered what was behind each door. Luis slid open the first door, revealing an old Nissan pickup truck that looked like it was used mostly for farm use. Next to it was a vehicle Chris had not seen since it had turned onto Ellwood Avenue and headed for the interstate about a year ago. Chico's Pajero!

"May I take that one?" Chris asked.

"Sure," Luis said while pulling the keys from a nail in a post.

Chris put his overnight bag into the back, slid into the front seat, and turned the key. It started right away.

Luis walked up to the car window and said, "If you turn left onto the dirt road in front of the stables, it will take you out the back of the property to another dirt road. Turn right on that road, and it will take you into town."

"Thanks," Chris said and started to back out.

Chris drove out of the property and turned onto the dirt road. It felt very odd driving Chico's old vehicle, knowing that he was gone, but it gave Chris a connection to the friend who had meant so much to him. He flew down the dirt road, leaving a giant trail of dust blowing out of the back of the vehicle like the contrails from a jet plane. Chris looked out onto the semi-arid desert opposite the Casa de la Guerra and noticed how the light cascaded throughout the live oaks and scrub brush, illuminating them as if from lights on some movie set. There were just a few shadows that morning, and the plants and trees seemed to glow, making their dull green color seem much brighter. The occasional yellow or red flower stood out from its backdrop as if in a painting. The sand glistened in the morning sun, making Chris squint as he looked over the vastness of the landscape. Chico had often mentioned how the desert light was different than the light anywhere else.

Turning onto the main road, Chris looked at the address he had written on the casita's stationery with the directions below: Laredo Police Department, 4712 Maher Ave. During the drive, he took note of how so many cities had become homogeneous, with the same fast-food places, strip malls, and giant box stores. They were all losing their individuality.

Pulling into the parking lot, Chris recognized that he didn't know where to go, didn't know what to ask, didn't even know if he would get to talk to anyone today. But he did know how charming and gregarious he could be. That was one of his best assets.

Entering the building, Chris approached the information desk, where a seemingly exasperated female officer was sitting, filling out paperwork.

"Good morning," Chris said with a smile. "Can you direct me to the homicide department?"

"Second floor. Elevators are down the hall," the officer said, not even glancing up at Chris.

"Thanks."

As Chris walked away, he thought, *Well, that was a waste of charm!*

Bypassing the elevators, he looked for the stairs. Chris quickly found the door, opened it, and walked up. His claustrophobia had long ago helped him develop a sixth sense for where the stairs were located.

Entering the second floor, he stopped for a moment to get his bearings. He saw quite a few police officers, some with guns in shoulder holsters, busily walking around with serious looks on their faces. There was a sense of importance with which they went about their duties. All were smartly dressed in police uniforms, save for a few that had the "detective" look about them. Coffee cups were everywhere, some showing signs of being freshly poured, others appearing to be empty.

This is what a police station should look like, Chris thought.

"You look lost." The friendly voice directed at Chris startled him.

Turning to his right, Chris saw a police officer with a broad smile on his face; it seemed at odds with the intensity he had just observed.

"I do?" Chris responded.

"I see that look on tourists' faces all the time." The officer's smile turned into a laugh.

Laughing with him, Chris said, "Thanks, I'm Chris Hamilton. I'm actually here to inquire about a friend of mine that has passed away."

"Oh, okay," the officer said, seemingly apologetic about his comedic introduction. "Maybe I can help you. Sit down."

Sitting in the adjacent wooden chair, Chris asked, "I wonder if you can tell me anything about his death?"

"I'll see what I can do. I'm Officer Lopez."

Chris got a feeling of genuine friendliness from the officer, and he had learned long ago to trust his instincts.

"Thank you, Officer Lopez. I really appreciate your help. I'm interested to find out how he died."

"Okay, I'll look him up on my computer and see what details are available about his death. What is his name?"

"Armando Guerra."

Officer Lopez's fingers paused almost imperceptibly at the keyboard, as if he had not heard Chris correctly, then proceeded to type in the name. After a few seconds, Officer Lopez said, "Mr. Hamilton, it says here that he died from natural causes."

Somewhat surprised by this answer, and sensing a feeling of uneasiness in Officer Lopez, Chris asked, "I see. Is that all you can tell me?"

"Perhaps you can speak to Detective Henderson. It says here the coroner referred the case to him."

"Okay, thank you," Chris said, sensing Officer Lopez's urgency to wash his hands of the issue. "Where can I find him?"

Officer Lopez stood up from his desk to look around the room. "I think he is in a squad meeting right now. I'll take you to where you can wait for him."

As they walked across the room, Officer Lopez asked, "Where are you from? You don't seem like a local."

"Virginia."

"Virginia?" the officer exclaimed. "Quite beautiful!"

"Oh, so you've been there?"

"No." The officer looked at Chris and smiled. He was either back to his natural ways or just relieved to be free of the situation.

Officer Lopez led Chris to a chair and said to another officer nearby, "When Detective Henderson comes out of the meeting, can you ask him if he has a few minutes to speak to Mr. Hamilton?"

He then gave Chris a friendly thumbs up and walked back to his desk.

As Chris sat there, he wondered why Officer Lopez had appeared taken aback by the name Armando Guerra. Did he just imagine his perceived gesture? Didn't his demeanor change also?

Looking around the room, Chris felt like an elementary school kid waiting for the principal. He noticed there were a couple of female officers, who always appeared to be more attractive in uniform. Just then, the door to the meeting room behind him opened, and a half dozen officers exited, with a tall, lean, dark-haired man leading the way. He was dressed in dark slacks and a pristine white shirt with a dark blue tie, a .38 neatly tucked under his arm in a shoulder holster. It looked to Chris like he was the stereotypical version of a detective.

As the detective walked past, the policeman whom Officer Lopez had charged with watching Chris looked up and said, "Detective, this man is here to see you," then pointed with his pencil at Chris.

Looking down at him, Detective Henderson said, "Morning. Give me just a minute to go to the bathroom and get some more coffee. It's been a busy morning." As he walked away, he turned back to ask, "Would you like some coffee, also?"

"No, thanks," Chris said.

There's something about him, Chris thought. *Aloof? Busy? Disinterested?*

The detective returned in a few minutes and, with a casual gesture, said, "Come on in." He motioned to his office over his shoulder.

"Where are you from?" Detective Henderson asked.

"Virginia. Why, is it that obvious?"

He smiled and said, "When you've lived here all your life, you can usually tell the visitors from the locals. What's your name?" As he asked this question, he sat on the edge of his desk and continued to smile, although it seemed forced.

"Chris Hamilton."

"Mr. Hamilton, I have to leave in a few minutes, but what can I do for you?" Chris realized this was why he sat on his desk, to signal the brevity of the meeting.

"I recently had a friend pass away, and I was curious about his death. There seems to be some question about how he died. I'm told it was one of your cases."

"And what was the name of your friend?"

"Armando Guerra."

As Chris said his name, he noticed a slight diminishing of the smile, now seemingly even more forced. "Are you familiar with the case?"

"Yes, I know the case." As the detective spoke, he now walked behind his desk to sit down. "But there is no mystery," he continued, the smile now returning. "He died of natural causes, the case has been closed."

"Can you tell me the circumstances of his death?"

"Well," he said, "it was very sad." He sat his coffee cup down on his desk and leaned back in his chair. "He apparently went walking in the desert and got lost. He was found about ten miles outside of town."

"Who found him?"

"Some young hikers. Apparently, he had been there for a couple of days. It was not pretty." Henderson gestured slightly with his hands as he spoke.

"Were there any signs of foul play?"

"Foul play? No, of course not. He died from the elements. Dehydration and the heat. He was seventy years old, after all. Perhaps he wandered away from his home and got lost. It happens." All traces of Henderson's smile were now completely gone.

"I was told he was murdered," Chris said, looking directly at Henderson and watching for any kind of reaction.

There was a moment, almost as if Detective Henderson was calculating how much Chris knew.

"Who told you such a preposterous thing?" he asked, his demeanor accusatory.

Chris knew he had entered a game of cat and mouse. He certainly was the mouse and thought it was best to defuse the line of questioning. He decided not to divulge that he knew the coroner had referred the case to the detective.

"Just a local. He said he had heard something," Chris said, shrugging.

"Yes, I understand. Locals have a tendency to create rumors. How long are you staying in our beautiful city?" The smile now returned to his face.

"Just a couple of days."

"Where are you staying?"

"I'm a guest at Casa de la Guerra. The señoras have invited me to stay."

"Then you must have been very close to Señor Guerra?"

"Yes, I was. He was a good friend of mine."

"Well, Mr. Hamilton," the detective said, rising from his chair, "I am very sorry for your loss. Please," he said, handing Chris a business card, "if you have any more questions while you are here, do not hesitate to call me." He proceeded to open his office door.

Chris shook his hand and said, "Thank you, detective." He walked back through the office and down the stairs. Officer Lopez was not at his desk.

As Chris was leaving the building, he walked past the information desk where the same female officer was still scribbling on a mound of papers.

"Excuse me," he asked her, "where is the public library?"

"1120 E. Carlton Road." She never looked up.

Why were Lopez and Henderson so anxious when they heard Chico's name? Was it just Chris's imagination? Was there anything to that? Was it just as Detective Henderson said: an unfortunate situation leading to an old man's demise? Was Eduardo being dramatic, or was he simply wrong? One thing swaying Chris's thinking was that he did not trust Detective Henderson. There was something to his demeanor that did not sit well with him. Chris felt he had given out more information than he had received.

As he pulled into the parking lot of the public library, Chris stopped and said, "You've got to be kidding me."

There, sitting in front of the building, was a six-foot-tall sign: "Joe A. Guerra Laredo Public Library."

Was this a relative? Possibly. He knew it certainly wasn't Chico's greedy brothers who had built this place.

As Chris was walking down the sidewalk, he knew if he was to get any information at the library, he would have to be extra charming, as his computer skills sucked. However, being six-foot-two with thick, dark hair and an athletic build had served him well over the years. He often thought of something his ex-wife had once told him: "You can be disgustingly charming when you want." Chris was hoping there would be a female librarian who could assist him, but then he remembered how ineffectual his so-called-charm had been at the police station.

Entering the library, he felt such a huge rush of cold air as he opened the door that it fogged his sunglasses. It felt refreshing against his skin, and he thought how wonderful air conditioning was, especially in the growing heat of the day.

Approaching the information desk, Chris noticed two attendants who were assisting people. One was a mid-forties Latino man who was almost assuredly gay. The other was a young woman, seemingly fresh out of college, with round glasses, her hair tied in a ponytail. She was plain-looking, wore little makeup, and had a pleasant disposition as she went about helping a group of young children who had just come in.

That one, Chris thought. *Besides, I like ponytails.*

Chris timed his approach to the desk so his choice of assistants wouldn't look too obvious. When his turn came, he switched on the charm, hoping to at least be acknowledged this time.

"Good morning. My name is Chris Hamilton, and I was hoping you could help me."

Chris could tell she was surprised by his presence. She probably helped mostly senior citizens and children all day.

"Well, I can certainly try," she said with a genuine smile. "My name's Lisa."

Chris understood by Lisa giving her name that he'd already had an effect.

"I had a friend of mine pass away recently, and I was trying to find out some information regarding his death. Perhaps some newspaper articles?" He left that last phrase hanging in the air, hoping for a volunteer.

"Well," Lisa said, "we have a microfiche room upstairs that probably has what you're looking for."

"Thank you, Lisa," Chris said. "Is there anyone up there that can assist me? I'm terrible with this sort of thing."

"No, it's a self-serve room," she said. Lisa then paused and looked at her watch. "You know, I get a lunch break in about fifteen minutes. I could help you." Her enthusiasm almost made Chris feel a little guilty, but he knew he truly would be useless alone.

"Lisa, I'd hate to take up your lunch break," Chris said in a meager attempt to make himself appear less obvious.

"Oh, I don't mind." Lisa was now smiling broadly.

"Thank you, Lisa, that's very kind of you. I'll see you up there."

In the fifteen minutes it took for Lisa to arrive, Chris had managed to find, with some silent cursing, files that were the approximate date after Chico's death. He had figured out how to turn on the machine, but that was about it.

When she walked in, Chris noticed how petite she was. She had a slim frame and wore a skirt that revealed she had nice legs and sandals on her feet. She had put on a sweater, knowing the room was a little cooler than the rest of the library. Chris thought perhaps she was all too aware of the effects a chilly room could have on women.

She enthusiastically sat down next to Chris and asked, "So, where are we?"

"I was just getting started," Chris said, slightly chagrined.

"Here, let me show you how to use this." Lisa gently picked up one of the files and inserted it into the already running machine. "Who are we looking for?" she added.

"My friend's name was Armando Guerra. I believe he died around September 10th."

Lisa scanned through several newspapers at amazing speed. As she looked through obituaries and related articles, Chris noticed she had very feminine hands. They were delicate, and she wore clear fingernail polish.

49

After about ten minutes checking all the papers from September 10th through September 17th, she'd found nothing.

"That's very odd," she said, perhaps more placating Chris than anything else.

"I don't think there is a requirement to have an obituary published in the paper," Chris said in response. "I just thought that would be a good starting place to find some more information about his death."

"What do you mean by more information? What are you specifically looking for?" Lisa asked, looking a little puzzled.

"Well," Chris paused a moment, wondering how much to reveal to someone so innocent. "What I'm trying to find out is…there seems to be some question as to how he died." Chris thought that was all he should share with her, then said, "I guess I'm back to square one."

"Well, maybe not," Lisa said. She had a knowing look on her face. "I believe all death certificates are notated as public record and should be available online. Perhaps that might contain more information."

"Do you know how I can do that?" Chris was once again looking for a volunteer.

Lisa looked at her watch. "I have about fifteen minutes left." She stood up, grabbed her purse, and said, "Follow me."

She walked out of the room and turned left down the hallway, going past the restrooms and a locked office. She stopped at a door marked "Research Room." She took a set of keys from her purse and opened the door, saying, "I do research for individuals who come in for assistance and for the library. I use this room a lot."

Inside, Chris saw four ordinary desks with computers sitting on each one. Lisa sat down at the closest one and turned it on. Within seconds, she was typing in information, the green from the computer screen reflecting off her glasses. Chris sat down in the chair at the desk next to hers, realizing just being quiet at this moment was the best course of action.

After a couple of minutes, Lisa turned to Chris and asked, "Armando Guerra?" She spelled it out to confirm the correct name.

"Yes," Chris replied, hoping she had found something.

"Look," she said, turning the screen toward him.

Chris read what was on the screen:

Death Certificate

Laredo, Texas

Deceased: Armando Chico Guerra

Age: 70

Address: 111 Flowering Cactus Drive, Laredo Texas

Race: Latino

Location: Off highway 305 between mile marker 103 and 104. Approx. 500 yards off the paved service.

Cause of death: Unnatural.

"Unnatural?" he said, the word radiating from the screen. "What does that mean?"

Chris realized he was staring at the screen while Lisa was patiently waiting, not knowing what to say.

He suddenly turned to her. "I'm sorry, you need to get back to work."

Lisa turned off the computer and started to leave with Chris, again glancing at her watch.

"I hope I have been of some help," she said as Chris opened the door.

"Yes, thank you, Lisa. You've been terrific, I really appreciate it." Chris's tone was sincere. He knew he would have found nothing without her help.

Walking down the hall, Lisa reached into her purse and pulled out a small piece of yellow paper that was folded in half. Handing it to Chris, she said, "I don't know how long you'll be in town, but if you'd like to get together, here's my number."

Chris took the piece of paper, aware that she had to have written it before she had even come upstairs. He was surprised that such a seemingly shy young woman would be so bold.

"Thank you, Lisa," he said as they started down the stairs. Lisa gave him a sideways glance and a shy smile.

Reaching the bottom, she said, "I really enjoyed helping you." Lisa then turned and walked toward the information desk. Chris knew the last line, timed with her exit, was done for dramatic effect. He knew young women enjoyed that; it was part of the game.

Perhaps I underestimated her, he thought. Neatly folding the piece of paper again so it would fit in his pocket, Chris walked outside.

"Ugh!" he said. The temperature had risen by what seemed like twenty degrees while he had been inside, and the coolness of the library had accentuated the difference. The reflection of the sun off the pavement and the windows made it even worse, and the heat hit him like someone had slapped him in the face.

Walking into the parking lot, already starting to sweat, Chris noticed a police cruiser with a tow truck nearby. As he approached them, he saw they were preparing to tow Chico's Pajero. Chris had learned long ago to keep his head and be respectful in these situations. Getting an attitude with the police can only escalate the situation.

"Morning, officer," Chris said as he approached, using his most cheerful tone. "Is there a problem with the way I parked?"

The police officer turned his way and very professionally inquired, "Is this your vehicle, sir?"

"It belongs to a friend of mine. I was using it for the day," Chris politely responded.

"I see," said the officer. "And can your friend verify this?"

Chris realized he had made a tactical error in what he had said. "Well, no, my friend is deceased."

"And your deceased friend said you could use his car?" said the officer, duly suspicious.

"No, of course not, officer." Chris reached for what would hopefully be an ace-in-the-hole. "I'm staying at the Casa de la Guerra, where my friend lived. His family was kind enough to let me use his car."

As Chris had hoped, this seemed to have some sort of effect on the officer. His suspicions seemed slightly diminished.

"Can you tell me the name of your friend?" the officer asked.

Chris had taken note of the officer's badge while he was asking the question.

"His name was Armando Guerra, Officer Hernandez." Chris mentioning the Guerras, along with addressing the officer by name, seemed to further relax him.

The officer studied Chris for just a moment, then said, "Yes, that is the name on the registration. And what is your name, sir?"

Chris reached for his wallet. "Shit!" He realized it was in Chico's car. "My identification is in the car," he said. "May I get it?"

"I'm sorry, sir. I cannot allow people to take items from a car that is being impounded."

"Impounded?" Chris was a little stunned but stayed polite. "May I ask why?"

"The vehicle has been reported as stolen, sir."

Chris now realized why the officer had been so suspicious of him using the car, but why was it reported as stolen?

"May I ask your name, sir?" the officer asked, repeating his question of a moment ago.

"Yes, of course. It's Chris Hamilton."

The officer then asked, "Do you have the keys to the car?"

Chris reached into his pocket and handed them to the officer. "Yes, here are the keys. The bag with my wallet inside is in the back."

The officer then walked over to the vehicle and unlocked it. Chris noticed his partner had now walked behind him and was standing nearby. Chris was wondering if he was in trouble or if this was all just a mistake. His claustrophobic feelings were starting to emerge; a jail cell was one of his worst nightmares.

The officer returned holding Chris's wallet. "What is your address, sir?"

"601 Red Maple Drive, Manakin-Sabot, Virginia," Chris responded.

"How did you know Mr. Guerra?" The officer seemed less suspicious now, almost friendly. Chris thought perhaps he knew what had happened to Chico and was becoming a little sympathetic.

"He was a friend of mine for years back in Virginia."

This answer seemed to appease the officer, and he asked one more question to further satisfy himself.

"What are his sisters' names?"

Chris was surprised by this question. Apparently, the cab driver had been right, and the family was revered in this town.

"Rosa and Isabella. I just met them yesterday." Chris then attempted to further the connection. "Do you know them?"

The officer smiled for the first time. "Yes, I know them. My mother used to work for them."

At this point, the officer's tone changed entirely, fully believing Chris was not a thief, or worse. In fact, he became helpful and understanding.

"Look, Mr. Hamilton, you were not driving the car, so technically, I can't charge you with an offense, and I believe your story. However, the vehicle is listed as stolen, so I must take it and all the contents."

Chris, relieved that he was not going to be jailed in a far-off city, decided to cut his losses and said, "I understand, officer. Can I have my wallet please?"

"Only the owner can remove articles from an impounded vehicle," Officer Hernandez dutifully said.

"Well, you know who the owner is, so that would be a bit difficult, wouldn't it?" Chris said, trying to minimize his sarcasm.

"You can go to the police department tomorrow and ask if it has been processed, but sometimes it can take a few days. I'm sorry, sir."

Chris knew full well he was just doing his job, and besides, Officer Hernandez had been nothing but professional. Chris knew when to fold his cards.

"Thank you, Officer Hernandez. I appreciate your understanding."

Officer Hernandez then reached into his shirt pocket and handed him a business card, saying, "If I can be of any help while you are here, please let me know."

Chris was sure the last gesture was due to the "Guerra effect," a reaction he was becoming familiar with, both good and bad.

Chapter 3

Curiouser and curiouser.

Chris thought as he walked back toward the library more or less because he had no other direction in mind. He wandered around to the shady side of the library and decided to sit on one of the concrete benches to take some personal inventory. "Now what?"

He began to think about his present situation. "I have no wallet, so no cash, credit cards, or identification. I have no plane ticket home. I have no change of clothes and, most importantly right now, no way of getting back to the temporary sanctuary of Casa de la Guerra."

He figured if he went there, he'd at least have a place to sleep and something to eat. Perhaps he could recover his belongings in the morning. He was sure Eduardo could be of assistance.

"Eat!" he said out loud. He remembered he had not eaten since dinner last night. Had it been his focus on finding out what had happened to Chico or the lingering effects of the pulque?

He reached into his pocket to pull out the contents. Seven dollars. He also noted that he had accumulated three business cards: one from a cab driver, two from police officers, and the phone number of a young and highly interested librarian. Not bad for twenty-four hours in Laredo. He couldn't help but laugh at the last observation.

"Lisa!" Perhaps he could get a ride from her after work? He looked at this watch: 1:15. He'd have to wait for several hours before she would leave work. "Besides," Chris reasoned, "I don't want to encourage her any further. She's too naive, too young, too willing, too…everything."

"But," he continued, "at least I can ask her if I can use the phone."

Walking back into the welcoming coolness of the library, Chris approached the information desk again. Lisa looked up and smiled, surely thinking that he had come back just to see her. Somehow, she seemed a little prettier to Chris than when he had first talked to her.

"Hi, Lisa. I seem to be having a problem with my car." Chris certainly didn't want to go into the details of what had really happened. "Is there a phone I can use?"

Lisa seemed a little disappointed; however, she maintained her smile and said, "Sure, there is one at the end of the counter."

"Is there one a little more private?"

Lisa turned around to look in the offices that were behind her. Selecting one, she said, "You can use Mr. Wilson's office. He's not in today." She walked him to the door and opened it so Chris could enter.

"Thanks," he said.

Sitting down at the desk, Chris pulled out the cab driver's card. It read:

Juan Eliseo – Cab Driver

Cell# 1-956-437-2965

As Chris dialed, he realized he was now getting very hungry. Perhaps Juan could suggest a place to eat nearby while Chris waited to be picked up.

"Hello, Juan here."

"Juan, this is Chris Hamilton. You gave me a ride yesterday from the airport."

"Sí. Hola, Chris. Are you heading back so soon?"

"No, Juan. I'm in a bit of a bind. I need a ride back to Casa de la Guerra. I've had an issue with the car I was driving."

"Okay," Juan said, "but perhaps you would like me to get my friend that has a tow truck." Chris knew that Juan was trying to be helpful.

"No, thanks, Juan," Chris said, then added, "Actually, it was impounded by the police."

There was a delay in Juan's response. "What happened, Señor?"

"It seems the car was reported stolen, which I find very strange."

There was an even longer pause this time. "Yes, that is strange." There was silence for a few seconds where Juan said nothing, then, "Señor, did the police tell you what day it was reported stolen?"

Chris was surprised by the question. What does that matter? "No, Juan," he said, "I never thought to ask that question."

"Mr. Hamilton," his tone grew more cautious, "where are you now?"

"I'm at the public library." Chris was becoming alarmed by the serious tone in Juan's voice.

"Where in the library?"

"I'm in an office behind the information desk. Why?"

"Good, stay there and call me back in five minutes." Juan hung up before answering Chris's question.

"What in the hell is going on?" Chris said out loud. It seemed like every move Chris had made in the last two days, every inquiry or action, had led to more questions and odd events. What had he stepped into here?

Chris looked up to see that Lisa had turned around to check on him, probably hearing what he said. He gave her a thumbs up like everything was okay, but it wasn't. Somehow, the events of the last two days added up to more than just the sum of their parts. He took the few minutes he had to piece together things to see how the puzzle looked.

How had a simple visit to pay his respects to his friend become so convoluted? Was Eduardo being melodramatic in saying Chico was murdered? Perhaps, but what did it mean on the death certificate where it said "Death: Unnatural"? Did he imagine the police having a reaction to the mere mentioning of Chico's name, or were his powers of observation off this time?

Why was Chico's obituary not in the paper? Maybe the family wanted to keep it private. That's plausible. But then there's the car. What were the odds that the first time it's on the road in weeks, it gets impounded? And who would have reported it as stolen? Certainly not Chico's sisters or Eduardo. Was it stolen before Chico died and Chico himself had reported it? Had the police

63

neglected to correct the records? Chris looked at his watch...five minutes. He picked up the phone and dialed again.

Juan answered quickly, startling Chris. "Juan?"

He started talking without answering Chris, "Mr. Hamilton, I think you are in danger."

The words seemed to strike Chris like a punch in the gut. In the back of his mind, he knew something was wrong, but he didn't want to believe it.

"What do you mean, Juan?"

"I will explain when I pick you up."

"Okay. Should I meet you out front?"

"No, stay in the room you are in. There is a loading dock on the side of the building that has a ramp, it is used for trucks to unload. I will be there in ten minutes. When I pull up, get in the back of the cab and stay down as we leave."

Chris was dismayed by the directions; however, Juan seemed very serious, so Chris thought it best to follow his lead.

"Okay, I'll find it." Chris hung up.

"What in the fuck?" Chris said loud enough for Lisa to turn around again.

Chris took the opportunity to walk to the door and open it. "Lisa," he asked, "where is the loading dock in the building?" She seemed a little surprised by the question but said, "You go down that hall and take the stairs. At the bottom of the stairs there's another door. Just open it and you're at the loading dock."

"Thanks," Chris said. He returned to the desk to get his business cards, then walked back to the open door. Walking past Lisa, he said, "Thanks for all your help."

"Wait," she said. "Are you leaving now?"

"Yes," he said, continuing to walk, hoping she wouldn't follow.

"You're in trouble, aren't you?"

Chris turned briefly to say "I don't know" and kept walking.

Walking down the stairs, Chris looked at his watch; five minutes until Juan arrived. He opened the door at the bottom to see there was a two-bay loading dock about twenty feet away. There were no workers in sight. Chris also noticed the bottom of the ramp was not visible from the street and assumed this area was used for loading books and furniture. He decided to stand in the hallway with the door opened just enough to see the ramp.

As he waited, he wondered if he had manipulated Lisa too much. He knew how charming he could be and how often women, especially young ones, found him attractive. Well, it wasn't the first time he had done it.

Just then a cab came leisurely driving down the loading ramp and stopped at the bottom. Chris quickly walked to the dock's edge, jumped down next to the cab, and got in the back. He crouched down into the back seat foot well. At the moment Chris got in, a man who had been hiding on the other side got up and sat in the seat. This startled Chris, but he assumed this was all part of Juan's plan.

From the front seat, Juan said, "This is Mando, he is my brother-in-law. Stay down and be quiet until I speak to you."

Chris felt the car backing up the ramp and turning onto the main road. He noticed Mando was quiet and looking out the window just as any passenger would; he did not look at Chris. He was dressed in an outfit that made him look like he was a maintenance man.

They drove for what seemed like five or six minutes, still at a casual pace, until the car came to a stop with the engine still idling.

"We are going to sit here for a few minutes to make sure we are not being followed." Juan spoke again from the front seat. Mando was now looking in both directions, still not paying any attention to Chris.

Chris knew not to speak or get up; he was sure they knew what they were doing. This was probably not their first time doing something like this. After a few more minutes, the car proceeded slowly again. Juan drove for a while, none of them speaking. Finally, Juan said, "You can get up now."

Chris rose and sat in the seat next to the still mute Mando, who for the first time looked at him.

Chris turned away to look out the window and saw that they were traveling down an empty two-lane highway. There were no cars in sight.

"Where would you like to go, Señor?" Juan asked, almost as a leading question.

"Can you take me to Casa de la Guerra?"

Mando then spoke for the first time, "You cannot go back there. There will be eyes on the house." He looked out the window as he spoke.

Chris felt a sense of foreboding from his comment. "What do you mean?"

"Your car that was reported as stolen? It was reported just this morning. There was a BOLO alert issued. Didn't you wonder how the police just happened to find you so quickly?" Mando turned toward Chris at this moment. "We think you are being followed, Señor."

"By whom?" Chris asked.

"We do not know," Mando said. "Tell me what you have done since Juan dropped you off yesterday."

"I had dinner at Casa de la Guerra last night, then went to bed," Chris said.

"And what about today?"

"I got up and drove into town to go to the police department."

"Shit!" Juan exclaimed from the front seat.

Mando seemed somewhat bemused at this. "You gringos," he said, "you fly into our town and you act like you are John Wayne or something. Did you speak to anyone in particular?"

"Yes," Chris said, "two different police officers, Lopez and Henderson."

"I know of Detective Henderson," Mando said. "What did you talk to them about?"

"I was inquiring about Armando Guerra's death."

"And what did they tell you?"

"That he died of natural causes."

"And do you believe them?" Mando raised an eyebrow as he asked this question.

Chris thought for a moment while looking out the window. "No."

He turned back toward Mando and asked, "So, are you telling me the police are hiding something, that they're corrupt?"

Mando made a dismissive gesture with his hand. "You speak of corruption too lightly, Señor. Sometimes there are connections, alliances—especially with powerful and influential people."

Understanding what Mando was saying, Chris replied, "If I was asking too many questions, if I was making people uncomfortable, why didn't they arrest me and say that I stole the car?"

Juan chimed in, looking at Chris in the rear-view mirror, "Because you are more vulnerable outside than inside, Señor."

"And there are too many witnesses in jail," Mando added.

Chris looked out the window for a moment, taking in what he had just heard. "So then, where are we going?"

Mando was more agreeable when he said, "We can drive you to San Antonio. You will be safe there. You can then take a plane home."

"I can't. When the police impounded the car, it had my wallet and plane ticket in there also."

"Shit!" Juan said.

"We are willing to help you, Señor, but we do not take risks for free," Mando said.

"So, you're like mercenaries?" Chris asked.

Juan laughed. "Sí, we are soldiers of fortune." He continued to laugh.

"We help many people, Señor. People are always getting into trouble." Mando was dispassionate in his speech. "If it just takes money to solve a problem, people are always willing to pay."

Chris decided Mando was the morose type, always calculating. He was the brains of their operation. Being a builder, Chris didn't mind dealing with someone looking to make a profit. *That's capitalism*, he thought.

The easiest contractors he worked with were not the ones who asked when or where or how but just how much, then they took care of the rest.

"Don't worry about the money part," Chris said. "As soon as I can get to a bank, I'll pay you."

"I believe you, Señor," Mando replied.

"How much were you going to charge me to go to San Antonio?" Chris asked.

"Fifteen hundred dollars," Mando said, unblinking.

Chris thought for just a moment. "That's fair."

"But San Antonio is not an option, is it, Señor? Where would you like to go?"

Chris looked out the window, weighing his options. Casa de la Guerra was too dangerous. In Laredo, he apparently had people looking for him, and he couldn't get a plane home or rent a car. He had no cash, no credit cards, no identification.

He thought about who he could call. The señoras? They certainly couldn't help. Eduardo? He probably couldn't do anything, and who's to say he wasn't the one who reported the car stolen anyway? His friends and family in Virginia were too far away to pick him up. They couldn't even send him money, and the only people he knew in all of Texas were the two men in the car with him and a naïve, sweet librarian.

No, that wasn't true. He *did* know someone else in Texas. However, he couldn't believe he was even contemplating that option. What in the world would be the reception? *Could he even help me?* he wondered. *What if I got there, and it was a waste of time?* Then he remembered a phrase he had once heard: "Desperate people do desperate things."

"How much to take me to Brownsville?"

"What?" Juan said. "Why go there?"

Mando, ever calculating, asked, "Do you know someone there?"

"Yes," Chris said. "If nothing else, I can get to a bank."

"Two thousand dollars," Mando said.

71

"If you get me there safely, I'll give you three thousand dollars."

Mando smiled for the first time.

Juan turned south from heading to San Antonio toward their new Brownsville destination. They drove in silence for a while, Chris thinking of what he would do once they reached Brownsville. He wasn't worried about getting the money for his newly hired saviors. He was sure he could convince a bank in Brownsville to let him call his branch in Virginia, where they knew him well.

The bank could wire him some of the thousands of dollars he had in one of his accounts. He was sure he could get his credit cards replaced, but that could take days. Getting new identification could be an issue.

Chris then realized the pulque he had drunk from the previous evening had released its final hold on him, and he was now ravenously hungry. He looked at his watch—2:30 in the afternoon.

"Can we stop to eat? I haven't had anything all day."

Juan responded, "We can stop in a little while. There is a café about twenty miles ahead. We should be safe there."

The car was silent again for a few minutes, then Chris asked Mando, "Why were you crouched down in the back seat when you came to pick me up?"

Mando, looking straight ahead while he talked, said, "We were fairly sure people were watching the library since your car was found so quickly. If they were to notice a cab entering the loading dock and leaving without a passenger, they would be suspicious and probably follow us. If it looked like an ordinary pickup and the passenger did not look like you, they would pay no attention. Juan has picked up many workers there."

"How did you know about the car being reported stolen just this morning?"

"We have relatives that work in the police department." Mando turned toward Chris, as if to emphasize his next statement, "Laredo can be very incestual. Blood supersedes all. It has been that way for generations."

Chris contemplated the last words Mando had spoken for a few moments, thinking how it also applied to the Guerras. There did seem to be a certain pride among locals when talking about the generations that existed before them. It was almost like a status symbol regarding how long one's family had been in the area.

Chris looked out onto the landscape and marveled at how flat the terrain was; it seemed to go on forever. There was a storm off in the distance, perhaps ten miles away, and the dark clouds looked more like rolling hills. They were the only thing breaking what appeared to be a limitless horizon. He could see the rain coming down in sheets, and occasionally he would see a bolt of lightning, and yet he was bathed in waves of sunshine that brilliantly illuminated all the trees and bushes. In the afternoon light, the sand almost glistened. Chris thought it was beautiful.

The cab pulled into what was the embodiment of a town that sat right in the middle of nowhere. A 1940s-style gas station with a surplus World War II Quonset hut as its garage was on one side of the highway, with an even older looking general store sitting directly across from it. The building had an old metal roof that was rusting, and the siding looked as if the sand had blasted most of the paint off years ago, the sun having now faded it into a silvery gray. Another building that was made from adobe-style bricks sat a couple of dozen yards away. It had an age-worn sign that was unreadable and appeared to be vacant. There were a couple of other buildings of undeterminable age and use set back from the road.

They parked next to the only structure that had any attendance, a cinderblock building with a generic sign outside saying "Café." It was painted a battleship gray and had a flat roof, with two old trucks and a rusted-out station wagon sitting in front.

Inside, three laborers were sitting together at one table looking like they had been baked by the sun every day. Two other men were sitting at separate tables staring into space, emotionless as they ate. Chris became aware he was the only white man in the café. Their waitress acted as if she would have preferred to be anywhere but where she was and begrudgingly took their orders.

After a few moments, Chris said, "Juan, when I was in the library and we were talking on the phone, when I mentioned the car being impounded…why did you see that as a red flag?"

"Because Señor, when I talked to you the first time in my cab, I thought there would be trouble. That's why I gave you my card."

"But you said it was out of respect for your father."

"Yes, it was. He would have wanted me to watch out for a friend of the Guerras." Juan smiled proudly at himself with this comment.

"But then, why did you think there would be trouble?"

"Because you are the kind of man that would want answers, and I figured you would want to find out what had happened to your friend."

"So, you were aware that Armando was murdered?"

Juan glanced at Mando for a split second, almost unperceptively, then said, "We hear things, rumors, gossip, myths.

75

I do not know for sure…sometimes you do not want to know." He gestured with his hands in a waving motion.

Chris contemplated his last comment for a moment while adjusting the salt and pepper shakers. "So, you figured I would go snooping around and possibly step on a few toes."

"That's what my instincts told me. You have to listen to your instincts, Señor."

Chris knew exactly what he meant.

The food arrived, and Chris thought it surprisingly good, but he was so hungry by that time he thought the sand outside would probably have tasted good. Mando didn't talk during lunch. He kept his eyes on the door, apparently concerned that something might happen to his three-thousand-dollar investment.

During lunch, Juan told the story of how his father knew the Guerras and what he used to do for them. His father had been a carpenter and helped with building structures on the property. Ironically, he was one of the men who had added the bathrooms to the casitas that Chris used that morning. Juan said his father had also helped to convert the stables into what is now the garage. He had passed away a few years ago.

Mando paid for lunch, and as they went out to the car, Chris asked him if he could have the back seat to himself. Mando shrugged indifferently and rode in the front with Juan as Chris laid down in the back trying to sleep. For a while, all he could do was stare at the stained headliner thinking about his upcoming and unexpected visit. Chris eventually closed his eyes.

Chapter 4

"What a shithole!"

Chris said, peering through the cab's rear window and looking out onto a rather unpleasant part of downtown Brownsville.

"Señor, we are here," Juan yelled from the front seat, unaware that his fare was now fully awake.

"Okay, thanks," Chris said as he looked at his watch, quite surprised that he had fallen asleep for almost two hours.

Pulque and Mexican food are kicking my ass, he thought.

Brownsville looked much older than Laredo to him. Palm trees and Spanish architecture were quite prevalent. Most of the two-story buildings had overhangs or balconies that protected the sidewalks from the relentless sun like he had seen in New Orleans. The downtown stores were right out of the 1940s and 50s, with the urban blight that had affected so many small-town business areas having ravaged here, too. Entire blocks of stores were vacant, displaying boarded-up windows, and there was the seminal signal

78

that the downtown area was dead: the local movie theater was closed.

There were some beautiful old Spanish-style buildings with historic markers in front that had become tourist attractions. It reminded Chris of a wonderful little town he had visited in Portugal years ago. It had been a wealthy fishing village but had fallen on hard times due to the changing socio-economic conditions. He did not remember its name.

"Do you know where you're going?" Chris asked Juan.

"Yes, I think so. I've been here a few times," Juan responded.

Driving for a few more minutes and passing through some more questionable areas, they turned down St. Charles Street. After a couple of blocks, the street became more of a commercial area with office buildings, hotels, and relatively upscaled restaurants and stores. They pulled up in front of a peculiar and rather out-of-place house. It was the only residential building in the area, thereby nullifying the towering skyline of the surrounding structures. It stuck out like an urban sore thumb. The house appeared to have had several additions to the original structure, with varying degrees of level and plumb. It was the only wood-sided structure that was visible, which accentuated its fragile nature amidst the concrete and brick monoliths.

There was an empty lot next door with a chain-link fence that had all but fallen over on all sides. Young boys were playing soccer in the field, dodging the clumps of weeds and broken bottles. It seemed like a picture from the 1940s, save for the adjacent buildings.

Most peculiar of all, there was a handful of people standing as if in prayer beneath a magnificent oak tree on the corner. Beneath the shade of the tree and the creeping shadows of the buildings, it was difficult to tell exactly what they were doing. Curiously, their actions seemed to be solemn and quiet.

"Are you sure this is the place?" Mando spoke up after a few moments of disbelief.

"Well, it's supposed to be," Chris said, wondering if the place was empty or even abandoned. What would he do if it was?

"Wait here," he said. "I'll be back in a minute."

Chris opened the rear car door and walked toward the house. He pushed aside an old gate that was hanging by just one hinge and walked across the uneven sidewalk. Through one of the windows, Chris could see a single light illuminated from the inside. *Somebody's here*, he thought.

As he stepped up onto the front porch, he saw several old metal chairs with badly faded paint. Beside one of the chairs was a standing ashtray that contained several dozen cigarette butts. Chris knocked on the door and waited. There was no noise from inside the house. He knocked again, this time louder. He heard the creaking of floorboards as someone slowly walked across the floor.

The door opened slightly, just enough for a voice to emanate. "I don't rent rooms anymore," said a disembodied voice, the door starting to close.

"I'm not here for a room," responded Chris in a rather urgent voice.

The door paused from closing entirely as Chris saw someone peer from behind the Venetian blinds that were attached to its upper section. It then began to open again, very slowly but farther this time.

In front of Chris stood someone of smaller frame than himself who looked a good thirty years older. He was not as tall; however, with the front porch being a few inches below the floor of the house, they stood eye to eye. Standing behind the shimmering of the silver screen in the door, and poorly illuminated by the light, the figure appeared faded, almost like an apparition.

"To what do I owe this inauspicious visit? Are your sisters and mother alright?" the shadow spoke through the screen.

"Yes, they're fine. That's not why I'm here." Chris paused for a moment, wondering how to explain his situation and, moreover, how to ask for help.

"Perhaps your visit has to do with your two friends in the cab?" the older man said before Chris could continue.

Surprised by his awareness, Chris spoke as he turned around to acknowledge Juan and Mando. "Yes, they brought me here..." He noticed they were no longer sitting in the car.

"They're over at the tree," he said to Chris. "The one on the corner. Come, I'll show you."

He opened the door and carefully stepped out onto the porch, the cautious steps of an elderly man. He seemed more frail when not blurred by the gauze-like filter of the screen. Holding onto the handrail, he walked down the three steps to the ground and gently stepped across the broken pieces of sidewalk, heaved and cracked by the years of expanding roots from the oak tree. He was not the same man Chris had seen just a few years ago, seeming to have aged twice as much in the time that had gone by.

Approaching the now heavily shaded tree in the advancing darkness, hurried by the tall buildings that towered above them, Chris saw that Juan and Mando were standing in complete silence before it, heads bowed as if in prayer. Under it were dozens of crosses ranging from a couple of inches tall to a few that were staked into the ground and measured two to three feet. At its broad base, over eight feet in diameter, were a myriad of pictures, flowers, and rosary beads.

Before Chris could ask about the reason for such an outpouring of colorful homage, his host turned to him and gestured to a place on the tree about ten feet from the ground, facing outward from the corner of the property.

"Look," he said, continuing to point to the spot.

When Chris looked up, he saw perhaps the most bizarre and unexpected thing he had ever witnessed. There, in the bark of the tree, as if some skilled craftsman had taken days to carve but had clearly grown naturally, was the unmistakable image of the Virgin Mary. Chris stood there in awe for a few seconds, staring at this amazing image.

It was then that Juan and Mando noticed them. They were quite reverent in their demeanor, Juan almost in tears. Chris, taken aback for a moment by these events, gathered himself enough to introduce everyone.

"Juan, Mando, I would like to introduce you to..." Chris stumbled for a second, mentally grasping for the appropriate words, since in his forty-two years of life he had never uttered them before, "…my father."

Chris was further dismayed by the enthusiasm with which Juan and Mando greeted him.

"Señor," Juan enthusiastically said, "I have heard of this most amazing thing! I thought it was a myth, but it is real!"

Mando uncharacteristically smiled and shook his hand. "Pleased to meet you, Señor. It is an honor."

"Please," Chris's father graciously said, "call me Michael."

Juan continued, "My cousin said he had visited here a few months ago. He told me how beautiful it was, but I thought he was loco! He said he had prayed for his wife to get pregnant. They had been trying for two years."

"So, what happened?" Michael asked.

"Oh, they are still trying, but she is trying more often now!" Juan burst into raucous laughter, then said, "That is a miracle in itself!" His laughter got even louder now, proud of his clever joke.

Chris looked at his watch and turned to Mando. "Obviously, we'll have to wait until morning to get your money."

Mando responded, "I knew that when we left the café. Juan and I have a relative who lives just outside of town, and we wish to visit them while we are here. It has been some time since we have seen them. We shall return in the morning at 9."

"Can you trust me until then?" Chris asked.

"Obviously, you and your father are men of integrity. You would not sacrifice something so valuable for something like money. Goodnight, señors."

Juan and Mando walked to the car and drove away.

As Chris and Michael watched them leave, Michael asked Chris, "How much do you owe them?"

"Three thousand dollars."

"That's an expensive cab ride."

"Apparently, I'm in a little trouble. They're more like hired mercenaries," Chris explained.

"That was smart. There's nothing more reliable than a man whose loyalty can be bought."

Michael started to walk toward the house, saying, "Come, let's sit down."

They walked back through the one-hinged gate and across the remaining pieces of sidewalk to where Michael gestured for Chris to sit down on one of the metal chairs on the front porch. "I'll be back in a minute," he said.

Chris sat in one of the chairs which felt somewhat unstable to him, as if the bolts that were holding it together could break loose at any moment. The kids' raucous soccer game next door was over, and there was little traffic on the downtown roads now; the frantic after-work exodus was over as well. An occasional service vehicle or late-night worker would drive by, but the streets were for the most part eerily quiet. It seemed a solemn time to sit on your out-of-place front porch and reflect on the events of the day. He thought this to be an appropriate setting to have the first one-on-one conversation with his father, albeit one born of such desperation.

Michael returned holding a pack of Camel cigarettes and a lighter in his hand. He sat on the chair where the almost full ashtray was, three chairs away from Chris's. Michael took out a cigarette and lit it with an old Zippo-style lighter. There was an insignia on the side of the lighter that had long ago become unreadable. Chris wondered how many packs Michael had gone through sitting on this front porch.

"So, what kind of trouble are you in?" Michael started.

"Well, I'm not really sure, to be honest. It appears I have pissed off some people while visiting a friend in Laredo."

"Okay, but there's more to the story than that. Why do you not have any money?"

Chris wondered how much to reveal. Would it offend Michael that he had come all this way to visit a deceased friend and yet had never taken the time to visit him?

"The car I was driving was impounded by the police, and my wallet was in the vehicle when it was towed."

"There must have been a reason they didn't let you take your wallet," Michael observed.

"The police said I could not be arrested since I wasn't driving. However, I couldn't take anything out of the car. One of the cab drivers said it was because they wanted me out on the streets."

"You have done more than piss someone off then. You must have scared them. That can be a dangerous thing if they are powerful enough. Why is your friend not helping you?"

Chris was concerned that this would be a contentious point, but he also figured this was not the time for lying.

"He's dead," he said. Chris noticed a look of concern on Michael's face and felt the need to further explain.

"He passed away a few weeks ago. I was here to pay my respects and to find out what had happened to him since there was so little information given to me."

"He must have been a good friend for you to have traveled so far," Michael replied.

Chris thought he sensed a tone of sorrow in Michael's comment. He was not sure if it was for the passing of his friend or if he was thinking about himself.

"He was a good man, and yes, a good friend," Chris responded.

Michael looked out into the yard for a moment as he took another drag of his cigarette, pondering what to ask next.

"Are these people chasing you?"

"No, I don't believe so. Mando doesn't think they followed us. I'm pretty sure they don't know where I am."

"So, you're safe here?" Michael said rhetorically. "That's good, that helps. And you have no cash, no identification, correct?"

"Yes, that's right."

Michael thought for a few moments and said, "You were wise not to go to the police station to try to get your belongings back."

"That's what Mando said, too. How do you know that?"

Michael just turned and gave a knowing smile. "I've seen these sorts of things for years. You were being pulled into a trap. There would have been people watching you or watching the police station, or more likely..." Michael paused for a second as if to underscore the impact of his comment, "the police are in on it."

88

Chris knew what he said was probably true, but he was also impressed that Michael was sharp enough to come to that conclusion.

"Do you know anyone at a bank?" Chris asked. "If I can get to one, I can at least get some cash and new credit cards."

Michael stared through the haze of smoke and, using the remains of the cigarette as if it was a pointer, directed it toward a building across the street.

"The Bank of Brownsville," Michael said. "I've known the president for years. I'll introduce you to him in the morning."

Chris was somewhat bemused with himself that he had been looking at the building, had even stood thirty feet from its front door when he was talking near the tree, and yet had never noticed it in the sea of surrounding structures.

"Thanks," he said. "That will help. At least I can pay off my saviors."

"Are you sure you can get money without identification?" Michael asked.

"I have a relationship with the people at my bank in Virginia. If I can get someone on the phone who knows me, they'll send me some money."

"But you still won't have any identification, will you?"

"No, that's going to be tricky. I can't go to the DMV without a birth certificate, passport...something."

Michael lit another cigarette and looked toward the oak tree on the corner, apparently contemplating what to say, as if he was about to divulge a secret.

"I know someone who can help you." He continued to stare at the tree.

"What do you mean? Someone in the government?" Chris asked.

Turning back toward Chris, Michael said, "You're in a border town. It's not like other towns throughout the United States where everything is done by the book." Michael gestured with his hand that was holding the cigarette, the glowing end leaving a trail of light like a firefly darting about in the darkness.

Chris wanted to believe him, since at this point there was no reason to doubt what he was saying, so he decided to wait and see.

Michael asked, "When did you discover your friend had been murdered?"

Chris was taken aback by this leap forward in the conversation and really didn't know how to react but said, "What do you mean? How did you know?"

"You told me," Michael responded.

"When, when did I tell you?"

Michael laughed with the unmistakable laugh that came from years of smoking. "Not by what you said, but by what you did. You see, if you knew he had been murdered before you went there, you would have called around from Virginia. You would have been more methodical about things before you left. Perhaps you would have contacted the police or hired someone to investigate if you didn't get satisfactory answers. So, you must have found out after you arrived.

"Then you clumsily went around trying to find out what had happened. That's an emotional reaction. If your friend had simply died of natural causes, you never would have reacted the way you did, and you wouldn't have created the situation you're in now."

Chris was impressed with his logic. What he said made perfect sense, and yes, Chris was in a "situation."

"And I'll tell you something else I know about you," Michael said, pointing his cigarette at Chris this time. "You're not going to let this go, are you?"

"I can't. I could never live with myself if I didn't find out what happened," Chris said, looking down at the old porch flooring.

"Is it worth getting killed for?" Michael asked while snuffing out the last remnants of his cigarette.

91

"Do you think that's a possibility?" Chris asked in a cautious tone.

"I'm not sure about that. I don't know enough about it yet. Maybe they're just trying to scare you or get you to go home sooner."

"I was supposed to go home tomorrow," Chris replied.

"Did they know that?"

"I don't know." Chris let his response linger in the air for a moment, then posed a more pressing question. "Can you let me stay for the night?"

"You said you weren't here for a room." Michael laughed hard at his comment, causing him to cough several times. After catching his breath, he rose slowly from his chair. The laughing and coughing seemed to take a good amount of energy from him. "Come on in," he said.

Chris walked into what would have been the sitting room for that era of house. It was full of old and worn furniture that looked as if no one had sat on them in a while. There was just the one light next to a reclining chair where Michael had been sitting while reading. The room smelled musty and was untidy, as if no one cared how it appeared.

There was a darkened hallway just to the right that was dimly lit from the outside light of other buildings, beckoning ominously. On the far side of the room was a desk piled with stacks of mail, letters, and unread newspapers. The floor squeaked vociferously as Michael walked across it, as if it might implode from the slightest pressure. The house was ripe with decay, showing obvious signs that no one had maintained it for a long time.

"I need to make a phone call," Chris said.

Michael walked to the desk and turned on a green lamp; it cast an eerie shadow on the walls and ceiling. There was cracked plaster and peeling paint everywhere. Michael picked up an old black phone buried beneath the newspapers and placed it in the middle of the desk. Chris went over to the phone and sat in the wood chair that creaked as he sat down. The phone had a rotary dial and looked like it was from the 1940s. He remembered the phone number he was calling, having a photographic memory for numbers. He could picture the piece of paper he had written it on back home in Virginia. As he dialed, he saw Michael turn on a light and walk toward what appeared to be the kitchen in the back of the house.

Chris called out, "I may need your help with this call." Michael turned around and retraced his steps.

When the phone rang, Chris recalled the sound from when he had called after Chico had passed, when he was desperately trying to find out what had happened. It was an odd ring, an old ring, like a woodpecker pecking against a metal shed. It had a forlorn sound to it. Chris was surprised when someone answered, but not at all surprised when the person spoke in an unintelligible Spanish accent.

Chris handed the phone to Michael and said, "Ask to speak to Eduardo."

Michael took the phone and, after a few seconds, asked in perfect Spanish if they could be so kind as to bring Eduardo to the phone. Chris knew full well that Michael spoke fluent Spanish, having lived in Brownsville most of his life. Chris understood Spanish but had great difficulty speaking the language.

Michael handed the receiver back to Chris and said, "He'll be here in a minute." Michael then continued his trip back to the kitchen.

There was silence on the phone, then after a minute or so, Chris heard the unmistakable light and quick footsteps announcing Eduardo.

"Hola, puedo ayudarlo?" he said.

"Eduardo, it's Chris."

94

"Señor Chris!" His voice was even more dramatic than normal. "We have been very worried about you. Luis said you borrowed the car this morning. It has been a long time since you've been gone, and we were concerned."

"I'm fine, Eduardo. I appreciate you worrying about me. I drove the car today to go see the police." There was a long pause on the phone.

"Eduardo?"

"The police? Señor, why would you do that?" Eduardo said. There was an ominous tone to his voice, then, as if to cover his dismay, he said, "The police are idiots. They know nothing. Please do not bother them."

"Thank you," Chris said, "but it may be too late for such advice."

"What do you mean, Señor?"

"Eduardo, have you or anyone you know reported the car stolen?"

"Stolen? Why would we do that?"

"The car was impounded by the police today. They said it had been reported as stolen."

Eduardo's tone changed again. "Señor, I beg you, do not involve yourself in these matters. You have no idea what you are getting into."

"Thank you, Eduardo, but I'm already involved."

"Señor." There was a pleading tone to his voice.

"I'll call you back in a couple of days."

Eduardo then asked, "Where are you staying, Señor?"

Chris paused for a moment, thinking of multiple scenarios and several appropriate answers.

"Out of town," he answered and hung up the phone.

Turning to Michael, he asked, "Is there a place I can sleep? I've had a long day."

Michael walked him down the darkened hallway, flipping on a light switch with a heavy click.

He opened one of the doors and turned on the overhead light that was excessively bright, since it had no shade on it; just a bare bulb in the socket. In the room was a twin-size bed with a crooked night table and a single chair orphaned from a long-lost dining room set. The bed was made and there was a small lamp on the nightstand.

"The bathroom is at the end of the hall. I'll see you in the morning," Michael said and closed the door.

Chris reached over to turn on the lamp, then turned off the beacon that was in the ceiling. He laid down on the bed, draping one arm over his forehead, and kicked off his shoes. He mused over how odd it was to be lying on a bed in his father's house...as ramshackle as it was.

He then thought how accommodating Michael had been, how he had listened to him when he knew he was in trouble, and how clever he had been in deciphering the sequence of events.

And then, for the second time that day, Chris closed his eyes and slept.

Chapter 5

"Damn! I hate the city!"

Chris said to himself as he heard the repeated banging of a garbage truck outside his window. *Why does the loudest vehicle on the road always start so early in the morning?* he thought.

He looked at his watch, which was still on his arm. He had not removed it before he fell asleep last night. "6:30," he said. It was a good hour later than he would usually rise, but then he remembered the time difference. "Can't fool Mother Nature," he said and laughed out loud at himself as he stretched.

Chris reached over to the uneven nightstand and turned off the lamp that had burned throughout the night. He had only been gone a couple of days, but he already missed his house in the rolling horse country of Manakin-Sabot, Virginia. The twenty acres where he lived was his true "Fortress of Solitude," always peaceful and welcoming. Even more than his home, he missed his dog. Somehow, Chris felt if his Aussie, Mick, was with him, he could help him figure things out. There was always a sense of comfort and contentment when his dog was at his side.

He sat up on the edge of the bed for a moment, thinking about what he had to accomplish that day. At the top of that list was his need to have three thousand dollars in his hands shortly after nine o'clock. He didn't think Juan and Mando were dangerous, but they wouldn't be happy coming all the way here and leaving empty-handed. Chris knew all too well how money can keep the peace.

He looked down at his shoes, which had been unceremoniously dumped onto the floor last night and were still lying on their sides.

"Clothes," he moaned. "Ugh, I don't have any clothes." Chris held his head in his hands, knowing how much he hated clothes shopping, but he mentally added that task to his to-do list.

He put on his shoes, then opened the door and walked down the hall to the bathroom. There were several steps that led up to the bathroom door, which seemed odd, and they were painted an unattractive chocolate brown. As he walked up the steps and turned the rust-stained doorknob, he got a shiver and a feeling of déjà vu. Chris stopped in the open doorway and wondered how that was possible. He had felt this only once in his life, a long time ago, and he had never been in this house before.

Shutting the door, he noticed the handle was loose and that he might not be able to open it again. He left the door ajar. There was a small hand towel hanging next to the sink. It looked like it had been recently placed there. Chris turned the faucet handles, and they squeaked in protest. He washed his face, used the heavily stained toilet that flushed at a sluggish pace, and went back down the steps. The house did not seem quite as dilapidated with the morning sun streaming through the windows, but it still felt empty and unloved, accentuated by the perpetual groaning of the floorboards.

Walking into the sitting room, he could see a couple of people outside standing in front of the tree. He watched them as they bowed their heads and prayed in unison, then silently crossed themselves before slowly turning away. Chris then heard some banging of metal coming from down the hallway that led to the kitchen. He followed the noise and, as he entered, saw Michael standing at a small gas stove busily cooking.

Michael turned, obviously hearing him walking down the noisy hallway, and asked, "Are you hungry?"

The kitchen was fully circa 1940s, with old linoleum flooring that had yellow and green flowers and a white porcelain-covered sink and countertop. The cabinets had several coats of paint on

100

them, with multiple chips and scratches displaying various colors beneath. There was an aqua-colored refrigerator that proudly displayed a large chrome badge with "NORGE" emblazoned across the front. An unused fireplace was on the far side of the kitchen that appeared to have had the hearth opening closed up many years ago with a different style of brick. The center of the room was occupied by a red and chrome dining table with four worn-out chairs. A grease-stained ceiling showed years of accumulation.

The aromatic scent of fried meat was in the air, and the sizzling sound from the pan atop the stove emphasized the savory smell.

"Sure," Chris responded, enthusiastically seating himself down at one of the table's place settings.

"You can have anything you want," Michael, sounding cheerful, said. "As long as it's what I'm cooking." He chuckled to himself.

"Whatever you're making is fine, as long as there's no pulque in it."

"Holy crap, who gave you pulque?" Michael asked, showing surprise that Chris even knew what it was.

"The man I spoke to on the phone last night," Chris said, gesturing down the hall. "He was celebrating with me as his newfound brother." Michael regretted saying this the second it came out.

"Well," Michael said, as he pondered the information, "I have had a few lady friends in these parts over the years, so it's entirely possible!" He then proceeded to laugh hard enough to induce another coughing spell.

Chris was relieved he had not taken the comment personally but was more concerned about Michael's bad cough. "Have you seen a doctor about your cough?"

"Yes," Michael responded, "and he has seen me." He then placed some scrambled eggs and a few strips of bacon onto Chris's plate. "I was thinking about your situation last night and what's happened. Don't worry, we'll figure it out. I've been in worse situations."

"I came here for a couple of days just to get some closure from a friend's passing," Chris said as he started eating, "And now, apparently, I have people after me, and I have no money or identification. I'm not off to a very good start with my plans to find the killer, am I?"

"Yes, that's all true," Michael said, sitting down in a chair across from him while lighting a cigarette. He continued, "But let's take a minute and look at what you've done so far that's good and

102

what assets you have to work with. You went to Laredo to pay respects to someone you cared about, which says a lot for you. Then you found out he was murdered, at least allegedly, but you didn't shrug your shoulders and go home. You did what a man is supposed to do and tried to find out what happened to him. That says a lot for you, too. Then, when you found yourself in some shit, you didn't panic. You kept your head and found a way to safety. A lesser man would have called it quits."

"I guess," Chris responded. "Perhaps I got a little lucky."

"Isn't it funny how smart people seem to have a lot of luck? It's more than a coincidence. So, where are you now?" Michael asked while playing with a gold glass ashtray on the table.

Feeling like a student being given a quiz by a teacher, Chris said, "Well, I'll have access to money. Hopefully, in a couple of hours."

"Yes, money seems to help almost every situation, doesn't it?" Michael chuckled. "What else do you have at your disposal right now?"

Chris said, "I was fortunate enough to know someone who could give me a room for the night." Chris found himself laughing for the first time in a couple of days.

"Yes, and that says a lot for you, too. I'm sure it wasn't easy showing up here, was it?"

"No," Chris said, looking at Michael as he spoke. "Honestly, I didn't know what kind of reception I would get."

"And what kind did you get?"

Chris thought for just a second, trying to be as honest as possible, then answered, "Better than I expected."

Michael stood up and took Chris's now empty plate to the sink. Chris thought he perceived an emotional reaction from his last comment but couldn't be sure.

It occurred to him that of all the strange things he had been through during the last two days—going to Casa de la Guerra to see Chico's grave and then, while drinking pulque with Eduardo, finding out that his friend had been murdered; going to the police station, then the library; the car being towed; and his impromptu trip here with his two rescuers—sitting in an old kitchen while being served breakfast and having a conversation with his father was by far the strangest.

"So," Michael said upon returning from depositing the plates in the porcelain sink, "we know what we have to work with. What do you want to do now?"

104

"Like I said yesterday, I want to find out what happened to Chico. If he was indeed murdered, I want to find the murderer."

"Okay, so you've thought about it and still want to do this. You're sure it's not just an emotional reaction?"

Chris, resolute in his look and tone, said, "No, it is not."

"Then how do we start?" Michael asked, sitting down and lighting another cigarette.

"I haven't quite got that far yet. Saving my own ass was my first priority." Chris paused for a moment and looked at Michael. "You have a suggestion, don't you?"

"Yes, I do," Michael said with a wry smile.

"You seem to understand it all so well, go on," Chris said, gesturing for him to continue.

"Your friends who brought you here, they seem to be profiteers. Do they have any connections in Laredo?"

"They said they had relatives in the police department, but I'm sure they have other sources also. From what they told me, they often deal with things like this."

"Good," Michael said, seemingly pleased. "Are you willing to pay them for information?"

"Yes, absolutely!" Chris said.

"If this had happened in Brownsville, I know many people who could help us. But I would be lost in Laredo. I wouldn't even know where to start," Michael said, shrugging.

"Are you suggesting I pay Juan and Mando for some recon work before we do anything else?" Chris asked.

"I can ask a few people I know here to put out some feelers, but I think that's the best place to start," Michael said, pointing at Chris.

"How much do you think they'll ask?" Chris was apprehensive about this statement. He already owed them three thousand dollars.

"Like with all things, it's supply and demand. It also depends on how difficult the information is to obtain and how much danger they'll put themselves in. If it's just a phone call for a name, a few hundred dollars. If it's difficult and very dangerous to ask questions about the matter, and you want who, what, when, where, and why…well, sometimes even money doesn't work." Michael emphasized this statement by extinguishing his cigarette in the ashtray.

"Okay," Chris said. "Let's talk to them after I pay them this morning. Once I put three thousand dollars in their hands, they may realize there's more where that came from."

"My thoughts exactly," Michael said, smiling in agreement.

Chris helped Michael clean up the kitchen from the morning's breakfast, then they walked out onto the front porch and sat down in the same chairs from the previous evening. Michael took out another cigarette and lit it with his old lighter as he looked out at the few people in front of the tree in prayer. Chris watched a car come to a halt on the corner as someone leaned out of the window to take a picture.

"When did this image appear?" Chris asked curiously.

"About six months ago, I saw a couple of men standing on the corner and pointing at the tree. I thought they were looking up at a bird or squirrel, but after a few minutes, others gathered around. I went out to see what they were looking at, and there was the image of the Virgin Mary. It's more prominent now, but it was definitely recognizable from the beginning. It's given me a new kind of status in this town," Michael said with a laugh.

"What kind of status is that?" Chris asked.

"I went from being the old man in the creepy old boarding house to being the enigmatic 'Holy Man.' Religion is a powerful force in this area. It has granted me different latitudes in this town, above and beyond the ones that I had been given through simple longevity alone.

"Your friends are indeed reliable," Michael continued, pointing to the street just as "Juan's Taxicab" pulled up. Chris looked at his watch. It was 8:57 a.m.

Chris walked out to the cab as Michael took a moment to extinguish his cigarette and then followed.

"Morning, gentlemen," Chris greeted them. "We're just about to go to the bank."

"Which bank are we going to?" Mando asked, a sense of urgency in his voice. Chris was aware of his use of "we," not "you."

Chris motioned with his finger over the top of the cab at the Bank of Brownsville, directly across the street.

"How convenient," Mando said.

Michael approached from behind Chris and, hearing the exchange, tried to reassure them by saying, "We shouldn't be too long, gentlemen. I know the president."

Michael and Chris crossed the street and walked up to the bank just as a young woman was unlocking the front door.

"Morning, Graciella. Is Herman in this morning?" Michael asked.

"Good morning, Mr. Hamilton. Give me just a moment, and I will let him know you are here."

Chris was not surprised Michael knew her by name. He was sure he visited the bank often. As they entered the building, Chris saw the interior was impressive while still being austere. There were tall granite columns with a poured terrazzo floor and heavy wooden partition walls with golden gates over the tellers' stations that were certainly more for decoration than protection. There were wooden desks on one side of the room facing the street for more personal transactions. A set of curving marble stairs led up to the rarefied air where the executives and wealthier customers transacted business. The ceilings were absurdly high and adorned with deeply stamped tin tiles. The sounds of business being conducted echoed off the polished structures. It was like a modern-day urban-styled temple. Chris had noticed the cornerstone upon entering: Erected 1929.

Graciella descended the grand staircase with her hand delicately holding the ornate wooden railing. As she approached the men, Chris observed that she had an elegant walk and an air of professionalism, both in attire and demeanor. *A nice-looking woman*, he thought.

"Mr. Montgomery said you may go up to his office," she said before she escorted them across the room and motioned them up the stairs.

The men walked down the hall toward the front of the bank. In the corner office sat the definitive bank manager—gray three-piece suit, round gold spectacles, and thinning gray hair. He looked like he was in his mid-sixties and wore a serious look on his face. Surprisingly, when the manager looked up and saw Michael, his facial expression completely changed, as if some instant metamorphosis had taken place.

"Michael, it's good to see you! How are you?" he said, rising from behind the rather large and intimidating oak desk. He approached them, continuing to smile, right hand extended.

"Herman, I'm doing fine." They shook hands in the manner that old friends shake hands in a formal setting, more for appearances than anything else.

Michael turned toward Chris and, motioning with his left hand, said, "I'd like you to meet my son, Chris."

As strange as Chris felt about the introduction, Herman was genuinely taken aback. "Your son!" he said, staring at Chris in astonishment.

"Nice to meet you, sir," Chris said as he shook his hand.

"So," Herman continued, having regained his banker's composure, "you are the famous baseball player?"

"Well, not so famous. But yes, I was a baseball player, sir."

"Around here, every baseball player is famous, at least to his father." Herman let out a huge laugh at his own joke, followed by Michael, showing the type of humor only two men who had shared a lot would understand. Michael stifled his cough as best he could.

"Come, sit down." Herman gestured toward two green leather wingback chairs in front of his desk as he walked back to his own chair.

"Herman, Chris has a bit of a problem, and we're hoping you can help," Michael said.

"Of course!" Herman responded. "What can I do for my friend's son?" He sat, ready at his desk, clasping his hands.

"Well, Mr. Montgomery," Chris started, "I was in Laredo and lost my wallet, so I need to call a Bank of America in Virginia and have them wire me some funds and send me new credit cards."

"That is no problem. Do you know someone at the bank?"

"Yes, I know several people. If I can get someone to find the number, I'll call them and make the arrangements."

"Excellent," Herman said. "Go back downstairs. I'll call Graciella and have her assist you. You should have your money in a very short time." He picked up the phone and started dialing.

"Thank you," Chris said.

Chris walked back down the stairs, leaving the two friends to talk. By the time he reached her desk, Herman had called Graciella, and she had the phone number ready for Chris when he sat down. He used her phone to place the call.

Someone Chris didn't know picked up the phone on the second ring, so Chris asked to be transferred to Scott Gaeser.

"Hello, Scott Gaeser," he said as he answered.

"Scott, good morning. This is Chris Hamilton."

"Hi, Chris. What can I do for you today?"

"Scott, I'm in Brownsville, Texas, at the Bank of Brownsville. I've lost my wallet with all my cash and credit cards, and I need you to wire me some cash to this bank and order me new credit cards."

"Sure, Chris, I can do that. It's Friday, so the cards will take a few days. How much cash do you want me to wire you?"

"Ten thousand dollars. See what you can do to expedite the cards. I'll pay to have them sent Federal Express."

"Okay," Scott said. "I'll transfer the money from your business checking account and see how quickly I can get the cards to you. I'll need a routing number to the bank."

Turning to Graciella, Chris said, "Can you give Scott your bank's routing number and address?"

112

"Yes, of course, sir," she said.

"Scott, I'm going to hand the phone to Graciella, and she can give you all the information. Send the cards here to the bank. It's right across the street from where I'm staying."

"Will do, Chris."

"Thanks," Chris said. He handed the phone to Graciella and sat looking out the window onto the street while she gave Scott all the necessary information.

Chris saw that Juan was standing outside the car smoking a cigarette while Mando was watching the people who were praying in front of the tree.

Graciella hung up the phone and said to Chris, "He's transferring the money now. How would you like it divided up, sir?"

"All in hundreds. Can you put three thousand in one envelope and seven in another?"

"Yes, sir."

"Thank you for your help, and please call me Chris," he said, thinking she made him feel old when she addressed him as "sir."

"Okay, Chris," she said, breaking her business face for the first time and smiling.

"I'm going back to Mr. Montgomery's office. Can you bring it up there?"

"Sure, Chris," she said, continuing to smile.

Chris ascended the lavish stairs again and walked back into Herman Montgomery's office as the two men were still talking. He then realized that Herman's office was at the front of the building, which allowed him to look directly out at the tree and Michael's front porch.

Looking up, Herman asked, "How did it go?"

"Fine, thank you. Graciella was a big help. She said she would bring the money up here."

"Excellent," Herman replied. "I'm delighted we could help you. Your father tells me you're visiting for a few days?"

"Yes, Mr. Montgomery, but I'm not sure how long at this point."

"Please, call me Herman. Your father and I have known each other for over thirty years," he said, holding up his hands in protest.

"Okay, Herman, thank you. By the way, I am having my new credit cards sent here. Can someone call, uh…my father when they arrive?" Chris hoped his verbal stumble was not too noticeable.

"Yes, of course," Herman said. "Where are you going to take your son while he's here, Michael?"

"We haven't made any plans yet," Michael said, looking at Chris. "He sort of showed up unannounced on my porch last night." Michael and Herman vigorously laughed at this comment, apparently sharing some inside joke like old friends do.

Graciella, displaying good timing and professionalism, walked in the door at that moment. She was carrying two light brown colored envelopes, one slightly thicker than the other, and she handed them to Chris.

"Is there anything else we can do for you…Chris?" She seemed to purposely pause before saying his name.

"No, and thank you again, Graciella," Chris said, then, turning to Herman, he asked, "How much do I owe you for the transaction today?"

Herman quickly spoke up, saying, "I told Graciella not to charge you. Our bank has a policy that allows customers' children to transfer up to ten thousand dollars for free…but only once every thirty years!"

Michael, Graciella, and Herman all broke into peals of laughter, Herman laughing the hardest at his joke. Chris also found it humorous but thought it spoke volumes about the relationship between the two men.

Standing up, Chris walked to the desk and shook Herman's hand, saying, "Thank you for your help, sir. It was an honor to meet you."

"It was a pleasure to meet my old friend's son finally. Please visit again before you leave our city."

Michael and Herman exchanged knowing nods as they exited the office. Graciella escorted the two men down the stairs and walked them to the door. Just before they left, she said, "I'll call you when your credit cards arrive...Chris," again pausing briefly before saying his name.

"Thank you," Chris said while sensing a certain tone in her voice. *I'm killing it with librarians and bankers in Texas,* he thought. He laughed at himself. Perhaps he was reading more into it than there was.

Michael and Chris walked across the street toward the cab. Mando was now tenuously leaning against a section of the fence next to the gate. Chris saw Juan had noticed that he was holding two brown envelopes in his hands. He dropped his cigarette, stepped on it, and approached.

"Who gets it?" Chris asked, holding out the smaller of the two envelopes while stuffing the other in his back pocket.

Mando stuck out his hand, saying, "I'll take that, Señor, thank you."

Chris took the opportunity to address what he and Michael had discussed over breakfast.

"Would you guys be interested in doing a little investigative work when you return to Laredo?"

Mando spoke up first, "What do you want to know?"

Chris sensed Mando had seen this opportunity coming. "See if you can find out anything about Armando Guerra's death."

Juan quickly joined the conversation, saying, "That could be dangerous to our health, Señor! We live in Laredo, and as you have seen, some people don't want anyone snooping around trying to find out what happened to him."

"I don't want you to get yourselves into trouble," Chris replied, "but you said you have connections in the police department, and you've already said you have heard some things."

"Señor," Mando started, "you are safe here, you now have money, and you are with your father. Enjoy yourself here for a few days, and then have a safe flight back home."

Michael, strategically weighing in, said, "We are willing to pay. Perhaps you can start with a name. That shouldn't be too dangerous."

"How much?" Mando shot back.

Michael continued, "Two thousand dollars for the name. Anything beyond that, and we can negotiate."

Mando said, "Excuse us for just a minute, Señor." Mando walked Juan down the fence line in the opposite direction of the tree.

Michael turned to Chris and whispered, "They'll do it. My guess is they already know something, they're just negotiating with us, pretending to be scared...probably."

"Do you think they really could put themselves in danger?" Chris asked.

"Yes," Michael whispered back.

Mando returned with Juan in tow. "Señors, we will try to get you a name for two thousand dollars. If we can get any more information, we will discuss it then. How can we contact you?"

Michael said, "Let me give you my phone number," then walked toward the cab, followed by Juan and Mando. Juan wrote down Michael's phone number on a pad he had in the car and gave Michael one of his business cards. Chris and Michael walked toward the house. As they did, Chris noticed Mando and Juan went back to the tree, where they bowed their heads and prayed briefly. He hoped what he asked them to do was not going to be dangerous, but he had to start somewhere, and they were his best bet, at least for now. As they reached the chairs on the front porch, the cab slowly left. Michael picked up his pack of Camels sitting down and pulled his lighter out of his pocket, lighting a cigarette with just one flick of the spark wheel.

"Did you notice they never counted the money?" Chris asked.

"It's the tree," Michael said, putting his lighter back into his pocket. "You should never underestimate the power of religion."

"Perhaps," Chris responded. "Do you really think it influences people in their everyday decision-making?"

"It's a powerful tool that has held sway over civilizations for centuries. Perception is reality."

"So, you think they trust us because of the tree?"

After taking a drag on his cigarette, Michael said, "I think they were dubious about looking into the matter any further, but now they believe they have faith on their side."

"But you said you think they already know something."

"Yes, I think they do. If they knew nothing, they would probably not be scared. But I think they have heard something,

119

either real or just a rumor. They are going to be very cautious in their approach."

"Do you think they'll get the name?" Chris asked.

Michael took another long drag on his cigarette, staring straight ahead. "I don't know. We'll have to give it a couple of days. Meanwhile, we have only solved one of your problems, haven't we?"

"Yes," Chris agreed. "I still need to get identification."

"Yes...our next Herculean task."

Chapter 6

"Oh My God!"

It was the fourth time Chris had said those words in the last thirty minutes. Not one prone to hyperbole, he was simply reacting to the situation.

The first time was when Michael showed him the vehicle they were going to drive. It was a 1979 Datsun pickup truck with almost every body panel dented, the last remnants of the silver paint barely discernible. It had severely worn tires, sagging seats that were beyond threadbare, and no windshield wipers. Chris also noticed the inspection sticker was expired. As Michael pulled it out of what was once a toolshed, he proudly proclaimed, "It don't look like much, but it's reliable as hell!"

The second time was during the short drive to their destination: Michael briefly told Chris about the man they were going to meet.

"He's my best and most reliable friend. I'd trust him with my life. Don't let his gregarious disposition fool you—he's as strong as

121

a bear and just as formidable. I once saw him kill a man with his bare hands."

The third time happened after pulling into the parking lot behind a giant department store with a sign reading "Garcia's!" The script incorporated small hand-painted sombreros in the letters. Chris verbally reacted as they entered the store as his senses were assaulted by the sight of mountains of tchotchkes.

From wall to wall and from floor to ceiling, every tacky, cheap piece of tourist crap was on display: t-shirts, bobble-headed animals, silk flowers, cheesy clothing, toys, fireworks, carved wooden figures, chocolates and candy, pottery, alcohol, blankets, salsa-by-the-gallon, and "authentic" Indian jewelry. Tejano music blasted from invisible speakers.

The fourth "Oh my God!" was perhaps his most heartfelt, emanating from him as he stood in front of a life-sized painting. Chris and Michael had been looking for the owner, who could possibly have been buried beneath the mountains of clothing or stuffed animals, when Chris's eyes were drawn to it, hanging next to the women's dressing room. In the painting was one of the sexiest, most alluring women Chris had ever seen. She was a young Latina girl in her late teens, wearing a white blouse with a peasant skirt that was striped in the red, green, and white colors of the

Mexican flag. She was barefoot, casually walking through a field with a basket of colorful flowers, her black hair flowing past her shoulders and down her back. There was nothing salacious about the painting, and very little skin was exposed, but Chris was mesmerized. He decided the model was either stunningly beautiful or the artist very talented.

After a few minutes of being separated from Michael, and not able to see over more than an aisle or two due to the amount of crap piled upon crap, Chris heard Michael calling his name. Attempting to locate the source, he navigated the walls of made-in-China, sold-by-Mexicans-to-American-tourists trinkets and knickknacks.

After finally discovering Michael, Chris saw him standing beside a fire hydrant of a man; short and squat, with a protruding waistline, he couldn't have been more than five-foot-three and must have weighed two hundred pounds. With his round face perched above his equally round torso, he looked like a Latino version of Frosty the Snowman. He may not have been physically imposing, but he radiated energy, enthusiastically waving his arms while he was engaged in conversation with Michael. Chris was tall enough to easily see the top of the man's head and how little hair was left. Like the rest of him, his scalp was heavily tanned.

123

Certainly, this was not the man Michael was talking about, the one who had killed someone with his hands. Maybe this was his brother or an employee.

Michael started his introductions. "Chris, this is my old friend Garcia." He paused a moment for dramatic effect. "Garcia, this is my son, Chris."

Garcia burst into animated gyrations, holding his head with his hands and bending backward like he was dancing. "Oh my God! Oh! My! God!" he shouted. "You DO exist!" Arms held out wide, he leaped forward, grabbed Chris's hand in his meaty paws, and gave him a most enthusiastic handshake. "I can't believe I'm finally meeting you!"

While shaking his hand, Chris could feel the strength of the man in front of him. "Nice to meet you, Mr. Garcia," he replied.

"Please, no mister. Just Garcia," he said, waving one hand in the air like a flamenco dancer. "Your father has said for years that he had a son, but he is getting old, and I did not want to embarrass him, so I say nothing. But here you are!" He accented the last comment by gesturing like a model showing off a new car and followed it with a huge belly laugh. Michael was smiling broadly at Garcia, thoroughly enjoying the display.

"Please, please, come sit down in our café," Garcia said, motioning for them to follow.

Michael and Chris followed as Garcia walked a couple of aisles over and turned a corner. Nearly hidden among the endless inventory was a café with seats for about a dozen people, complete with a small counter and a couple of booths. The color scheme was just like a 1950's diner—candy apple red with white stripes, black and white checkerboard flooring, lots of chrome, and it was all as cheesy. The menu was also "All-American," with hot dogs, burgers, fries, and milkshakes the only items available. The three men sat down in a booth, Garcia's prominent belly pushing against the tabletop as he slid into the bench-style seat.

"Michael, we must take him fishing on South Padre Island while he is here," Garcia started, then, abruptly turning to Chris, he asked, "Have you ever heard of Boca Chica Beach? It is a very beautiful place."

"No," Chris said. "I hope I have time to see both."

"How long are you staying? There is so much to do," Garcia said, his attitude still as effusive as when Michael had introduced them.

Michael chimed in, "Well, we will have to see. Right now, he has an opened-ended plane ticket. But we have a couple of

125

problems to solve before we can have any fun." He removed a cigarette from its pack and, cradling it in his fingers, left the lighter in his pocket.

"What kind of problems?" Garcia asked, his eyes lowering like an animal preparing to fight, allowing Chris to catch a glimpse of Garcia's formidable side.

"Let's start with the easiest two," Michael said. "He needs to buy some new clothes, and then he needs a new driver's license and passport."

Garcia's facial expression relaxed. "Clothes are no problem. We have clothes here!" he said, proudly raising his hands and gesturing to include the entire store. Chris groaned inwardly at the thought of buying clothing from this tourist Mecca.

"I was hoping you could take him to see Antonio," Michael said.

"Antonio? Yes, but he will want cash today. When do you need them?"

Chris interjected, saying, "I'd like them as soon as possible. I feel a little naked walking around without any ID."

"Antonio will want more money for a speedy delivery, of course."

"How much?" Chris asked Garcia.

126

"Five hundred dollars for both if you want them by tomorrow," Garcia responded.

"That's fine," Chris said.

"I was hoping you could go there with him," Michael said, looking directly at Garcia. "I have a doctor's appointment."

"On a Saturday?" Chris asked and turned to look at Michael, somewhat surprised.

"Of course, of course!" Garcia responded in his usual over-the-top fashion before Michael could answer. "I'd love to go with him!"

"Good," Michael said, getting up to leave. "I'll be back in a couple of hours. Is that enough time?"

It took Garcia a few seconds to unwedge himself from the booth, then he said, "Yes, that should be enough time. If we are not back, wait here for us in one of the booths."

Michael walked away, disappearing behind a wall of teddy bears wearing colorful Mexican sombreros.

Chris turned to Garcia and asked, "Is it okay for you to leave the store for a little while?"

"Oh yes, that is not a problem. I have very good workers, and I often have to leave to run errands. Give me just a moment to talk to them. The men's clothes are just around the corner. I will meet you there." Garcia pointed in a different direction from the one Michael had left and walked away, leaving Chris to find his way to the clothing.

After a few wrong turns, Chris found the men's clothing section and, to his amazement, discovered some fairly nice clothes. The shelves and racks contained linen shirts, Levi's jeans, socks, shoes, and even underwear. Garcia returned after a few minutes and asked abruptly, "How much money do you have on you?"

"A thousand dollars," Chris responded without flinching.

"Give it to me," Garcia said as he sat on a small bench and took off his shoes.

Chris reached into his pocket and pulled out ten one-hundred-dollar bills he had taken from the bank envelope that morning. Garcia split them in half, putting five in each shoe. Reaching into his pocket, he retrieved and handed Chris two twenty-dollar bills and said, "Put one in each of your pockets. If someone approaches you for money, give one to them and keep walking. They won't hassle you if they get something, but if you stiff them, they could get violent."

"Where are we going?" Chris asked.

"Matamoros, just across the border," he said.

"But I have no passport. They won't let me across," Chris said apprehensively.

"Just stay next to me," Garcia said, rising from the bench. "And it will be fine. The border guards see me almost every day. All we need to do is walk across and pay a one-dollar toll."

Exiting the store through the back, the two men walked down an alley for about a block, then turned onto a side street that was a mixture of houses and stores. The street was lined with large oak trees, which helped deflect some of the sun's rays, at least partially diminishing the rising heat of the day.

Chris found Garcia a comfortable man to be with, even though they had just met. He seemed wise and confident, the kind of man you wanted on your side in a tough situation. He was pleased Michael had such a man as his best friend. As they walked, Garcia lit a cigarette. Chris noticed he smoked the same cigarette as Michael.

Garcia told him how he had met Michael while serving in World War II at North Camp Hood. They were in basic training together. He told Chris the story of his two failed attempts to join the army because he was an inch too short. On his third attempt, an officer recognized him from his previous efforts. The officer asked him why he was so adamant about joining the service.

"I told him I wanted to personally find the son of a bitch that killed my older brother and slit his throat from ear to ear. The officer told the doctors to change my height status from 5'3" to 5'4", and they let me in. I became an EOD specialist, Explosive Ordinance Disposal."

He told Chris that Michael had joined the Army Air Force because he had always wanted to learn to fly, and they desperately needed pilots at the time. When he graduated from flight school, he was considered one of the best pilots in his class and had been sent to advanced flight school to learn to be an instructor. Michael ended up training pilots in Texas and Oklahoma for a year before they finally let him go to Europe, flying P-51 Mustangs as a bomber escort.

Chris knew Michael had flown as a pilot in WWII because his sisters had shown him some old flight schoolbooks, but he didn't know he had flown the Mustangs, Chris's favorite WWII plane.

Garcia surprised Chris with something else about Michael. He told him Michael had been an Ace during the war. Not just any Ace, but a triple Ace with 16 1/2 verified kills. It all happened long before Chris was born, and since his father had left when he was two, it was something he had never known about.

The two men turned onto the main road, about a hundred yards from the walking bridge that led across the Rio Grande River and into Mexico. There was a fair amount of foot traffic in both directions since it was Saturday, a big tourist shopping day. Chris wondered how many people going in the opposite direction would end up at Garcia's store.

Garcia walked up to a window like the tellers at a drive-thru bank, purchased two tokens for the turnstiles, and gave one to Chris. They each inserted one into a turnstile and entered Matamoros, Mexico. They continued walking as if they did it every day.

"That was easy," Chris said.

"Yes," Garcia responded, "that was the easy part. But now we are in Matamoros, and things are not the same here. No one will bother me. It's you I'm worried about."

"Do I look that much like a tourist?" Chris asked sarcastically.

Garcia looked at Chris over the top of his sunglasses and said, "Son, you look like a neon light."

They traveled down the street in silence for a block, then turned into an alley. The paving there had been partially washed away, leaving cavernous ruts they had to carefully negotiate, forcing them to take a rather sinuous route. Endless numbers of trash cans, cardboard boxes, and pallets made their journey more like an obstacle course run than a walk down an alley. A small beat-up car roared past, causing Chris and Garcia to quickly sidestep behind a wall.

After a few more blocks of scurrying about, Garcia approached a nondescript building's rear entrance. The structure was identical to others they had passed, just dark cinder blocks with a metal door embedded in the back wall. Garcia knocked heavily on the door, then he took a step back.

A few seconds later, a small man with thick glasses wearing a dirty apron stuck his head out the door.

"What do you want?" the head asked.

"I need your skills, Antonio," Garcia replied.

Pushing his glasses farther up his nose, the man raised his head a little and said, "Garcia." He opened the door and let them inside.

Small and poorly lit, the room smelled of ink and turpentine. Chris had expected a roomful of printing presses and copiers; instead, he saw only a few hand tools and various pieces of paper scattered about. There were three different stools next to individual workstations, each illuminated by a single desk lamp. There was no phone Chris could see.

As Antonio shuffled about his room, he asked, "What can I do for you, Garcia?" He did not make eye contact and seemed to have a permanent hunch to his posture.

"I need some identification for my friend here," Garcia said.

"I'm busy, very busy. I couldn't get to it for a week or so," he said, putting tools away as he spoke, never looking up.

"Yes, you are always busy, Antonio, but we need them right away. He has come a long way to visit his father and he needs to return soon."

"That's nice," Antonio said somewhat indifferently. Then to Chris, he asked, "Who's your father?"

Chris spoke up promptly after receiving his cue, "Michael Hamilton, sir."

Antonio stopped putting his tools away and looked up. As he did, he directed one of the lamps onto Chris. "Well, what do you know," he said.

He stared at Chris, seemingly in disbelief for a couple of seconds, then said, "I've known your father for a long time. He's a good man."

"Thank you, sir," Chris said.

"What happened to your identification?" Antonio asked, continuing to fiddle with his tools.

133

"I lost it in Laredo, sir."

"Laredo! What the hell were you doing in Laredo? You kids nowadays, always gallivanting around. You'd lose your heads if they weren't screwed on," he said, mostly to himself while walking around the room picking up some of the paper items. "You got five hundred dollars?"

"I have the money, Antonio," Garcia said.

"All right. Come over here and sit down," he said reluctantly, "I've got to get your picture."

Chris sat down in front of a blue screen as Antonio collected an old-looking camera and turned on an overhead light. He placed the camera on an ancient yet very sturdy-looking tripod and then took a couple of pictures after giving Chris a brief warning. He then had Chris fill out a couple of forms asking for detailed information such as name, address, the state that issued his license, height, weight, date of birth, eye color, hair color, etc. Chris thought it odd that the form looked even more professional than the ones at the DMV and asked more questions than the official version. The form Antonio gave him for his passport was equally detailed.

After Chris filled out the forms, he handed them to Antonio and asked, "Is there anything else you need from me?"

"No, that's it," he said, waving his hand to dismiss Chris. "You can pick them up tomorrow afternoon." He was once again shuffling papers and tools around.

"Do you want me to pay you now?" Chris politely asked.

"I have already taken care of that," Garcia interjected. "Let's go." He started for the door, Chris following right behind.

Upon entering the alley, Chris said, "Thanks for your help, Garcia. Antonio seems like an odd fellow."

"He is a true artist, the last of the old school artisans. Sadly he has been reduced to making fake IDs," Garcia said, making large gestures with his arms. "He would have been a magnificent forger of paintings. He has a brilliant eye."

Garcia took out his pack of Camels and lit one. As he did, Chris noticed it was the same style of lighter as Michael's, with a similarly worn insignia on the side.

Adeptly sliding the cigarette pack into his shirt pocket with one hand and the lighter into his pants pocket with the other, he turned to Chris and asked him, "Tell me about these other problems you have." His demeanor instantly switched into serious mode.

Chris was impressed that Garcia strategically knew when to ask questions. He had helped Chris get his identification, so he was now indebted to him. He asked the question when no one else was around, not even Michael, so if it was personal, it could remain between the two of them. He even calculated asking early in their return journey so they would have time to discuss it.

Chris began, "It started with me going to Laredo to pay my respects to a friend who recently passed away."

Chris recounted the events that had transpired during the last few days, telling him about going to Casa de la Guerra, finding out his friend was murdered, and going to the police department and library. He told him about the car getting impounded and why, his getaway in the taxi, his trip to Brownsville, and meeting Michael. Finally, he told him about the two cab drivers he had sent to Laredo to hopefully discover the name of the killer. Garcia listened intently to his tale, never interrupting. Chris recognized the level of focus the man possessed. This was, after all, a man who had worked with explosives; he was no ordinary man. Michael was right. Garcia was formidable, and Chris found himself hoping he was going to be on his side. After Chris finished telling his entire story, they walked in silence for about a block as Garcia contemplated how to respond.

"I have a suggestion for you," Garcia finally said, breaking his silence. "Tomorrow, you will have your identification back. After we get it, come enjoy some fishing with us. We will visit some beautiful places, and then you should go home."

"That's what everyone keeps suggesting," Chris said in frustration.

"So why do you not listen to them? Look, you are my best friend's son. I know all about your relationship, about him leaving when you were young, about him visiting you a few years ago. Michael has told me everything. He is a very complex man and has had many issues over the years, but we all have. He may not have been the best father, and I know he regrets that, but I also know he would not want to see you hurt for anything. A father always wants to protect their son, regardless of their past."

"Do you have any children, Garcia?" Chris asked.

"I have three daughters."

"If you had a son and someone murdered you, would you want him to go after the killer?"

"I would not want him to put himself in danger over something he cannot change," Garcia said with more exaggerated hand movements.

"'I don't want to put myself in danger, either, because I have a daughter, too. Since you are fully aware of my relationship with Michael, you won't be surprised when I say the friend I lost was the closest thing I've had to a real father in my life. I can't just walk away and do nothing. I believe a man of your experience knows what I mean."

Garcia and Chris were approaching the border turnstiles again. Garcia paid their tolls, and Chris stayed close behind him, glad to be back across the border. After getting out of earshot of some giddy tourists returning with their shopping booty, Garcia asked, "Does Michael know how you feel about your friend?"

"Yes. I've told him everything, and he knows I'll do this alone if I have to." Chris was resolute in his statement.

"And what happens when you find this person? What then? Will you kill him?" Garcia turned and looked at Chris over his sunglasses, then said, "You are no killer."

Looking ahead and making his now familiar hand gestures, he asked Chris, "Are you going to tell the police? What good would that do? The police probably already know who did it, and it appears they don't give a shit."

"I don't know, Garcia. I've asked myself those same questions. I guess we'll have to wait and see what happens."

Looking over the top of his sunglasses again, Garcia said, "Not much of a plan."

They had turned down the tree-lined street and were only a couple of blocks away from "Garcia's."

"When we get back to the store," Garcia said, "you go buy your clothes and let me talk to your father. Let me feel him out to see what he thinks."

"Okay." Chris was thankful for his willingness to take the time and listen.

Garcia's was abuzz with shoppers when they entered, screaming children running up and down the aisles, knocking over bits and pieces of everything. Garcia took no notice as he and Chris walked over to the diner area, where Michael was sitting at one of the booths drinking a strawberry milkshake. "God damn, these are good, Garcia!" he said as the two approached.

"I'll be back in a few minutes," Chris said, walking toward the men's clothing section as Garcia wedged himself into the booth.

Chris bought a couple of pairs of jeans, two linen shirts, two t-shirts, underwear, and a pair of very comfortable sneakers. On his way to the register, he made a point to stop by the painting of the Mexican girl he had seen before. *Damn! She's sexy!* he thought.

Chris paid for his clothing and walked through the store, blending in with the other shoppers as he carried the two shopping bags emblazoned with "Garcia's" on the side in little orange sombreros. Sitting down at the table with Michael and Garcia, Chris noticed Garcia seemed to have regained his jovial mood. He joked about how he felt like he was "taking out my two boys for some shopping and milkshakes," laughing heavily at his joke.

After Chris settled into the booth, Michael said, "Garcia and I have talked about your situation, and we have some suggestions."

"Okay, what are they?" he asked, curious as to what they had come up with in such a short time.

Garcia jumped in, saying, "We do not feel your cab-driving friends will get much information. They seem to know some things already but are too scared to investigate further. You see, they live in the same town, so they are vulnerable. They have children, wives, businesses. Yes, they have contacts, but contacts can work for both sides."

Michael continued, "We want you to go somewhere with us this afternoon. There are a couple of men we want to see, men who know how to get very useful information. These men are not afraid to ask questions if the money is right."

Garcia then gave Chris an earnest look and said, "Look, when we get there, you cannot talk to anyone. You cannot even walk around on your own. You must stay with your father and me at all times. This is a place of business, but it can also be a place of danger."

"What's the name of this place?" Chris asked with a sense of apprehension.

"The Thieves Market."

Chapter 7

It's like being in a third-world country!

Chris thought when they arrived. There, in the seediest part of an industrial area and hidden by massive warehouses set up on an abandoned loading dock, was the Thieves Market.

The twenty-five or so merchants were guarded by two overtly armed men who patrolled each end of the dock. There was a haphazardly installed railing several feet off the ground where the trucks would unload, and only a ramp at each end allowed access to the merchandise. It was clear no one would be able to grab anything and run before meeting their demise.

Purveyors of the finest stolen merchandise, you could purchase anything from a single ring to a truck full of goods, and the salesmen were as diverse as the items they sold: Asians selling various electronics, Mexicans selling jewelry and antiquities, an Australian selling paintings and various pieces of art, Americans selling cigarettes and guns, a Brazilian-looking man selling what appeared to be gemstones and "authentic" watches, and even one person of indeterminable race selling an entire truckload of furniture. This place was clearly not for the tourist crowd. Each person walking up the ramp had to be approved for entry, as if being let into some hip dance club. There were no women among these shoppers.

Garcia had driven separately and was already walking among the crowd when Michael and Chris were given permission to enter. Chris noticed how the atmosphere was quiet and serious, and he now understood the warning he had been given. There were multiple handwritten signs saying "No Pesos." The roof above kept the midday sun from melting the customers and merchants, which seemed to add to the clandestine feeling of the location.

Garcia approached Michael and Chris and said in a low volume, "I see Gonzalez, but I don't see Speedy."

"Do you want to talk to him first?" Michael responded.

"Yeah, at least we can find out if he's interested," Garcia said.

"Which one is Gonzalez?" Chris whispered.

Without pointing or turning around, Michael said to him, "He's the one selling the Indian jewelry."

Chris looked over his shoulder to see a man with several tables of turquoise and silver jewelry, including bracelets, rings, and necklaces. It all looked expensive and hand-crafted as emphasized by a sign reading "Top Quality Turquoise and Silver."

As they turned and walked toward the table, Chris noticed a few men nodding and pointing at Michael. When asked, Michael said, "It's the tree."

Chris stood a couple of steps away and let Michael and Garcia talk to their contact. He was a serious-looking man with a permanent scowl on his dark-skinned face. He had very thick black hair that seemed to grow straight up out of his head. Of stocky build with broad shoulders, he looked like quite a powerful man. He gave Chris the impression of someone who had been in many fights over the years, having won most of them. He did not shake hands with Michael or Garcia and, after initially recognizing them, never made eye contact again, preferring to perpetually rearrange his wares. During the brief conversation, he shook his head "no" many times, giving the impression he was not interested, or that he didn't know anything. After a final shake of the head, Garcia and Michael motioned for Chris to follow them to a more secluded corner of the docks.

"He doesn't have any contacts in Laredo," Garcia said, "and he didn't seem interested in going there and digging up any dirt."

"Okay, so where does that leave us?" Chris asked.

"We need to find Speedy," Michael said. "I think he has contacts there. He might be the only one that can help if your friends don't come through."

"Where can we find him?" Chris asked. "Does he have an office or a phone?"

Garcia raised his eyebrows, held up his hands, and said, "Wait here a minute." He then quickly walked off toward one of the ramp entrances.

"Do you come here often?" Chris asked Michael, half joking.

"I used to sell stuff here," Michael said with a wry smile.

"Really? When? What did you sell?"

"It was a long time ago. It's a long story," Michael said, dismissing any further questions with a wave of his hand.

Garcia returned at that moment, clapping his hands together once as he approached. "I've got his phone number. He has a cell phone, and that's the only way to reach him."

None of the three men had a cell phone, so they decided to drive to a better part of town to find a pay phone. After reaching a graffiti-laden phone booth a dozen blocks away, Garcia placed the

145

call. Michael and Chris watched from the old truck as he had a brief conversation on the phone.

Garcia hung up and walked over to them. "He said he will meet us at Madison Avenue and 5th Street in ten minutes."

"Seems an odd place to meet," Michael said. "Do you know where it is?"

"Yeah, I know it," Garcia said with a bemused look on his face.

"Okay, let's go," he said, cocking his head while shrugging his shoulders.

Michael and Chris left, with Garcia closely in tow. "Where are we meeting him?" Chris asked.

"You'll see," Michael said as he fumbled to light a cigarette while he drove. "We're only a few minutes away."

"What do we do if he's not willing to help us?" Chris asked.

"Well, if Speedy doesn't want the job and your cab-driving friends crap out, we can snoop around some ourselves, but you see how well that went before." Michael looked at Chris after his last statement with a definitively wary look.

Pulling up to the corner of Madison Avenue and 5th Street, Chris saw what Michael and Garcia were referencing as an "odd place to meet." It was the entrance to The Brownsville City Cemetery.

"You've got to be kidding me," Chris said.

"Some people have a sense of the dramatic...or the macabre," Michael responded.

They parked the truck and walked past the entrance gates with Garcia just a few steps behind.

"Did he say to meet him here at the entrance?" Michael asked.

"Yes," Garcia said while looking at his watch. "He'll be here in a minute. He has always been reliable if nothing else."

Chris didn't ask what "if nothing else" meant and didn't want to know.

Just then, crossing from a few dozen gravesites away, a man appeared from behind a small mausoleum. Walking rather hurriedly as if he was late for work, he made a beeline for the three men.

He was about five-foot-six and sinewy in his build. He had a very tight buzz haircut, and Chris assumed this was to hide his obviously receding hairline. He fidgeted with his hands as he walked, not as if he was nervous by nature but more like he had drunk several cups of espresso. He wore tan slacks that hung loosely on his thin waist, and his black Hawaiian shirt was adorned with lots of yellow Hibiscus flowers. As he got closer, Chris noticed he also wore a gold necklace, a heavy gold bracelet on his right wrist, and a big gold watch on his left, as well as several rings. Not exactly the incognito attire he had expected to see on this sleuth-for-hire.

"Gentlemen," he said as he got within a few feet of them. He stood just far enough away so as not to warrant a handshake. "Shall we take a walk?" He motioned for them to follow him down one of the gravel walkways.

The cemetery was a maze of paths made from light brown pebble stones. There were thousands of gravesites, from small worn-down crosses and eroded gravestones to newly constructed monoliths and gleaming granite headstones shining brightly in the late afternoon sun. There was the occasional large oak tree that gave some respite to the burdensome heat. Chris saw only a handful of patrons throughout the cemetery.

"How do you like my office?" Speedy asked, holding up his hands.

"Seems like an odd place to conduct business," Garcia responded.

"Oh, no, it is wonderful! I get to take lovely walks with my clients, it is very private, and the rent is reasonable. Plus, as you know, dead men tell no tales." He emphasized this last comment with a toothy grin. "What can I do for you gentlemen today?" Speedy asked.

Michael started, "Do you have any contacts in Laredo?"

"Yes," Speedy nodded his head. "I know many people there. Some better than others. What is it about Laredo that interests you?"

"I had a good friend that lived there," Chris said, deciding to move things along. "I went there to visit his family after he had passed away, and then I found out he was murdered."

Speedy nodded in acknowledgment. "What was your friend's name?" he asked.

"Armando Guerra," Chris responded. "Do you know him?"

"No," Speedy said. "I may have heard the family name years ago, but I do not know that particular name."

Chris was somewhat surprised since the mention of the Guerras had elicited such reactions in the past.

Speedy continued, "So, I'm assuming you desire to find out who did this killing of your friend?"

Michael said, "We have a couple of people checking on the name, but we don't have confidence in them."

"And what do we want besides the name? Do we want to know why? Are you going to the police? Planning on some kind of retaliation?" Speedy asked.

"That depends," Garcia said. "We want to know who and why first. That may come later, but we are not killers."

"I see," said Speedy. "If I had a name before I went to Laredo, that would be very helpful. I can go there in a couple of days. I charge five-hundred dollars a day, and I get a thousand-dollar bonus for getting results."

"That's expensive, don't you think?" Garcia asked.

"Yes, but you know I am very good at what I do, and we are not talking petty crimes here. There may be some risk involved."

"That's fine," Chris interjected. "We'll call you if we know anything before you go."

"Good," Speedy said. "I'll look forward to hearing from you. You have my cell number."

Speedy walked off in a different direction as if to take a shortcut somewhere, still not shaking hands. The three men walked back toward their vehicles. Chris thought how odd and yet competent Speedy appeared. He asked the right questions, listened intently, and seemed to understand the situation. And yet, he exuded the personality of a used car salesman rather than a thief or informant.

"What do you guys know about this man?" Chris asked.

"He's known to get results," Michael answered. "He may seem a little peculiar, but he knows what he's doing."

"Besides, we do not have a lot of options at this time," Garcia added.

Arriving back at their vehicles, they went their separate ways—Garcia wanting to check on the store, and Michael wanting to go home to rest for a while. During the drive home, Michael smoked a cigarette contemplatively as Chris thought of what they could do next besides wait. As they pulled in behind the house, there were two to three dozen people at the base of the tree holding what was apparently some sort of a religious ceremony.

"They're Seventh Day Adventists," Michael said. "They pray on Saturday and rest on Sundays."

"Why so late in the day?" Chris asked.

"They do this in groups all day. We even get some Jewish people here on Saturdays. They try and take turns."

The two men walked past the outdoor churchgoers, having to veer into the street to do so, then climbed the stairs into the house. Chris noticed Michael struggled more than usual with going up the front steps. *Perhaps he's tired. It's been a long day for him,* he thought.

Michael went to rest in his bedroom while Chris sat at the antiquated phone to make some calls. He called his building supervisor, Jim Payette, to let him know he would be a few days later getting back than he had planned. They spoke about a few business situations, but Jim said he had everything under control. "Get back when you can. I'm on top of everything," he said through the old speaker.

Chris had often thought of Jim as more of a brother than an employee. After all, he had known him for almost twenty years and found him to be one of the most honest people he had ever known. He also thought Jim was one of the few people in the construction business who equaled Chris in people skills. He pushed himself away from the desk, the old wooden rollers on the chair legs more sliding than rolling, and walked across the floor and down the hall while attempting to keep the squeaking of the floor to a minimum so as not to disturb Michael. He walked up the brown bathroom steps, again being struck with a feeling of déjà vu.

He now noticed that the door to the bathroom did not match the rest of the house. It was an exterior door, solid and much heavier. It had sharp edges, since it had been planed down to fit the opening. The door handles were very loose on both sides, the knobs needing to be tightened onto the metal rod. Since there was no window in the bathroom and Chris felt the handle could slip off, he left the door ajar so he wouldn't get locked in, his claustrophobia once again dictating his actions. As Chris was exiting the bathroom, he heard some noise coming from the front porch. It sounded like a woman screaming and something pounding on the walls. Chris rushed down the hall and pulled open the front door.

"Malditos cigarrillos, malditos cigarrillos!" screamed the woman as she pushed Michael's stand-up ashtray to the porch floor, sending cigarette butts flying in various directions.

"What in the hell are you doing?" Chris asked tersely.

Spinning around without missing a beat, the woman held up one of the cigarette butts and said, "He is not supposed to be smoking!" There was both anger and concern in her voice. "Why do you let him smoke?"

Chris, completely taken aback by the accusation, just said, "You mean Michael?"

"Idiota! Yes, of course, Michael. Where is he?"

Composing himself after the onslaught of her tirade, Chris said, "He's sleeping. May I ask who you are?"

"I'm Garcia's daughter. I come by to check on him every couple of days." With a calmer, more measured tone, she said, "He is not supposed to be smoking." She said this while looking at the cigarette butt she was holding.

Chris, sensing a tinge of sadness in her voice, said, "Please come in."

Chris opened the door and led her inside. "May I get you something to drink?" he asked.

"May I have some water, please?" she responded. Chris felt she wanted a moment to calm herself, perhaps slightly embarrassed by her actions on the porch.

Chris went into the kitchen and returned with a glass of water. As he entered the room, he saw her standing in front of the windows, backlit by the setting sun. Without her anger as a mask, Chris could now see what a natural beauty she was. She wore almost no makeup, as if to minimize her attractiveness. Her black hair was brushed straight back, framing her face. Her white skirt fell just below her knees, her green and red blouse rising almost to her neckline. Only her arms, calves, and feet protruded from her garments, strangely making her more enticing. There was an air of

154

confidence and innocence that radiated from her all at once. But as alluring as all that made her, there was something else...her sensuality. It flowed from her like water, as if drawn from some hidden reservoir that gushed through miles of pipes, it seethed from her pores. Chris had no doubt she was fully aware of her effect on men.

As he handed her the glass of water, she said, "I'm sorry I called you an idiot."

Chris laughed it off and replied, "You're not the first, and you won't be the last."

She smiled at his comment and asked, "May I sit down?"

"Of course," Chris said, turning an old wing-backed chair toward her.

She sat sideways in the chair, casually draping her legs over one of the arms. Chris sat in the chair Michael had used for reading, about ten feet away.

"Perhaps we should start the conversation over. I'll start with introducing myself. My name is Chris Hamilton."

"Yes, I know. My name is Sophia."

"And how did you know who I am?"

"My father told me the long-lost son was in town when I went by the store today. He told me you'd be here after I said I was coming to check in on Michael."

"Well, I wasn't exactly lost."

"It's just a figure of speech." Sophia made a dismissive gesture while saying this. Chris resisted the urge to flirt with her. Her legs hanging seductively over the side of the chair wasn't helping.

"Tell me about Michael. Why do you have to come by and check on him?"

"So, I guess you don't know. He hasn't told you yet?"

"I just got here a couple of days ago. He hasn't mentioned anything regarding his health."

Sophia turned away to look out the window as she spoke. "I've known Michael a long time. He knew my father before I was born." Turning back to Chris, she said, "I even know about you and your sisters." She paused for a minute and took a sip of water. "A few months ago, he was diagnosed with stage IV lung cancer. He does not always remember to take his medicine, and sometimes he misses his chemotherapy. And he still smokes those damn cigarettes."

"He does seem like he has aged quite a bit since I last saw him," Chris responded. "I was unaware that he wasn't supposed to be smoking. Why didn't your father say something to me?"

Sophia rolled her dark brown eyes while saying, "My father...he would never betray Michael. Their bond is unbreakable. He often talks about how much they have done together and how many times Michael has saved his life."

"What do you mean by that?" Chris asked.

"I'm not sure, he has never told me the actual stories. Something happened in the war and then a couple of other times. It was before I was born."

Chris found himself trying to guess her age. Dark-skinned women were always so difficult, they did not show the lines on their faces as so many Caucasian women did. He thought she was probably in her late twenties to early thirties. Regardless of age, she was truly beautiful. But surely this could not be Garcia's daughter as she had stated. She was not anything like her father in facial features or body frame. They were the antithesis of each other.

"Do you know anything else about Michael's diagnosis?" Chris asked.

"It's not good, that's all I know." Sophia swung her legs from the arm of the chair and stood up. She walked to the window overlooking the front yard, still talking. "Do you know about the tree?" she asked, now looking out the window.

"I know it has the image of the Virgin Mary on it, and people seem to think it's a religious symbol."

Sophia continued to gaze out the window. "It appeared the day after Michael was diagnosed with cancer. That's a little strange, don't you think?"

"Yes, very strange. No one told me that." Chris was genuinely surprised by what she said and wondered what significance it held.

"My father says it will go away when Michael dies." Sophia walked back to the chair and sat down, obviously sad from her statement.

"That seems almost like a superstition," Chris said.

Sophia looked at Chris and said, "Perhaps you are right, but my father seems to know things."

Chris enjoyed listening to her talk. She had a soft, mellifluous voice that was very feminine. She seemed to be a kindhearted and sincere woman, as unique inside as out. But the two things Chris had learned regarding beautiful women were caution and not to behave in an obsequious manner. He had known more than his fair share of attractive and sexy women, and they were all a major pain in the ass. Their entitled attitudes with endless opportunities made dating them a nightmare, and they were used to men fawning over them, so he had stopped long ago.

Besides, this was the daughter of a man who had killed someone with his bare hands. Chris was attracted to her, as he was sure almost all men were, but he knew he should keep his distance. This was another dangerous situation he needed to avoid.

Chris asked if she wanted him to check on Michael since he had not come out of his bedroom.

"Yes, please. I would like to see how much of his medicine he has taken over the last few days."

Chris walked down the hallway as quietly as possible, gently opening the door just enough to peer inside. In the darkening room, he could see Michael was fast asleep. After returning to the front room, he saw the shadows on the floor were quite long now, announcing the approach of the gloaming on the outside. As he sat back down in his chair, he reached up and turned on the reading light, which cast a yellowish light across the room. Somehow this made Sophia's face even more attractive, softening her features as if she was illuminated by the glow of a candle.

"He's still asleep," Chris said.

"That means he's probably taken his medicine," she said, seemingly relieved. "How long are you going to be in town?"

159

"I don't know. It depends on several things." Chris emphasized his remark with a shrug of his shoulders.

"May I ask you another question?" Sophia said with raised eyebrows.

"Sure."

"Why are you here?" Sophia seemed to make this a particularly pointed question, filled with different connotations.

"Didn't your father tell you?"

"My father doesn't share other people's information. He'll take many secrets to his grave." Sophia looked down at the floor with this comment.

"Well, Sophia, it's kind of a long story."

"Does it go back to when your father left you when you were two? Or does it go back to when he came to see you five years ago to ask forgiveness?" She was polite in her questioning but also assertive.

Chris was completely disarmed by her questions and struggled to give a proper response. "It actually has nothing to do with either of those situations. I'm curious as to how you knew that?"

"Michael tells me everything. He's not like my father in that way. I've known about you since I was a child." She looked at Chris knowingly.

"I ended up here because of a sequence of events that put me in some danger, and quite frankly, I had nowhere else to go. I will say this: I'm not here to find riches or cause Michael any problems. To be honest, I'm actually quite surprised how willing he's been to help me."

"I thought you might be searching for a will or something." Sophia was obviously relieved by Chris's admission.

"No, hardly. From what I see, he doesn't have much anyway."

"I wouldn't know anything about that." Then, looking up at Chris, she said, "My father tells me you have never been to South Padre Island."

"I've never even heard of it."

"It's a very beautiful place. He suggested I take you to go see it."

"Are you asking me to go because your father wants you to take me, or do you want to take me?"

Smiling for the first time, Sophia said, "I would like to take you. Can you go tomorrow?"

Chris paused for a moment, just for effect, then said, "Sounds like fun, but you'll have to drive. I don't have a car here."

"I'll bring my dad's jeep. You can drive on the beach there." She stood up to leave, and Chris escorted her to the door.

Standing at the door for a moment, Sophia said, "Remember when I said my father knows things?"

"Yes."

"He told me you were a good and honest man," she said while looking into his eyes for a reaction. "I think he was right."

She then stood on her toes and gently kissed him on the cheek. "I'll see you at nine."

Chris opened the door for her to leave and watched her walk down the sidewalk. As she got into her car, he said to himself in a very low tone,

"Oh, shit."

Chapter 8

"What in the holy hell?"

Chris said loudly as he was suddenly awakened by strange noises outside his window...again. This time, it wasn't trash trucks, it was a policeman blowing a whistle while directing traffic and the loud banging of metal together.

Pulling back the curtain sheers that blocked a minimal amount of sunlight, he looked out the window to see what all the commotion was about. There were city workers stringing caution tape across the far end of the street and a Brownsville Police cruiser being utilized as an additional obstacle. Looking in the other direction, he saw that the intersecting streets in front of the tree had also been blocked off, and there were two policemen standing in the middle of the road.

What is going on? An accident? A fire nearby? Was there a parade today?

Chris got dressed and headed to the front door. As he walked down the hall, he heard Michael making cooking noises in the kitchen. When he opened the door, he could see there had been a small wooden stage erected in front of the tree with an ornate pulpit set on it. In the middle of the intersection, there were aluminum bleachers being assembled, just like he used to see at his Little League games. The entire block was cordoned off in all four directions, with police cars at the end of each street.

"They make quite a production on Sundays, don't they?" Michael said, coming through the door that Chris had left open.

"You mean they have religious services here?"

"They have four of them, at eight, nine, ten, and eleven," Michael said as he sipped his coffee. "I've sat out here and listened to all four sermons at times."

"And the city allows this?" Chris asked.

"They were the ones that started closing the streets. I mean, it is Sunday, after all. Not much traffic down here today. They thought it would be better than just having people standing in the streets."

"How many people will show up today?" Chris asked.

"Probably a few hundred...depends. They also sell t-shirts," Michael said proudly.

164

"So, no one at all can drive down the street?"

"No, they close the streets until the afternoon," Michael said while sitting in his usual chair. Chris noticed his knocked-over ashtray was upright again. "Why? Are you expecting someone?" Michael said in a leading sort of way, like he already knew the answer.

"Sophia is supposed to pick me up this morning to take me to some beach. Is that going to be a problem for you?" Chris asked as he sat down in his now accustomed chair, three away from Michael.

Michael laughed his raspy laugh and shook his head at the same time. "You kids think us old folk have never done any of the things you do. I've had girls sneak out while their boyfriends were sleeping to come see me." He laughed again. "I expected that when you two met you would be attracted to each other...it's only natural. I've noticed how the girls look at you."

"Yes, but this isn't just any girl, is it? She's your best friend's daughter."

"Do you think Garcia knows?" Michael asked.

"From what she told me, I think he suggested it."

Michael had an extended laugh and coughing spell at this last comment, having to catch his breath before finally saying, "That son of a bitch. He's always planning some shit. I bet he was checking you out when he took you to get your identification."

"You mean he was deciding if he wanted me to meet her?"

"You bet your ass! If he didn't like you, he never would have allowed her to come over here last night."

Chris, somewhat surprised, said, "So, you knew she was here?"

"Yes, I heard you talking in the living room." He took a sip of coffee before continuing, "Look, it's a little late to give you the 'Birds and Bees' talk now. You're two grown people who can make your own decisions. Sophia has a good heart and is a very smart woman, it's just..." Michael paused, searching for the most benevolent way of phrasing what he was about to say. "She has a certain effect on men."

"Yes, I am fully aware of that. Don't worry, I've had some experience with very attractive women." Chris was simultaneously bragging and reassuring Michael.

Michael chuckled at this statement. "Yes, I'm sure you have. It's funny how genetics works, isn't it? Even though I didn't raise you, we have a lot of similarities because of that."

"What do you mean?"

"Women, for instance. Have you ever had trouble meeting women?"

"No, not really."

"Neither did I. Do women often approach you? Do they ask you out sometimes?"

"Yes."

"Friday at the bank, did you notice how attentive Graciella was with you? Were you aware of how she looked at you, and spoke to you? I used to get that look in women's eyes when they looked at me, especially when I was a pilot."

"Women do love a man in uniform, don't they?" Chris said, encouraging Michael.

"You're damn right they do!" He said emphatically, pointing his finger at Chris. "When I was in the service, my buddies would say my problem was that I loved chasing women. I told them the only problem I had was that they would let me catch them!"

Chris and Michael both laughed at this, with Michael again coughing extensively afterward. Chris noticed Michael had not smoked any cigarettes that morning, unsure if it was because he had heard Sophia's rant last night or because he knew she was coming over this morning. He decided this was not a good time to have that conversation.

Looking at his watch, Chris saw that it was almost eight. "I guess I had better go get ready," he said, rising to go back in the house.

"I made some eggs if you want some," Michael called after him.

Chris showered in the old rust-stained tub, once again leaving the bathroom door ajar. He put on one of the pairs of jeans he had bought at Garcia's, along with a white linen shirt. He had also bought some blue slip-on sneakers he thought were a little too nautical looking for him, but they were the most appropriate shoes for the occasion. He then took out the five-hundred dollars from his other pair of pants that Garcia had returned to him after they had safely returned to the store.

Chris ate some of the now-cold eggs Michael had cooked, then went outside to sit on the porch and watch the Sunday morning show. The first service was about to begin, and the aluminum bleachers were almost full now. There were a couple of men setting up a microphone at the podium.

The sun had not yet risen high enough to cast its light onto the brick and steel canyon walls as the attendees sat quietly, resplendent in their Sunday meeting clothing. There were many shades of green, yellow, and blue dresses, and dotted among them were the darker grays, browns, and blacks of the men's clothing.

Although the churchgoers were shaded by the buildings and the expansive oak tree, they still fanned themselves in the growing heat as they waited for the services to begin.

Promptly at nine, a salt-and-pepper-haired African American minister dressed in a black suit and red tie stepped up to the microphone and announced "Good Morning" to the gathered crowd. He started into his prepared sermon as a few stragglers sat down in the bleachers.

"They always comment on how they feel blessed to preach on such hallowed grounds, like they're in the Vatican," Michael commented as he stared out at the crowd.

Chris then saw Sophia coming down the street, walking in front of the empty field. Her black hair was in a ponytail, and it bounced up and down as she walked. She had on a red baseball cap with "Garcia's" written across the front in gold script.

She opened the gate and walked up the broken sidewalk, then stopped just before she reached the stairs and said, "Maybe I should come back later. You guys look like you're in desperate need of salvation this morning." She smiled her brilliant smile, proud of her comment.

"Salvation can be delivered in many forms and in a multitude of temples," Michael replied.

"This is true, sir," Sophia responded, continuing to smile.

"What temple are we attending today?" Chris asked Sophia.

"South Padre Island. It's quite the beautiful place."

"Well, you kids have a good time. Keep an eye on him, Sophia. He's new around here and might get lost." Michael chuckled at himself.

"I'll take good care of him, sir. Does he need to be home before dinner?" Sophia joined Michael in laughter.

"You two are killing me," Chris said wryly as he went down the stairs to meet Sophia. "Good morning."

"Good morning," she said, looking up at him. "Are you ready?"

"Sure, let's go."

They both waved goodbye to Michael, walked through the gate, and turned right past the open field.

"How far away did you have to park?" Chris asked.

"About four blocks. I forgot how crazy it can be down here on a Sunday morning."

"I was quite surprised when I woke up this morning. I had no idea." Chris glanced back toward the house and noticed Michael was already lighting a cigarette. He made sure Sophia did not see.

"Michael loves it," she said. "He usually sits on the porch for all the services. Sometimes people even stop by and talk to him after the sermons. My father has been there a couple of times, but he is more dubious than Michael."

"They seem to have a unique friendship, yet it appears to be a genuine one," Chris said.

Sophia looked up at Chris, saying, "They have a connection like no other I have ever seen. They would kill for each other. They have been friends for over fifty years through war, marriages, children, businesses. Even I don't know everything about them."

They finally reached Garcia's car: a 1994 Jeep Wrangler painted dark green. The soft top was already down, and the windows were still up. It had a winch on the front, and Chris thought it a perfect vehicle to take to the beach.

As they got in, Sophia said, "I'd let you drive, but you don't have a license, do you?" She said this with a knowing smile.

"It's a long story," Chris said with a bit of exasperation. "But how do you know that?"

"My father said we should stop by the store later today because he is sending someone to pick up your identification in Matamoros."

"Oh, that's great," Chris said happily.

"You seem to have a lot of long stories, don't you?"

Chris chuckled. "No, not really. I have nothing to hide. I just haven't had time to tell you everything."

"Well," she said, putting on her sunglasses, "we have all day, don't we?"

Sophia gunned the jeep and took off past the parked cars. She drove rather fast through the all-but-empty downtown streets this Sunday morning. At a stoplight, she reached into the glove box and pulled out a small bag. Handing it to Chris, she said, "Here's a present from my dad."

Chris opened the bag to find a pair of Ray-Ban sunglasses, a baseball cap that said "Brownsville, Texas" on it, and suntan lotion. He laughed and said, "That's perfect. I lost my sunglasses." Chris put on both the glasses and cap and asked Sophia, "How do I look?"

Sophia glanced over at him, gave an impish smile, and said, "Not bad. Are your lost glasses another long story?"

Chris responded, "What about you? You know a hell of a lot more about me than I do about you."

Slightly defensive, Sophia said, "What do you want to know?"

"Let's start with the basics...ever been married? Have any children? What do you do?"

172

Sophia became a little more serious in her demeanor. "I was married when I was very young. I was nineteen. He was just a boy, twenty-two going on sixteen. My father said that we were too young. He was right. It only lasted a few years."

"No kids?" Chris asked.

She fidgeted with her hands on the steering wheel before she answered, "No, no kids."

"What do you do?" Chris asked.

Sophia flashed her brilliant smile again, looked at him, and said, "Guess!"

Chris sat back contemplatively in his seat. "Okay, let me see. You're too smart for an ordinary job like retail, and I can't see you as a secretary or as an attorney." Sophia laughed at this. "And you're definitely not a nurse or in the medical field."

"Why do you say that?"

"Because you didn't speak about Michael's condition like someone in the medical field would," Chris answered. Then continuing, "You have a bit of an attitude. It seems like you enjoy being in charge and you're educated." He stopped for a second and looked at Sophia with a smirk and said, "You're a teacher."

This brought peals of laughter from Sophia and for the first time, Chris saw her really laugh out loud.

173

"You're right!" Sophia said. "I teach history."

They were now approaching the Queen Isabella Bridge that crossed from Port Isabella to South Padre Island. The bridge and barrier island reminded him of Assateague Island in Virginia, where wild horses that were descendants of Spanish horses still run free. He remembered spending a weekend with a beautiful woman there long ago. They walked on the beach and ate crab during the day; at night, they sat on the deck and watched the sunset and listened to the insects playing their instruments. He was pretty sure she had been a good lover...but he couldn't recall her name.

The Queen Isabella Bridge was almost three miles long and provided a spectacular view of boats entering and leaving the port. There was an old wooden schooner with a beautiful teak deck sailing south, probably destined for some private alcove in the Caribbean. Several colorful catamarans skipped across the green water, leaving a trail of white foam in their wake. A large cruise ship was wallowing slowly through the water with hundreds of enthusiastic customers waving to no one in particular. But mostly, there were the fishing boats, filled with girthy men from all over the country in search of the big one that didn't get away. Their boats were stuffed with rods and reels, bait and food, and vast quantities of beer, already on full display to all passersby.

Entering South Padre Island, it appeared to Chris that the island was in the "calm-before-the-storm" phase of construction. Hotels were dotted here and there along the beaches, with the occasional restaurant appendage, but the real building boom was sure to come. Soon, there would be the chain tourist eateries, beach themed hotels, water parks and putt-putt courses, t-shirt outlets, and crapola stores like Garcia's. The same thing had happened to many undeveloped places he had seen in the past; it seemed as inevitable as barnacles on a ship's hull.

"Where are we going?" Chris asked.

"I thought we could drive on the beach before it gets too busy," Sophia said.

"Do you know a good spot?"

"All of it is a good spot. You can drive for miles here. You'll see."

Sophia turned a couple of blocks ahead where a sign said "Beach Access."

They drove for a couple hundred yards between two hotels and then suddenly were on the beach.

There were already several cars driving in both directions—pickup trucks, jeeps, and a minivan that was stuck in soft sand. Sophia turned left and headed away from most of the activity. The

175

water was a different color here on the ocean side. It was not the crystal blue water of the Caribbean but more of a rich deep green, like the color of emeralds. The sun's rays accentuated the color variations, with some sections reflecting a lighter shade, like seafoam, and then other deeper parts the color of viridian. The sand was a brilliant white, a stark contrast to the water's multiple shades.

Sophia drove along the surf, sending up spray from the wheels as they ran through the shallow water, obviously thoroughly enjoying herself. Chris was quite sure she had come here often.

"You're different today," Chris said to her.

"What do you mean?" Sophia had to speak louder due to the noise from the surf and tires.

"You seem much more at ease, less wary."

Sophia glanced at Chris for a moment and said, "I couldn't trust you yesterday. Even my father was a little skeptical at first. We didn't know why you would show up out of the blue, didn't know what you wanted."

"And yet your dad was so accommodating, so happy to meet me," Chris said.

"That's his way of charming people into giving themselves away. He's very clever like that. He also reads people very well. Apparently, something you did or said put him at ease."

"You were still suspicious when you came over last night, weren't you?"

"Yes. I mean, he could have been wrong, or you could be a good liar. I didn't know."

"What changed your mind?" Chris asked.

"Nothing specific." She glanced over at him. "You just seemed to be a straight shooter, an honest guy. I don't think you bullshit people." Sophia gave him a sincere look with her comment.

"You could be wrong," Chris said with a roguish grin.

"Yes, but I'm not," she said. "I trust my instincts. I've learned to read men pretty well since my divorce. I can tell within a few minutes what they're like and what they want."

"Really? What do I want?" Chris said as he gave her a curious look.

"Only what people can offer. I mean, you don't have an agenda. You take what people can give you. You know asking anything more is foolish or dangerous."

"Okay. I won't argue with your analysis. How often do you see that quality in men?"

"Very rarely, as often as I find a rainbow-colored unicorn." Sophia flashed her brilliant smile once again as if it were an exclamation point to her comment.

Driving past several campers and RVs that had parked for the night, they were about a mile from the initial beach access.

There were less people on this part of the beach, as it widened and narrowed along the surf. At some places, it was only enough for two cars to pass each other; at others, it was nearly a hundred yards wide.

"There's a great place to walk up ahead," Sophia said, pointing to a pier-like structure jutting out into the water.

She pulled out of the surf and parked near the grassy dunes. There were just a few vehicles parked near them.

"Come on," Sophia said, "but stay out of the grassy area."

"Why?" Chris asked.

"Rattlesnakes."

There were two parallel jetties protruding out into the water about a quarter of a mile apart, both approximately two hundred yards long. Fishermen were dotted among the rocks, each trying to cast their lines as far out as possible. The structures were made of rectangular blocks, about three feet wide by eight feet long, and it seemed like there were millions of them. It was as if a giant pyramid had toppled over into the water and these were the remnants.

The stones were not laid flat, nor set in any kind of pattern. They were haphazardly dropped into place, making walking on them slightly treacherous. A person had to pay attention or they could easily fall into the surf or between the rocks.

The water was more a blue-green here, more like the color turquoise than the emerald green they had driven through. Chris and Sophia stepped onto the jetty's stones and carefully walked and jumped from one to another, heading out to the end. Sophia stumbled about fifty yards into their journey and Chris grabbed her hand. They continued to hold hands as they walked.

"I guess this is a good time to tell you how I ended up here," Chris said.

"If you want to, Chris. I don't want to pry into your personal affairs," Sophia said, cautiously jumping onto another stone.

Chris noticed this was the first time she had spoken his name. "Thank you, I appreciate that. It's kind of a bizarre story."

As they reached the end of the jetty, there was an older man packing up his fishing gear. Walking past them, he nodded, leaving them all alone on the tip of the outcropping. Sitting next to each other, Sophia let her feet dangle in the cooling waters as Chris began his story.

He started by describing who Chico was: the kind, intellectual man who had taught him so much during his post-baseball career, how he knew him in Richmond, and how he had become a father figure during those years. He recounted his trip to Laredo, the meeting with Eduardo, and discovering that Chico had been murdered. This seemed to elicit a sense of sadness from Sophia, showing an empathetic side to her. He told her about his trip to the police station and the car being impounded with his bag inside, which explained his need for new identification, and how he had to more or less escape from the library and his subsequent cab ride to Brownsville.

Sophia listened intently, allowing Chris to tell his story without interruption, which did not go unnoticed by him.

"My trip to Brownsville wasn't to visit Michael or to offer forgiveness for the past, and it certainly was not because I knew he was ill. It was one born out of necessity. I literally had nowhere else to go. It was simply a serendipitous event."

Sophia, who had been looking out onto the waters, turned to ask Chris, "What will you do now?"

"I've told Michael, and your dad, that I want to find out what happened to my friend. I have to."

"What did they say?" Sophia asked.

"After they realized I was serious, they've both been very helpful, surprisingly so. They understand how important this is for me."

"Are you aware of the irony of the situation?" Sophia asked. "You have engaged your estranged biological father to find out who killed your surrogate father."

"Yes," Chris said contemplatively, "that fact has not escaped me."

"I have a sense of foreboding about this, Chris," Sophia said, looking back out onto the blue-green waves. "These kinds of quests always seem to have unintended consequences."

"I'm aware there's an element of danger, but sometimes you have to accept that risk in life," Chris responded. "I've had to weigh several different responsibilities."

Sophia stood up and held out her hand. "Come on, let's go walk in the water."

They backtracked across the jetty and onto the sand. Chris rolled up his pants legs on his jeans and waded into the water. Sophia was wearing white shorts and a red tank top. She took off her sandals and frolicked even deeper into the water. Chris had noticed how shapely her legs were, something not often found on a woman who was just five-foot-four. He also appreciated how well-proportioned the rest of her body was. She was truly a very sexy woman. She was now walking knee-deep in the pulsating blue-green waters, tempting Chris to venture further than the rolling up of his pants allowed without them getting soaked.

"The water's so warm," she teased. "Don't worry, your pants will dry." She kicked up the foaming water at him with her feet and said, "You Virginia boys are such pussies."

Chris darted after her. She tried to run, but he caught her before she could take two steps. He adroitly picked her up, put her over his right shoulder, and walked deeper into the surf. While Sophia playfully screamed sounds of protest, he tossed her farther into the water, where she landed with a resounding splat. She popped up to the surface like a ball that had been held underwater, laughing and pulling her soaking black hair back. She swam over to Chris, who was standing chest-deep in the ocean, with the waves surging up to his neck. Sophia's feet did not touch the bottom. After treading water for a few seconds, staring at his eyes that were an even deeper blue than the waters, she put her arms around his neck, pulled herself closer, and kissed him. Chris's strong arms held her body against his, her feet still dangling in the water. Her kisses were soft and gentle, given with restrained passion, the taste of salt from the water making it even more erotic. They stood alone in the ocean, enveloped by the warm waters, and continued kissing. Chris slowly pulled away and looked into her eyes. He could tell she had been aroused by his manhandling of her; he knew all too well the effect that had on women.

He carried her back to the shore and softly set her down on the sand, both exiting the ocean completely soaked from head to toe. Sophia held onto his hand as they walked back toward the jeep. Handing Chris the keys, she said, "You drive."

After adjusting the seat, he revved the engine and took off down the beach. Sophia stood up in the passenger seat while holding onto the jeep's roll bar, her hair swirling in the wind. "This is a great way to dry off," she screamed, holding out her arms.

Chris drove down the beach, passing several other cars with people yelling and waving at the beautiful dark-haired woman standing on the seat, arms out as a child would do. She seemed so happy and innocent at this moment, Chris thought, and he acknowledged to himself that she had signs of being as beautiful inside as out. She was insightful, compassionate, intelligent, and fun. He remained cautious, however; too many lessons in his past taught him to know better.

"About a mile down the beach, there's a place called Louie's. We can eat lunch there," Sophia yelled from above. "It has blue umbrellas you can see from the beach."

A few minutes later Chris saw the blue umbrellas ahead and pulled onto the access road to enter the parking lot. Sophia jumped out while giggling.

"That was fun." She was completely dry, but Chris was still soaking wet. They chose an outside table under one of the umbrellas that overlooked the beach. Chris took out the soaking wet one hundred-dollar bills he had in his pocket and set them under a salsa bottle on the table to allow them to dry.

"I thought you were broke," Sophia said with a smirk.

"No, don't worry. I have money, I just don't have my credit cards and identification yet," Chris replied.

"Damn, and here I thought you were one of those starving artist types, sleeping on other people's couches and stealing food from friends." Sophia was clearly enjoying needling him.

"Sorry to burst your bubble, lady, but I have my own business, a house, and even my own couch," Chris shot back at her.

"Ugh! Just like any other guy: boring!" Sophia smiled and winked at Chris.

When the waitress came over, Chris ordered two beers for them while they waited for their food. They spent the next hour and a half sharing stories of their lives and how they had arrived in the places each were now. Chris told her about his twelve-year-old daughter and how she loved riding horses. Sophia talked about her life growing up in the area and shared about the passing of her mother a few years ago.

"My father was madly in love with her, but she was too free-spirited and hardheaded to appreciate how good he was to her. She drove him crazy until he finally gave up. He still has a painting of her in the store."

"That was your mother?" Chris said, astonished. "I thought that was you!"

"Thank you. She was very beautiful, wasn't she? My father told me she was pregnant with me when the painting was done."

They both shared tales of dating, with Sophia admitting she had received two marriage proposals since her divorce. "It was just not the right man either time. It's so easy to compromise, isn't it? Is it too much to ask to have some romance? I feel so often I am the man in the relationship. Women want to be able to feel like a

185

woman." She expressed complete frustration with this last statement.

Chris told her he had dated some over the last couple of years but had not met anyone he felt a real connection with, no one that he wanted to see every day. He had focused mostly on his work and his daughter.

He found it easy to make Sofia laugh and was surprised how effortless she was to be with. Relaxed and comfortable, she could hold her own in a conversation, and he was smitten with her charm and femininity.

It was midafternoon now. Chris paid for lunch, the hundred-dollar bills drying off faster than he did, and they headed back to the jeep, with Sophia driving this time. "I want to show you one more thing before we go by Garcia's," she said.

They went back across the bridge to Port Isabella where Sophia pulled into the parking lot of the old lighthouse. It was the tallest building in the town, and its pristine white paint was gleaming in the afternoon sun.

After Chris purchased two tickets, they walked inside the structure where there was a unique set of metal spiral stairs beckoning them to climb all the way to the top. Sophia started up the stairs, and Chris followed behind as they traversed the eighty or so steps to the summit. During the three-minute trip up, he had a close-up view of her beautiful brown tanned legs and shapely butt. He was quite sure this was intentional.

After reaching the landing where the giant light was kept, they stepped out onto an exterior walkway that went around the building. Sophia pointed out several buildings in the town, and they watched some of the boats entering and exiting the harbor.

While admiring the view, Chris moved behind Sophia and put his arms on each side of her as he held onto the railings. She leaned back against him, resting her head on his chest.

"It's been great getting to know you, Chris. I've had a wonderful time today," Sophia said while looking out over the sparkling waters that surrounded the quaint little town.

"Thank you. I've enjoyed it as well," Chris said. He could smell the fragrance of her hair.

"You have good eyes," she said. "They are not kind, but they're sincere and they don't miss much or look away. I've been looking for eyes like that."

Chris was startled by her candidness, and before he could respond, Sophia asked, her voice almost a whisper, "Can you do one thing for me before we go?"

"Yes, what is it?" Chris said.

"You haven't spoken my name all day. I want to hear you say it."

Chris leaned down and softly spoke into her ear in a low tone, "Sophia."

She slowly turned around and kissed him deeply, putting her arms around his neck. This kiss was more passionate and longer than the first one. It was interrupted after just a few seconds by a family who had climbed the stairs. The kids were now running around the circular walkway.

Chris and Sophia retreated down the stairs, laughing the entire way that one of the kids had pointed to them as they were kissing. They took off in the jeep toward Garcia's. While driving, Chris played with her hair, which she seemed to thoroughly enjoy, almost to the point where she was purring.

"Every guy I've gone out with in the last several years spends half the time telling me I'm beautiful or how attracted they are to me. It drives me crazy. Why do men do that?"

"Beauty is a distraction to men. It's hard to get past it sometimes. It's like seeing flashing lights on a machine and not looking beyond that. Most men are easily dazzled."

"But you're not like that, are you?"

"I've dated beautiful women before, and almost without exception they were shallow and narcissistic. Because they have been given the gift that men so desire, they never develop themselves, never seem to understand that there is a deeper connection that men also look for. Beauty is like a perfume: it's wonderful—even intoxicating—but it will eventually wear off."

"Is that how you see me?" Sophia asked, still not turning her head as Chris ran his fingers through her hair.

Chris looked at her and said, "No, not at all."

Sophia pulled in behind Garcia's store. It was just a few minutes before closing time. They found him behind one of the registers checking out some of the final Sunday shoppers. Sophia told him they would wait in the café.

They had been sitting there just a few minutes sharing a milkshake Sophia made for them when Garcia came over and handed Chris a manila envelope. Inside was his new Virginia driver's license and passport. Not only did they look completely original, but they also had an appropriate amount of wear on them. Chris was impressed.

"Your friend really is an artist, Garcia," Chris said.

"He is a dying breed," Garcia said with a wave of his hand. "Did my daughter give you the tour of South Padre Island?"

"Yes," Chris said, looking at her. "It's quite beautiful, we had a great time."

"Where are you off to now?" Garcia asked with raised eyebrows.

"We're going to go check on Michael," Sophia said. "He's been by himself all day."

"Oh, he has probably had many visitors today. He loves Sundays," Garcia said, laughing.

Sophia and Chris left the store and drove back toward Michael's house. The streets were eerily empty again, especially after all the early morning revelry.

As they parked in front of the house, all signs of Sunday service, bleachers, tape, and pulpit were long gone. There was no one standing in front of the tree, and it was quiet.

After walking through the gate and across the uneven sidewalk, Chris saw a note had been taped to the front door. He quickly climbed up the steps and pulled it off. It was scribbled in a man's sloppy handwriting:

Juan and Mando called – they have the name.

Chapter 9

"I promise I'll be careful,"

Chris had said, giving final words of assurance before Sophia had left last night. She had expressed concern that he and Michael were off on some journey that was sure to be mired in danger. Even though his promise was genuine, he shared her trepidation of what potential peril may lie ahead. He was touched by her sincere concern. *She really does have a good heart*, he thought.

After she left, he had checked in on Michael and made a couple of work-related phone calls to his supervisor Jim to see if he had everything under control for the coming week. He then called his ex-wife to make sure she was able to keep their daughter Kendall during his unplanned extended stay. He was once again thankful that they had remained on amicable terms since their divorce years ago. There had been many occasions when schedules had to be modified, and neither party ever complained about the inconvenience. In many ways, they had a better relationship now than when they were married.

Chris had been lying in his bed thinking about yesterday evening, but now his thoughts turned to today. What was going to happen next? Did Juan and Mando really have the name of Chico's killer? Did they find out the reason behind his murder? What would he do with the information? How was he going to get the name from them? Surely, they'd want to get paid first.

Chris heard floorboards creaking down the hall, coming toward his room, then there was a gentle tapping at the door. "You awake?" It was Michael's early morning raspy voice.

Chris rose from his bed and opened the door. "Morning," he said.

"You want some breakfast?" Michael asked.

"Sure, thanks," Chris answered.

Michael headed off toward the kitchen while Chris took a shower, again leaving the door slightly open.

After dressing, he walked into the kitchen where Michael was standing next to the stove making some scrambled eggs and toast.

"How was your date?" Michael asked with a grin.

"It was fun...and a little surprising."

"What was surprising about it?"

"Umm..." Chris was caught off guard, wishing he had not elaborated. "I found Sophia to be more interesting than I expected."

Michael walked to the table and scooped some eggs onto his plate. "She's special, isn't she?"

"You're as bad as Garcia," Chris said dismissively. "Tell me about the phone call yesterday."

Michael sat down and reached for a cigarette that was already burning in the old glass ashtray.

"Mando called yesterday and said they want to meet us in Laredo this afternoon. He said they have the name of the person that murdered your friend, so bring two thousand dollars. I guess that means that's all they have at this point."

"That's all he said? What do you make of that?"

"I'm guessing they got the name and want no part of any further digging. I'd be willing to bet they wish they didn't even find out who did it, but they did. They just want to get their two thousand dollars and wash their hands of the situation."

"So, when we get the name, then what?" Chris asked.

"It depends on the name. We'll have to decide on our actions after that."

"When are we supposed to meet them?"

Michael put out the last remnants of his cigarette while saying, "Two o'clock."

"I'd like to get my credit cards before we go," Chris said.

"Okay. I'll call Herman when they open this morning and check on their status."

"Should I rent a car for the trip?" Chris asked, hoping not to have to drive Michael's beat-up truck.

"I know the truck don't look like much, but I promise she'll make it there and back. Besides, if we are to do some scouting, we'll be invisible in that truck. No one looks at beat-up old cars or who's inside."

"All right," Chris said, with some resignation. "Let me go get ready."

"I think you should pack all your stuff. We may be staying the night in Laredo," Michael called after him. "There's a suitcase in the bedroom next to yours."

Chris went to his room and packed the limited amount of clothing he had after retrieving a scuffed-up brown and tan leather suitcase from the adjacent room. It looked like it was from the 1940s. He took the six thousand, two hundred dollars he had remaining and put two thousand dollars in his left pocket, two hundred dollars in his right pocket, and the other four thousand dollars in his shoes. He then went to find Michael who was sitting on the front porch smoking another cigarette.

Setting down his suitcase next to a similar one Michael had packed, he said, "I understand you're not supposed to be smoking."

"Doctors don't know everything," Michael said, staring out at the tree. "How much longer will I live if I don't smoke? Some things are out of our hands."

"How long have you known?" Chris asked.

"Since they told me, but I've suspected for a while."

"Why didn't you tell me?"

Michael turned to look at Chris. "Because I didn't know you then." He got up from his chair as he extinguished his cigarette and went inside to call the bank.

Chris waited on the porch, watching the Monday morning rush to work for the downtown crowd. Men in suits and polished shoes carrying secrets in their leather cases, women in business outfits and comfortable sneakers carrying their indoor footwear in bags. One woman was stopped at the light on the corner while frantically trying to put on her makeup at the last minute.

Michael came back out and sat down, saying, "Herman said your cards will be here at ten. That gives us time to gas up and go by Garcia's."

195

"Why do we need to go there?" Chris asked.

"I told him I would let him know about any progress we made, and I want to let him know that we're leaving town."

Michael went inside and locked all the doors, then they took their suitcases out to where the truck was parked in the makeshift garage, placing them in the back. Michael handed the keys to Chris and said, "You drive."

Chris stopped at an Exxon gas station a couple of blocks away before heading to Garcia's. When they walked in, Garcia was already busy reorganizing the manhandled merchandise from Sunday's throng of shoppers.

"Morning, gentlemen," he said, extending his arms out as he spoke in his usual cheery tone. "Some early morning shopping?"

The three men sat at one of the diner's booths again as Michael informed Garcia they had received a call from the cabbies informing them they had the name of the murderer. He told Garcia they were driving up to Laredo and may come back tonight or tomorrow.

Garcia expressed concern, saying, "Some information is not given with impunity."

"That's very true," Chris said, "but we've come this far. We'll let you know what happens."

Michael and Chris left, drove the few blocks to the bank, and parked out front. Chris glanced at Michael's house and noticed it seemed even more dilapidated from a distance; the broken fencing, the sagging sections of the house, and unkept exterior made it look as though it was abandoned.

They entered, and Chris was met by Graciella's welcoming smile as she waved to them from her desk. She walked over and invited them to sit down on the sofa and two chairs in their entrance for a minute while she went to find the Fed-Ex package. She returned shortly and helped Chris open the box that contained his credit cards.

"Thank you," Chris said politely. "I feel normal again."

"You're welcome, Chris," she said, smiling broadly. "Here's my card if I can be of any further service." She handed him a business card with her name and title smartly embossed on the front.

As they left, Chris noticed there was something additional on the back, with "Home #" written by hand above the seven numbers. Michael saw this also, and as they opened the doors to exit, he said, "I told you."

Chris inserted the credit cards in his new wallet, alongside his ever-growing collection of business cards, and headed out of town following Michael's directions.

"We should be in Laredo by about 1:30," Michael said. "They said to call Juan's cell phone when we get there."

"I think it's time I bought a cell phone," Chris said. "If cabbies and criminals are using them, I need one, too. I have a feeling it will come in handy in the near future."

Michael agreed with the potential value it could hold and said they could get one in Laredo. Then he lit a cigarette as they turned onto Highway 83. Michael stared out the window as he smoked, seemingly deep in thought. Chris looked out onto the flat, almost endless landscape on each side of the highway.

Even though it was the rainy season in Brownsville, it had not rained since Chris arrived. The overcast skies and darkening horizon forecast an inevitable change in that situation. The low, gray clouds made the terrain appear as if it was underwater; there was no reflection of sunshine, no discernable shadows, and the wind made the plants move as if they were in the ebb and flow of the waves. The sandy soil was easily imagined as the bottom of an ocean as the flat lighting from overhead appeared to give the surrounding air buoyancy. Only the fish were absent to complete the optical illusion.

Michael had finished smoking and leaned back in his seat, quickly falling asleep. Chris presumed this was caused by his medicine he had taken, or maybe from being a passenger in the truck. The straight, flat highway seemed to roll on forever to the horizon; it was a tedious drive. There was what appeared to be a bluish-gray wall intersecting the highway ahead. Chris was unsure of the distance since the monotonous asphalt was difficult to gauge. As the wall grew larger in the windshield, he soon realized as they moved that it was moving toward them. He could see the curtain of water pelting the road, and traffic coming in the opposite direction had their wipers frantically moving across the glass. He then remembered that there was something the truck was missing...windshield wipers!

The wall was now only a few seconds away. There was no place to pull off onto the shoulder, and no exits nearby. Spotting a tractor-trailer truck up ahead, Chris asked the lethargic engine for everything it had. Just as the torrential rain hit them, he pulled in behind the truck, only able to make out the taillights that were all too close. The rain sounded like a thousand little metal hammers hitting the truck as if they were trying to beat off what paint was left. Chris stayed close to the truck hoping the driver would not slow down or suddenly brake, as the ten or so feet between the vehicles would never be enough time to stop. He was hyper-focused on the glowing red lights ahead, the two little beacons showing him the way like a lighthouse would a ship in a storm. He stayed like this for almost five minutes, hunched over the tightly gripped steering wheel, when suddenly, as quickly as it came, the storm was gone. The sunlight shone brightly like someone had turned on a giant light switch in the sky and yellow light gloriously beamed down through the trailing clouds.

Chris slowed down and receded back behind the truck to a safe distance. After a minute, he changed lanes and passed the truck. As he did so, the trucker gave him a thumbs up, apparently signifying he knew they were behind him the whole time. Michael had slept during the entire storm. Chris wondered if this was the most dangerous event they would encounter on their trip or if this was an omen of the many obstacles that might lie ahead.

For the next twenty minutes, Michael slept while Chris drove. He spent the time thinking about questions he had long wanted to ask him, as well as some more recent ones. He knew there was probably no delicate way to broach these topics, but he also knew he would probably never get a better opportunity.

When Michael awoke, he asked how far away from Laredo they were. "About two hours or so," Chris responded. Michael lit another cigarette and Chris continued, "Do you mind if I ask you some questions?"

"I knew you would, sooner or later. What took you so long?" Michael said with a chuckle.

"First, I want to thank you for all your help. I really did not know what to expect when I showed up at your door."

"Neither did I," Michael responded. "I'm sure there was mutual apprehension. Go on."

"You probably don't have an answer for this one, but something has happened since I've been staying with you. Twice I've walked up the stairs to the bathroom and got a feeling of déjà vu. How is that possible?"

"Because you have been there before," Michael said, evoking a questioning look from Chris. "When you were about four or five, your mother drove down from Virginia with you and your two sisters and stayed in the same room you are in now. We had talked briefly about reconciling, but that was our love doing the thinking, not our brains."

"What does that mean?" Chris said, wanting more information.

"I had not stopped drinking, even though I told her I had. I couldn't even stop for the few days she was here." Michael was looking off into the distance as he spoke. "We loved each other very much when I was sober, but those times became more infrequent. She packed up and left in the night while I was passed out on the couch, just like before."

"What do you mean, just like before?"

Michael turned to Chris and said, "She never told you?"

"Mom never said a bad word about you that I ever heard. Even when you came back to see us a few years ago, she never showed any animosity of any kind. She was genuinely glad to see you."

Michael again looked out the window and said, "She was a damn fine woman, had a heart of gold." Turning back to Chris, he said, "If you ever find a woman like that, hold on to her with all ten fingers."

"So, what happened? You said, she never told you?" Chris said, pursuing the answer.

"I came home one evening, absolutely stinking drunk. I don't even know where I'd been. It was one of hundreds of times I had done this, but…this night was different…"

"What do you mean?"

"Your mother forgave me for a lot of transgressions, but this was the time she'd had enough because…I hit her." Michael seemed to be reliving the moment in his head, as if it had happened recently. He could not look at Chris. There was a pause before he could continue.

"So, in the middle of the night, she packed up an infant, a three-year-old, and a four-year-old, put all the belongings she could get into our old station wagon, and drove an hour and a half to your grandmother's house. She left a note saying she was done and asked me to leave her alone. The next thing I remember, I was back in Brownsville."

There was a deafening silence inside the cab of the truck for a few minutes before Chris spoke up, asking, "What happened to you after that?"

"I'm told I drank even more, if that's possible. I was staying at the house I live in now because my mother needed help maintaining the place. I was the resident drunk handyman for many years."

"Did you communicate at all with her?"

"She would send the occasional letter telling me about you kids, I think more out of courtesy than anything else. But besides the one trip she made down here, we didn't see each other for almost thirty years. I would occasionally send her money. I had very little at the time, but she would always send it back. Whatever you kids have become, you owe it all to her."

Chris knew he had delved enough into the past for the time being and could feel the emotional pain Michael was so poorly trying to hide. Deciding to change the subject, Chris waited for a few minutes, then asked about how he knew Garcia.

"I met him at Camp Wolters during basic training. We had known each other a little in high school, but Mexicans and whites didn't socialize much back then. He went on to train to be an aircraft mechanic, and I wanted to be an aviator, so we were both sent to Randolph Field after boot camp. I was learning to fly, and he was turning into a fine mechanic. He had a real feel for the planes, was great with his hands, and had amazing focus when he worked. We often talked about how we were going to kick the Germans' asses once we were sent to Europe.

"Well, apparently some army geniuses needed people for their new EOD program since the Germans had placed land mines throughout Europe by the thousands. They interviewed hundreds of army personnel, from mechanics to technicians to metal fabricators, anybody that was skilled with their hands and had high concentration skills. Garcia was a perfect candidate for the job, so they sent him to Aberdeen, Maryland. The next time I heard from him, he was heading to North Africa. He worked there for a year before being sent to England to prepare for the D-Day invasion."

Chris was in awe of this statement, seeing as he was an amateur historian of WWII. "Was he actually part of the landing?"

"He went in on Omaha Beach."

"Wow!" Chris responded, "they took the worst beating."

"He was considered to be what they referred to as 'Protected Personnel.' He was there to defuse bombs on the beach, on the roads, and in the hedgerow countryside once they got there. Garcia was one of the last to land. He said the water he waded through was red with all the blood from dead and wounded soldiers. He dragged several wounded soldiers to safety from drowning as the tide started to rise. Once the beach was secured, it was his job to dismantle landmines and magnetic mines in the water so they could install the Mulberries, allowing all those thousands of trucks and tanks access to the beach. He was shot in the leg his first week and never stopped working. He knew the men were relying on him."

"Damn, he was one tough son of a bitch," Chris said, thoroughly impressed.

"He received a purple heart and a bronze star. He's the only man I have ever said I would trust with my life."

"Did you really see him kill a man with his bare hands?" Chris asked apprehensively.

Michael took a minute to light another cigarette and to recall the memories in preparation for his tale.

205

"He was in Bastogne, Belgium, and I was serving my second tour of duty at an airfield about fifteen miles away. It was in February 1945. We had the Germans on the run after the Battle of the Bulge. I had a two-day pass and drove into the town with a couple of other pilots.

"We were looking for booze and girls, but all we found was bombed-out buildings and worn-out soldiers. They were still rooting out a few Germans who had captured families and been forced to hide them. The first night, Garcia, my buddies, and I were walking to a tavern that was still intact when we heard yelling down an alley. We ran in the direction to find a Belgian man in a knife fight with a German soldier. We found out later the man had discovered the soldier had been raping his daughter. Garcia ran toward the two men as the German stabbed the father. Garcia picked up the lid of a trashcan as he approached him and used it to defend himself from the German's knife. He pushed the soldier against a building, pinning him there. We ran over to help, but Garcia had wrestled him to the ground and started strangling him. By the time we reached them, he had crushed his neck and the soldier had stopped breathing, not that we would have stopped him.

"Garcia and I took the Belgian man to the hospital while my buddies checked on the family. The man was released from the hospital after they patched him up, and the next night his family invited all four of us to have dinner at their home. I remember the young daughter crying while hugging Garcia and speaking in French. She said, 'Tu es mon sauveur.'"

Chris contemplated the story, trying to reconcile the roly-poly retailer that had such a happy disposition and friendly smile with the cold-blooded killer he had just heard about. It was an amazing war story, to be sure, but also a tale of a man with a possible Jekyll and Hyde personality. Ultimately, Chris came to an obvious conclusion. "I guess war makes people do strange things," he said.

"You have no idea," Michael responded while looking out onto the black ribbon of highway stretched in front of them.

The two men sat in silence for a period of time, Chris sensing that Michael had spent a good deal of emotional energy reliving the experiences from so long ago. Michael finally spoke up, asking, "Do you think we should call them soon?"

Chris looked at his watch and said, "We're still about forty minutes away, but I'll stop at a phone in a few minutes and let them know where we are. Did they tell you where we're meeting?"

"No, they said to call them and they'll let us know then."

A few miles later, Chris took an exit that had multiple gas stations and fast-food stops. He pulled up to a pay phone and called Juan, who answered immediately.

"Hola," he said.

"Juan, it's Chris Hamilton. I'm calling you to let you know we're about thirty-five minutes from Laredo."

"What road are you on?" Juan asked.

"Highway 83."

"In about fifteen minutes, you will come to a town called Rio Bravo. Meet us behind the Webb County Water Utilities building. We'll be there in about twenty minutes." Juan hung up and left Chris with the distinct feeling that he had not wanted to prolong the conversation.

He got back in the truck and told Michael the plan and meeting place. Michael responded, "I know where it is. We used to go fishing near there. It's on a desolate road near nothing."

"Any idea why they'd pick a place like that?" Chris asked.

"Yes," Michael responded. "It's far enough away from Laredo and isolated enough that they'll feel safe. Like I said, I think they're scared."

They pulled back onto the highway and drove the fifteen minutes before exiting into the town of Rio Bravo. There were just a few stores on the main road and one McDonald's. About three minutes past the stores, they turned down a road that had a sign saying "Water Utilities Building." Half a mile down the road was a one-story building with a flat roof made of brown stone with light blue stone accents. A tall blue water tower stood ominously in a field behind the building. There were a couple of white vans parked on one side of the building, and it was obvious they had been there for a while. Chris turned into the parking lot and pulled in behind the building. He did not see anyone or any evidence of activity.

He parked the truck and stepped out to stretch his legs as Michael sat inside and lit another cigarette. Chris stood in the parking lot looking out over the marshland that surrounded the water tower, wondering what the next few minutes would hold.

Shortly, the familiar Studebaker cab with "Juan's Taxi" written on the side came pulling up beside the truck. Michael stood up, dropping his half-finished cigarette to the ground, and stepped on it.

Juan and Mando both got out and approached Chris and Michael. Chris noticed they looked around as they walked toward them, checking for any prying eyes.

"Hola, gentlemen," Juan greeted them. "I hope you have been well." He was a little more reserved than he had been in the past.

"Did you bring the money?" Mando asked, ever the businessman.

"What do you have for us?" Michael interjected.

Mando proudly replied, "Like I told you on the phone, we have the name for you."

"We also talked about finding out what, when, where, and why," Michael said firmly.

"We have the name, and that's all we're going to get," Mando replied emphatically. "We have put ourselves at great risk just getting the name. If we had known who it was before we agreed to our deal, we would not have done anything!"

Chris, sensing rising tensions, said, "I've brought the money, guys, and we appreciate what you've done. I owe you a lot."

Juan then chimed in, "Look, Señor, we really like you, and we try to help you out because you are friends with the Guerras, but I think now you take the name and go home. Do not pursue this any farther."

"Thank you, Juan. I guess we'll have to make that decision." He then reached into his pocket and handed Mando the two thousand dollars.

Juan retrieved a business card from his pocket and handed it to Chris. "The name is written on the back, Señor."

Chris turned over the card in his hand and read the name out loud, "Villatoro Sacarras."

"He is known as El Loco Diablo," Juan added, almost in a whisper.

Michael seemed shaken by the announcement of the name. He looked at Mando and asked, "How sure are you of your information?"

"I am one hundred percent positive of my source and the accuracy of the information. I would not give you such a name impulsively," Mando said, steadfast in his belief.

"Well, thank you, then," Michael said as he turned and walked away.

Chris thanked Mando and Juan again and shook their hands as he said goodbye. They went to their cab and slowly drove off. Chris turned to see Michael was looking out onto the same marshland he had and was in the process of lighting another cigarette.

Chris walked up behind him and stood there for a moment before speaking. "You seem upset. Do you know this man?"

Michael took a deep drag on his cigarette and answered, "I knew that name a long time ago. It was a time—and a person—I have tried very hard to forget."

"Who is he?" Chris asked, wondering why Michael had been so affected by the mere mention of this man's name.

Michael was slow in his response, eventually saying, "He is an evil man. He has no morals, no principles, he only cares about himself. I was praying he was long ago dead."

Chris slid the card into his pocket, half hoping the gesture would alleviate some of his anguish. Michael seemed to be held in a trance, just looking into the distance, not even smoking his cigarette. He stayed like that for several minutes as Chris grew increasingly concerned. Michael suddenly turned and said, "We need to go buy a cell phone." Then he walked to the car and got inside.

Chris followed him to the truck and drove back down the empty road toward the interstate, then turned toward Laredo. Michael was deep in thought, so Chris kept quiet and just drove, speculating he was trying to figure out a way to extricate himself from their quest or formulate some kind of plan.

After about twenty minutes, they entered the outskirts of Laredo. Chris thought briefly about how he had recently exited this city and how it seemed more like a few weeks than just a few days ago. He turned onto one of the busiest streets, the kind that had all the mini-malls and fast-food chains. He drove while scouting for a place to buy a cell phone, eventually spotting a Radio Shack that was tucked into one of the ubiquitous strip malls. Chris parked, and before he turned off the engine, Michael said, "I'll wait here."

Inside the store he found a young and very helpful kid standing behind the counter. He was exactly what you'd expect to find at this kind of store; nerdy with black-rimmed glasses, a white short-sleeved shirt with a cheap clip-on tie, and three pens in his breast pocket. He was quite knowledgeable about cell phones, which Chris thought was perhaps a status symbol among his peers: knowing all about the latest technical gadgets.

After spending a few minutes listening to the young kid's advice, Chris bought a Motorola cell phone and signed up for a monthly service. After a brief tutorial on charging, turning it on, dialing, etc., Chris left the store with his new toy. He had debated whether he should have bought one back in Virginia but had always thought the phone he had installed in his truck was more than sufficient. Besides, he didn't like the idea of being always accessible. Things were now different here in Laredo.

Chris sat in the truck and plugged the phone's charger into the cigarette lighter.

"The first thing we need to do is call Speedy," Michael said, surprising Chris. "We need to tell him we have the name and see what he can find out. Then we need to find a place to stay."

"So, you have a plan?" Chris asked.

"Not really, just the beginnings of one. We need a lot more information before we can make a plan."

Chris dug out Speedy's number from his drenched suitcase. Fortunately, the old girl had kept the contents mostly dry.

It took a minute to dial, then Speedy answered immediately. After Chris told him they had the name, Speedy repeated his charges for his services, agreeing to meet the next morning. Chris gave him his new cell phone number, and Speedy said he would call when he arrived.

"How much faith do you have in this guy?" Chris asked Michael after he hung up.

"Don't judge a book by its cover," Michael said. "Speedy is an ex-cop."

Chris was completely taken off guard by the revelation. "You're shitting me!"

"No. He was good, too, but he didn't like playing by the rules. He thought police were way underpaid, so he augmented his salary." Michael let the words hang in the air.

"He was into taking bribes, stealing, what?"

"He was into shortcuts," Michael said with a chuckle. "I think you'll be surprised by the results he achieves. He has always impressed me and Garcia."

"I hope so," Chris said, then turned and looked intently at Michael.

"What?" Michael asked.

"Do I have to ask? Do I need to ask you about the elephant in the room?" Chris continued, "We get the name we have been waiting for, one I paid good money to get, and it elicits such a reaction from you that you don't talk to me for twenty minutes. Are you not going to tell me what you know about this man?"

"I guess you find it a little strange that I would know the man that killed your friend?"

"No shit, Sherlock," Chris said in a demonstrative tone.

Michael took out a cigarette and lit it, something Chris noticed he often did when he reminisced. He stuffed his lighter back in his pants and began.

"After the war, lots of pilots that came back home were looking for work in aviation. I tried crop dusting, mail delivery, commercial pilot, even giving flying lessons, but it was hard to make a living at any of those things. I had started drinking a lot after the war, so that didn't help. The flying industry had stagnated in America during the war, and it took years before it caught up. Lots of good pilots who fought for this country couldn't find work. I knew an old buddy who had gotten involved with flying contraband across the Mexican border. He was working for a group of men that had pickups in Mexico that were delivered to various places in America. They didn't smuggle drugs back then, it was different. We flew in items like stolen merchandise that was too hot to fence in Mexico, wealthy people taking large amounts of cash across the border, products that were heavily taxed by U.S. Customs, medicine that was not approved in the States, people escaping from prison, large amounts of gold and silver, jewels, everything. I even once flew in a couple of Nazis who had made a deal with the C.I.A. to live in America for being double agents during the war.

"We would usually fly at night, landing on every kind of runway in all sorts of out-of-the-way places. And we'd have to fly in all types of weather, and we didn't have radar back then. It was exciting, dangerous, and it paid very well. I was a damn good pilot, so I was never afraid, but some guys couldn't hack it.

"One day I got a flight to go pick up what I was told was stolen Aztec antiquities that had been looted from a museum in Monterrey, Mexico. It was for Sacarras.

"I had flown in some cargo for his father before, but he had been killed in some duel or something. His father was a son of a bitch, but his two sons were worse. Nobody liked them. They were obsessed with the occult, and there were all sorts of rumors about them being into all kinds of crazy shit and doing really perverse stuff. I didn't want the job, but I was young and dumb and needed the money. They offered me a thousand dollars for a day's work, which was a hell of a lot in 1950.

"When I flew in, it was late in the day. I had met a truck outside Monterrey at some old airfield. Well, the bastards kept shoving things into the cargo hold, some of it very heavy. All kinds of boxes of stuff—gold, silver, jewelry, antiquities. They even had items in the passenger seats. I found out later they were stolen items from a museum and a bank, and it was too much for me to safely haul in one load. When I took off, I was probably five hundred pounds over my limit, and I was flying back at night. I barely got off the ground, and I could never get enough altitude, but I managed to get within thirty miles of Brownsville before I ran into a storm. I couldn't fly above it, so I tried to go through. I kept losing altitude and had to land in the desert. When I came down, the weight caused the landing gear to break, and the nose of the plane dug into the sand. When I finally stopped, the propeller was bent, the landing gear gone, and my left ankle was broken.

"I drank whiskey and ate aspirin all night for the pain. Come sunup, I left the plane and tried to find help. I found two sticks in the desert I used as a makeshift crutch. Somehow, I made it to a road and laid there until a farmer picked me up and took me to a doctor."

Michael had stopped telling his story for a moment as if he was unsure where to pick up the tale again.

"So, you were safe. You ended up okay, right?" Chris asked.

"No, not really. Two days later, Garcia came to get me. I had been in a hospital bed with a cast on my foot and suffering from dehydration. When we drove out to where the plane had crashed, everything in the plane was gone. The plane was there, but all the cargo was completely gone."

"What happened then?" Chris asked.

"I found out later Sacarras thought I was responsible. He blamed me for him not getting his precious artifacts, and he didn't care that I was almost killed. He sent men looking for me. He wanted his Aztec junk, which he was sure I had taken, or have them kill me. I hid out for a few days, then left town and went to Florida for a while. By the time I returned to Brownsville, I guess they had either found the stuff or given up searching."

Once again, Michael seemed emotionally drained, so Chris let him lean against the window and close his eyes. He soon fell asleep.

Chris was debating where they should stay for the evening and what to do with this information about Sacarras. He drove aimlessly for a while, then suddenly had an idea. "I need to make a phone call," he said to himself, then pulled over.

Chapter 10

"I need to talk to you,"

Chris said while thinking how odd it was to be using such a technologically advanced device to call an old rotary phone sitting at the top of the stairs in a centuries-old house.

"Where are you?" Eduardo asked, not showing surprise by the out-of-the-blue phone call.

"I'm in Laredo. I have some important information about Chico. Are you available this afternoon?"

"Yes, I would like to hear what you have to say. What time can you be here?"

Chris looked at his watch. It was 3:30. "I can be there in about half an hour."

"Yes, that will be fine. Do you remember how to get here?" Eduardo asked.

"Yes," Chris said. "See you soon."

Chris walked back to the car. Michael was still asleep. He drove toward the part of town that he was somewhat familiar with to get his bearings. Once there, he recognized some landmarks and turned toward his destination. Michael woke up and looked around, asking, "Where in the hell are we going?"

"I have someone I want you to meet," Chris said. "I think you will find this very interesting."

Michael lit a cigarette as Chris drove on. He soon turned off the main road and down Flowering Cactus Drive. Michael looked out his window at the lavish homes with their well-manicured landscaping and commented, "You didn't tell me your friend lived in the slums."

At the end of the street, Chris pulled into the large circular driveway and turned off the engine. The two men got out of the truck just as Eduardo appeared at the top of the stairs.

"Hola, my brother," he said as he descended the steps to greet them. "I am so glad to see you."

He walked over to Chris and fervently shook his hand, grinning broadly as he looked at him. "I have been so worried about you since your last call."

"Thank you. I apologize for my abrupt ending. I was very tired, it had been a long day."

Eduardo stood back and held up his hands, gesturing. "Please, there is no need to apologize, my friend."

"Eduardo," Chris said, turning toward Michael, "I would like you to meet Michael...my father."

Eduardo was visibly surprised at this announcement and took a second to regain his usual demeanor, eventually saying, "Welcome, Michael. This is quite an honor." He walked over to shake his hand. Eduardo was clearly confused, not just by the fact that Chris had a father, but about why he would bring him here. However, his social graces intervened in the situation, and he behaved in his usual courteous fashion.

"Thank you, Eduardo," Michael said.

"Please come and sit down. You have much to tell me, I'm sure." Eduardo gestured for the men to follow him as he walked up the stairs.

He led Chris and Michael through the courtyard, the first floor of the house, and out onto the patio where Chris had last seen the two señoras having breakfast. The afternoon sun was now setting behind the tall hedges and the wisteria that enveloped the wooden arbor keeping the patio cool and shaded. As they walked, Michael looked at his surroundings, clearly impressed with the house and grounds, but said nothing. They sat down in large comfortable

222

chairs next to a wooden table, opposite to where the señoras had tea when Chris was previously at Casa de la Guerra. The fountain in the center splashed loudly.

"Have the police contacted you about returning the Pajero?" Chris started out.

"No, we have heard nothing since you told us it was impounded," Eduardo said, raising his hands again. "But I will look into it. I find it very strange that someone would report it as stolen. I can't understand why."

"I can," Michael interjected. "I think Chris was asking too many questions about something certain people thought had been forgotten, and someone got scared."

Eduardo spoke, talking to Chris, "When I told you that Armando had been murdered, I did it out of respect. I thought you should know since he meant so much to you."

"And I appreciate that, Eduardo, but I couldn't leave town without some answers. It's just not something you can let go. I'm sure you understand that," Chris replied.

"Yes, of course, but now you say you are in danger. I wish I had never said anything." Eduardo seemed sincere in his concerns, making large gestures with his hands.

"You didn't know I would pursue the issue, and even if you did, you certainly couldn't have suspected it would cause problems." Chris was trying to placate his newly found friend.

Michael interjected again, asking, "How did you find out he had been murdered?"

Eduardo took a deep breath and looked down at the table. "About a week after the funeral, we received a letter in the mail. It was typed on a computer and had no return address. It was written to the señoras. All it said was, 'Your brother was murdered.'"

"Were you surprised by that?" Michael asked.

"No, not really," Eduardo said, looking up at him while leaning back in his chair. "I did not believe the police when they said he had just wandered into the desert and died from the elements." Eduardo made a motion dismissing their story.

"Which leads me to why I came to see you today." Chris spoke in a matter-of-fact tone.

Eduardo's eyes grew narrower and he asked, "Yes, what is it you wish to talk about?" His voice was calm and measured.

"Have you ever heard the name Villatoro Sacarras?" Chris asked.

Eduardo looked at Chris with a blank stare, as if trying to remember some old tale. He then looked at Michael, and after a moment he stood up and walked a few steps away, his back to the men.

Michael gave Chris a perplexed look, and Chris shrugged. Looking over his shoulder, Eduardo spoke in a slow, choppy cadence. "It was a name I heard when I was a boy. I never knew why, but it was always whispered in hushed tones, like they were talking about something evil. I remember when his father died, there were rumors… I really don't know much, I was very young. But that name has always been inside of my head." He turned back and looked at Chris. "Why do you ask such a question?" He seemed to know the answer but was apprehensive.

"Because," Chris said, "we have been told he was the one who murdered Chico."

Eduardo looked down at the paving in the patio and took a few steps back toward Chris and Michael. Looking directly into Chris's eyes, he asked, "Are you sure?"

"Yes," Chris said, resolute in his tone.

Eduardo turned his stare back to the patio. "There is someone who can tell you much more than I can," he said, "but I do not know if they will talk to you."

"You mean the señoras?" Chris asked, understanding his apprehension. "But they don't know you told me Chico was murdered, do they?"

"I have told them about our conversation," Eduardo said with a slight sigh. "They are very private and did not want such matters known, but they agreed it is what Armando would have wanted."

Eduardo had walked back toward the table. "Where are you staying tonight?"

"We don't know, we haven't made plans yet," Chris replied while glancing at Michael.

Eduardo's personality returned to him enthusiastically, and he said, "Then you must stay here! Yes, I will have the casitas prepared for you. We can have dinner, and I will talk to the señoras." Eduardo immediately started waving his hands, dismissing any objections. "I do not want to hear what you have to say. You are staying here!"

Michael and Chris laughed at his demonstrative display, and both said, "Thank you."

Eduardo excused himself to have someone get their luggage and have a maid prepare their rooms. He said he would return shortly.

Michael looked at Chris and took out his lighter and cigarettes, then said, "I let you stay at my house, and this is how you repay me? By having us stay at this piece of shit place?" He laughed his familiar, gravelly laugh.

"What do you make of what he said?" Chris asked.

"Well," Michael said, lighting his cigarette, "I think he's a bit taken aback by your Quixotic adventure."

"What do you mean?"

"I think he had suspicions. They could even have been subconscious, but you have confirmed his worst fears," Michael said, putting away his trusty lighter.

"You think he intentionally planted a seed when he told me Chico was murdered? Do you think he was hoping I would investigate further?" Chris asked.

"I don't think so. He seems too genuine of a person. I do think he now regrets getting you involved, even if it was unintentional," Michael said, leaning back in his chair. "But his reaction to Sacarras was interesting, and the rumors he heard when he was young that have stuck in his head all these years. For some reason, I don't think he was completely surprised when you said his name. Do you think the señoras will talk to us?"

"I don't know," Chris responded. "They are not communicative at all. As Eduardo said, they are very private people."

"Well," Michael said, pointing at the house with his cigarette, "they probably know a lot of Sacarrass's history, and anything they can tell us will be helpful if we move against him."

"Are we going to move against him?" Chris asked, surprised at this announcement.

"Damn right, we are!"

Eduardo returned and escorted Chris and Michael to the casitas, along the way giving Michael a quick tour of the house and property. Chris thought Eduardo must feel obligated to give every new visitor at least an overview of the estate, like a tour guide at a historical site. He wondered how often he had done this throughout his life and how infrequently he got to proudly tell visitors about Casa de la Guerra these days.

Upon reaching the patio where Chris had dined a few days earlier, Eduardo directed each man to their awaiting casita. Chris was in the same one he had previously stayed in, and Michael was in the adjacent one, their luggage was sitting on their beds. Eduardo informed them that dinner would be served on the patio at 7:30 and left to attend to other matters. Michael told Chris he was going to take a nap and asked him to wake him at 7. Chris took the time to plug in his new cell phone and make a few calls, checking in with his supervisor, Jim Payette, and calling his daughter, Kendall, to apologize for having to switch weeks with her mother. He promised to take her horseback riding when he returned.

After unpacking a few items, he walked across the patio to awaken Michael. The torches that surrounded the patio had been lit and provided dancing shadows of the many plants and flowers as the sun was beginning to set over the massive hedges that surrounded their small enclave. Michael came to the door still a little dazed and said he would join them outside at 7:30.

Chris was just leaving his casita as the servants were bringing the food. Michael followed a couple minutes later. Eduardo soon arrived wearing black pants and a long-sleeved black shirt. Chris thought he looked quite dashing in all-black and noticed how his graying temples contrasted against his dark attire, dark skin, and coal black hair, like an artist had added just a splash of color to this handsome Latino.

As the men ate, the topics of conversation were much lighter and freewheeling than the day's earlier interrogations. Eduardo regaled the two men with stories of growing up on the property and some of the hunting trips he took while riding the many horses they used to have. He seemed quite nostalgic about those days. He told Michael a few stories about Armando and their travels together but was wise enough not to go on with the tales for too long. In turn, Michael shared a few of his endless war stories; what it was like to be a pilot in WWII and some of the planes he flew. Eduardo appeared fascinated and surprised them both by being so knowledgeable about the planes. Michael said he had flown to Laredo many times as a pilot delivering passengers or when he was crop dusting, but he said he never really got to see the town. He did not mention any of his illegal flights across the border. The men thoroughly enjoyed their time dining together, Chris acknowledging this was the first time he had socialized with Michael. Up until now all their conversations had been of a more serious nature.

A short time after they had finished dining and the plates and silverware had been removed, from just outside the flickering light of the fire lamps appeared two small figures. They walked from the shadows quietly and gently, like entering a church. Even in the darkness, Chris recognized the petite and frail figures of the señoras. As they neared, Eduardo rose from his chair and pulled out the one next to it, allowing a graceful approach for them.

Michael rose first, then Chris, as the señoras walked to the table. All three men remained standing until the señoras were seated. Eduardo, graciously and dutifully, took a moment to introduce Rosa and Isabella to Michael, who nodded, sensing these were women that required respect even without speaking.

"Eduardo tells us that you may have put yourself in danger in the attempt to find out what happened to our brother," Rosa started out saying.

"It seems I have upset a few people in the search for some answers," Chris respectfully responded.

"We do not include outsiders in family affairs," she continued, "it has been that way since we have lived here." She paused for a second. "But things are different now." Rosa trailed off with her last remark, momentarily losing eye contact. "Our brother was very fond of you, and Eduardo believes you are a man of honor. My sister and I also appreciate what you have done, and Armando would have wanted us to help you any way we can."

Chris was surprised by this opening, and he scrambled to ask the appropriate question. "We have been given information, that we believe is accurate, about the man that killed Armando. We would like to know more about him."

Isabella spoke for the first time. "Yes, Eduardo has informed us about the man of whom you speak. We believe this is quite possible. However, his story goes back many decades and includes much history from both families. We do not share such knowledge easily."

Michael and Chris, aware they were being sworn to some secret pact, acknowledged this and both nodded in agreement.

Rosa then spoke. "We were rival families a long time ago. One family tried to do good for the people, the other tried to corrupt and pervert. There was much bad blood. Many of the local families were forced to take sides, some did so at their own peril. The grandfathers tried to make peace between the families, but there was always something—blood feuds, money, women, or government officials—that kept us from having peace. Eventually, our father and the father of the Sacarras family settled disputes that were decades old. Then...there was a girl."

Isabella took up the story. "She was a young girl that lived in the town, her name was Adela. She was very fond of Armando, as he was of her. It was said her family had arranged a marriage with the Sacarras family, and there was much money to be paid to them. However, when Adela met the man she was to marry, Villatoro, she refused. Her family did not care and planned for the wedding without her consent. She fled to Armando for safety. Villatoro found out she was hiding here and the bad blood between the two families erupted again. Villatoro's father did not want to go to war over a young woman, but Villatoro was obsessed. There was a fight one night as they argued, and Villatoro shot him and killed him.

"Armando and Adela fled when the story reached them. There was no controlling Villatoro now, and they were both afraid for their lives. Villatoro went crazy when he found they had left. He killed Adela's father and burned down their house. He was not foolish enough to attempt anything with our family. However, he swore he would have his revenge on Armando."

"What happened to Armando and Adela after they left?" Michael asked.

"We would get the occasional letter from Armando," Rosa said. "They were traveling the world together. He loved to travel. We would send him money from time to time. They never married, and sadly, she was killed in a car accident some years later. But Armando did not want to return home. Perhaps he was still concerned for his life, perhaps it was his love for Adela kept him away. He never said, even when he eventually came back."

Chris spoke up. "Do you ladies know anything about Villatoro now?"

"He used to live in a section of Laredo called Aztecca," Isabella said. "The neighborhood was named after their estate. When their father died, they did not manage the money well and had to sell their land, which is why they live among the houses now."

"Is there anything else you can tell us about the man?" Michael asked.

"His family has always been obsessed with the Aztec culture and history," Rosa now spoke. "They believe they are descendants of Aztec kings. That is why they named their estate Azteca."

"Señoras, we greatly appreciate you sharing this information," Chris said politely. "I would like to ask one more question. When I discovered the car had been impounded, I was told not to return here because it was not thought at the time to be safe. Am I inviting potential danger to Casa de la Guerra by being here?"

"He would not dare to set foot on this property or even have his minions do so," Isabella stated emphatically. "This is considered consecrated ground. Even the devil himself has respect."

"There is one thing we would like to tell you before we leave," Rosa said. "You are a grown man, and what you do is your own business. If you decide to pursue this further, you have our respect and blessings, but do so knowing there is great risk you may incur.

Our beloved brother cannot be brought back, so remember, retribution is only for the living."

Eduardo stepped forward to pull back their chairs with Chris and Michael standing as they left. Eduardo whispered "I'll return shortly" and hurried off to escort the señoras to the house.

Chris turned and looked at Michael, who spoke as he pulled out his pack of cigarettes, "That's one hell of a story: tragic and romantic all at the same time."

"What do you make of it?" Chris asked. He had noticed Michael had not smoked the entire time the señoras were there.

"I think it's just like I thought...we're dealing with one crazy son of a bitch!" Michael said in exasperation. "Anyone who kills their own father, is obsessed with a woman who doesn't want to marry him..." His voice trailed off as he shook his head.

"I noticed that Eduardo had a similar reaction to yours when he heard the name," Chris said.

"Yes, so did I. I guess when you cross paths with such a person, even when it was so long ago, it's a shock to the system not just to hear their name but realize you have to wrestle with them again," Michael said.

"You were really shaken when I read the name Villatoro Sacarras on the card, weren't you?" Chris asked.

"I'll be honest, I fought almost three years in the war, and I've done some pretty hairy things since then—some of them I'm not proud of—but the only time I was scared in my life was when I was hiding out from him. I guess it's because I wasn't in control and someone else had my life in their hands."

"If Sacarras really thought you had something to do with the looting of the plane, why did they eventually leave you alone?" Chris asked.

"I heard later he was only interested in the Aztec antiquities. The gold and other items from the bank were someone else's stuff, and that guy was murdered a few weeks later. Perhaps Villatoro realized I didn't take it, or they found it or..."

He sat for a minute, tapping his pack of cigarettes against the table, deep in thought. He looked at Chris after breaking his trance and said, "I think I have an idea. Where is your cell phone?"

"It's charging in my room, why?"

"I want to call Speedy and ask him to bring something with him when he comes up here tomorrow."

"Do you want to tell him the name while you're talking to him? Perhaps it will give him a head start," Chris suggested.

"Yes, that's a good idea," Michael replied, pointing his lit cigarette at him.

Chris retrieved his phone and Speedy's number and returned to the table just as Eduardo returned holding a bottle of tequila and three glasses. Michael excused himself and went into his casita to call Speedy, leaving Chris and Eduardo at the table.

"Eduardo," Chris started, "Michael is a recovering alcoholic, so don't be offended if he doesn't drink when he returns."

"Should we not drink in front of him?" Eduardo was concerned he had upset his guest.

"I don't think he'll mind. He just went to his room to make a call. But I'll be happy to have some tequila with you. It will probably affect me less than the pulque you served me the last time."

Eduardo smiled his beaming smile, saying, "Pulque is an acquired taste."

"I don't think I'll be here long enough to develop that," Chris said, laughing, while pouring some tequila into two of the glasses. "Thank you for asking the señoras to tell us about the Sacarras."

"I was very surprised when they agreed to speak to you. The name seemed to affect them as it did me. Opening old wounds can be very painful."

"Yes, that is very true, Eduardo," Chris said. "So, tell me, why did hearing the name Villatoro Sacarras affect you the way it did?"

Eduardo sat in his chair looking at his hand holding the glass while slowly swirling the golden liquid. "I think I was half hoping it was just a random killing, something that had no explanation, no reason. I do not know why. But when I heard it was someone from out of the past, this near-mythical person that I remembered from my childhood, it was very personal. To think there was someone who had waited so long to kill my friend was...difficult."

Chris had poured tequila into both their glasses, but they had not drunk yet, so he took the opportunity to cheer up his friend. Lifting his glass, Chris said, "To finding justice for our friend and mentor, Armando Guerra."

The two men clinked their glasses together, as they had a few days ago with the pulque, and took a long drink of the tequila.

Michael exited his casita and returned the phone to Chris. "Speedy said he would make a few calls tonight and meet us at ten in the morning."

"I guess we are off and running," Chris acknowledged.

Michael, still standing, turned to Eduardo and asked, "Is there anything else you can add to what the señoras have told us about Sacarras?"

"I was too young to remember anything about the man," he replied. "I do not recall ever meeting him. But I will tell you this: If

238

he does live in Aztecca, as the señoras say, it is an appropriate place for such an evil man."

Chapter 11

"This is the calm before the storm."

Those were the first words that crossed Chris's mind when he awoke the next morning. Just like the rainstorm the day before on the drive to Laredo, he felt there was a giant wall of water heading his way, and there was no turning back now. He briefly thought of the people he had engaged with over the last week in his journey—Juan, Eduardo, Detective Henderson, Lisa, Mando, Michael, Garcia, Speedy, and Sophia. One thing Chris was resolute with regarding their attempt at retaliation was that Sophia was not to have the slightest involvement in anything he and Michael attempted. She wasn't even to know what, if anything, they did. Her father could make his own decision if he wanted to join them.

Before he left the comforts of the bed, he gave thanks he only had one glass of tequila after dinner last night. He got the distinct feeling that Eduardo could out-drink anyone, drinking anything, and he needed a clear head today.

Chris rose and showered, then called Jim again to check on work back home. He gave him his new cell phone number in case anything came up that was important. Looking at the phone, Chris wondered if it was a blessing or a curse to be always available to the whims of someone calling. Whichever one it became, he knew it was going to be an essential tool over the next few days.

He left his casita to discover Michael sitting at the same table where they had dinner last night. He was smoking a cigarette while staring at the main house. As Chris approached, Michael said, "What a wonderful place this must have been growing up as a child."

"Yes, I'm sure there was always something exciting going on here," Chris replied while sitting down.

As Michael extinguished his cigarette, he said, "Look, I know we've had some intense conversations since you showed up at my front door, but I just realized that I had not taken the time to say I'm sorry you lost such a close friend."

"Thank you. I appreciate that." Chris was moved by his comment.

"He must have been an interesting man."

"He was," Chris replied. "It's unfortunate you two could not have met."

The old woman who had served them the night before walked across the patio to their table and said, "Good morning, gentlemen. Eduardo asked that we serve you breakfast this morning, it will be out in a few minutes."

"Is Eduardo joining us this morning?" Chris asked.

"He said to tell you that he is tending to house matters this morning but will see you before you leave." She walked back toward the house.

"I guess today is an important day, isn't it?" Chris asked Michael.

"It is if we want to find out some information about this guy."

"Do you think Speedy will come up with something useful?"

"He always has," Michael replied, "and he's always fast. Why do you think he's called Speedy?"

"That would be great," Chris replied. "Is there anything specific you think we should be looking out for with this guy?"

"Weakness," Michael said.

The woman returned with their breakfast and placed all the food and silverware on the table, she then retrieved a large pitcher of orange juice. The day seemed to have the makings of being much hotter than yesterday, and the idea of driving around in a beat-up old truck without air conditioning was not a pleasant one for Chris.

"Do you think we should drive to Azteca and look around after we meet Speedy?" Chris asked.

"Yes, that's as good of a place to start as any. When I was stationed in England and France, whenever you wanted to get information, whether it was places to eat, girls, or about the locals, you always went to the bars. In Europe, the bars are a combination of townhall, restaurant, and newspaper. It's just the same here."

"You said you'd be looking for weakness. Do you mean vulnerability?" Chris asked.

"We have to think about the end game here. What are we trying to accomplish? Are we going to kill this guy? No. We are not hit men, and Speedy isn't, either. So, are we trying to get him to confess? Never happen, and even if he did, this man seems to have the police by the balls. We have to find out what we can exploit with this guy, what avenues we have for some retribution, whatever form that may take."

"I guess I never thought it all the way through," Chris said, somewhat chagrined. "I was so obsessed with getting his name I never thought what would come after that."

"I knew your intentions were honorable. Finding the murderer was important, even if it just gave you and your friends some solace, but I don't think it did. It asked even more questions and dug up some skeletons that were long ago buried." Michael finished eating and began to light another cigarette.

"I think finding out who it was had another unexpected effect," Chris said with a wry smile.

"What would that be?" Michael asked.

"Up until we got the name, you were just helping me. But it became a little more personal for you after we discovered who it was, didn't it?"

Michael fondled his cigarette in his fingers reflectively, then said, "I won't deny that getting back at the only man I have feared in my life has its own value."

Two women appeared and removed all the remnants of breakfast. One of the women said, "Eduardo wanted to know when you were leaving."

Chris looked at his watch. It was now nine. "We'll be leaving in about twenty minutes," he replied. "We have to meet someone."

The men went back to their casitas and packed their belongings. Chris left twenty dollars for the women that were to clean the rooms, thinking they were probably the same women who had served them breakfast. He did so even though Eduardo would probably have been offended by his gesture.

Michael and Chris were walking toward the house just as Eduardo appeared. "Good morning, my friends!" he greeted them with his usual level of enthusiasm.

He escorted them through the house and upon entering the courtyard, he said to Chris, "I hope this is not a goodbye, my friend."

"No, Eduardo, this is just a 'so long for now.' I'll see you again very soon, hopefully with some good news," Chris responded.

As they reached the truck, Chris placed their luggage in the back. Eduardo turned to Michael and said, "Mr. Hamilton, it was a great honor to meet you. You are welcome here anytime."

"Thank you, Eduardo, and thank the señoras, too," Michael responded, getting in the passenger's side.

Eduardo turned to Chris and said, "May your journey be safe, my brother," surprising him with an enthusiastic hug.

Chris, touched by the uncommon gesture, said, "Thank you. I'll keep you updated, I promise."

He got in, started the engine, and slowly drove away. As he did, he thought he caught a glimpse of two figures in an upstairs window.

"I guess we should call Speedy and see what he's up to and where he wants to meet," Michael said.

Chris handed him the phone and the number, saying, "Call him."

As Chris drove back down Flowering Cactus Drive, he wondered how long it would be, if ever, before he saw it again. He had become fond of the place and the people who lived there.

Michael spoke to Speedy on the phone for just a minute, then hung up, chuckling.

"What's so funny?" Chris asked.

"This guy has a thing for cemeteries. He said to meet him just south of the city, off Highway 83, at a place called Old Forgotten Cemetery."

"Why am I not surprised?" Chris said as he took the phone and placed it on the seat.

He was just a mile from Highway 83. Once there, he turned south. A few miles outside of town, there was a small sign that said "Old Forgotten Cemetery." It pointed to an access road running parallel with Highway 83. The sign could have easily been missed, and the arrow pointing in its direction was vague. After driving for a few more minutes, the men decided that an overgrown and seemingly empty field was their destination. It contained a couple dozen weather-worn and cracked headstones, with the remnants of a foundation from an old church that had been torn down years ago. There were no fences, no signs, no registry. It was indeed a forgotten cemetery. Chris wondered about the last time anyone had paid a visit to one of its residents. Michael had just enough time to exit the truck and light a cigarette before Speedy came driving up; quickly, of course. It was exactly ten o'clock.

"Good morning," he said as he exited a black innocuous jellybean of a car. Chris thought it was an excellent car to use; it was so generic it would be invisible to anyone.

"Morning," Michael said to Speedy as he walked toward their truck. "We have some information for you."

Michael and Chris took a few minutes to tell him about the story the señoras had shared with them the previous evening. Speedy listened intently and even took a few notes. Chris was impressed with his focus.

"Good, thank you, this could help. Having some background information can be very useful," Speedy said. "Now, let me share with you what I found out last night and this morning."

"How did you find out stuff already?" Chris asked.

"I made a few calls after Michael gave me the name." Speedy fidgeted with his hands as he spoke. "First, there's a few people

247

willing to share information about him, as long as it's confidential and there is money involved. Sacarras has kept people silent over the years by intimidation and fear, but he is getting old, and he is not as powerful as he once was. The police seem to think he is more trouble than he is worth because he is so erratic. They prefer just to look the other way, but it is said he still has connections inside the department. I already have two people that I am meeting this morning who are going to want to get paid today."

"How much do you need?" Chris asked.

"Probably a thousand dollars," he replied.

Chris reached in his pocket and gave Speedy ten one-hundred-dollar bills and asked, "What else did you find out?"

"He has a bodyguard that goes everywhere with him. If we are to make any kind of plans, we need to consider him as an obstacle. So, I know we discussed this before, but what are we trying to do here? None of us are killers, and going to the police will probably lead to nothing. If you are going to set him up, he's the kind of man that if he knows he has been taken, he will hit you back, and hard. So, in my opinion, he must not know."

"Yes, that's exactly what I thought," Michael said. "Did you bring the box?"

Speedy walked back to his car and opened the rear door to retrieve a dark green box lying on the back seat. It was about ten inches long, eight inches tall, and four inches deep. It looked like an ammo box from WWII. Michael took the box and walked to the back of the truck and let down the tailgate, then set the box down. He opened the safety latches and removed a rolled-up towel from inside, then placed it on the truck bed. He gently unrolled the towel to expose its contents; it was a Pre-Colombian figure of an Aztec god carved in jade. It was only about three inches tall and two inches wide, but gleaming in the sun for the first time in years, it was a sight to behold. Chris thought it was one of the most beautiful things he had ever seen. Michael then reached into the box and removed a dozen Polaroid pictures of other pieces of Aztec jewelry—necklaces, rings, figurines, and medallions.

"What would you like for me to do with this?" Speedy asked.

"Use it as bait," Michael said. "We know he's obsessed with Aztec antiquities. If you can meet with him or one of his men, tell them these items are for sale. He's surely going to be interested."

"I cannot promise that will happen," Speedy said. "There's a lot left to chance. But if I do meet someone, what should I tell them about how I knew Sacarras would be interested?"

Michael answered, "Tell them you heard from someone at the Thieves Market that he was an admirer of all things Aztecan, and you sought him out because you thought he would appreciate such a collection. Make sure you tell him the items are located in Brownsville, and if he wants to view them and make an offer, he has to go there. He has too many allies here in Laredo. If we can get him to Brownsville, the odds will be even."

"I'll see what I can do. I promise to take good care of your piece of jade. I will not let it out of my hands," Speedy said as Michael repacked the box and handed it to him.

They walked to Speedy's car. He said he would call them as soon as he had some news and headed in the direction of Laredo.

Chris and Michael got back in the truck and started in the same direction. As they drove north on highway 83, Chris asked, "Tell me what you are planning. I mean, this was originally my idea, so it would be nice to know what the hell is going on."

"We can't do anything about Sacarras in Laredo. This is his home base. He knows too many people, the cops are scared of him, and he has a bodyguard. The only hope we have is to get him to come to Brownsville," Michael explained.

"Do you think the Aztec pieces will lure him there?" Chris asked.

Michael lit a cigarette and said, "I do."

"And then what? As Speedy said, we are not killers. Even if we were, I don't want to risk going to prison over this, and I don't want his men coming after me," Chris emphatically stated.

"We're not going to be killing anyone, don't worry. I'm hoping Sacarras will buy the Aztec pieces when he comes to Brownsville, and then we can report him." Michael was looking out the window, something Chris noticed he often did when he was planning something in the gray areas of life.

"Report him for what? Is owning Mexican antiquities illegal?" Chris asked.

"They are if they're stolen," Michael responded.

"Stolen? Stolen from where?" Chris exclaimed.

"From a museum in Monterey, Mexico, about 45 years ago."

"Wait, you mean the stuff you were carrying when your plane crashed?" Chris was raising his voice for the first time at Michael.

Still looking out the window, Michael calmly said, "Yes, I took a few pieces as insurance, just in case they refused to pay me. They were the sons a bitches that overloaded the plane and almost killed me. I took some pieces that were easy to carry and stuffed them in an old army bag I had with me."

Chris took a minute to think, a hundred questions running through his head. "How come Sacarras's men never found them?"

"I gave them to Garcia. They didn't know I knew him, and we avoided contacting each other for a while."

"Garcia's had them all these years?" Chris asked.

"Yes."

"Is that the plan? For him to buy the stolen Aztec pieces, we report him, and he goes to prison?"

"Yes, that's the best I can come up with, unless you have any other ideas." Michael turned back to look at Chris. "It's just very important he gets caught in Brownsville."

"How long do you think he would go to prison?" Chris asked.

"It depends. If he gets caught by the local police, very little to none. But, if he gets caught by the F.B.I., he'll get five years, maybe."

"How will we manage to bring in the F.B.I.?" Chris asked.

"I know someone," Michael replied. "If they can pick him up right after he buys the stuff, he'll go to prison for sure. The trick is, he can't know we had a hand in him getting caught, that is going to be the hard part."

Chris drove on for a while, thinking about Michael's plan and how they would be able to pull it off. He was concerned with the element of danger involved and was trying to think of any alternative schemes that would be less risky. Perhaps after they had some more information, they could make a plan B, or even a new plan A, since Chris had a feeling of trepidation about the first one.

After a few minutes, Chris broke the silence by saying, "You know how ironic this sting would be if the stolen Aztec antiquities that you were supposed to deliver to him forty-five years ago were the same antiquities that put him in prison?"

Michael broke into a smirk and answered, "That thought had occurred to me."

As they entered the Laredo city limits, Michael suggested they find out where Azteca was and do some scouting there and try to find someone willing to talk. Chris pulled into a gas station to fill up the truck. While he did, Michael asked one of the mechanics for directions. Chris noted how people always seemed willing to talk to Michael; he had a knack of engaging them in a comfortable, non-threatening way. He wondered if certain traits, like being gregarious and having people skills, were genetic, since he had the same skill set.

Michael returned to the truck and told Chris the mechanic said to stay straight on the road for three miles, then turn left just after they went under the interstate overpass. The neighborhood would be on the right.

The men followed the mechanic's directions, and after turning when they went under the interstate, they saw an old brown wooden sign with the word "AZTECA." The lettering was at one time painted gold, but the paint was all but worn away, making the letters blend into the sign and difficult to read.

After driving for just a few blocks, it was clear to Chris that, although the neighborhood was not the worst he had ever seen, it was surely a forgotten and forsaken part of town. He thought, while there may be more dangerous parts of the city, none could be more forlorn.

The area was bounded on three sides by the interstate, an industrial area, and a large culvert that was overgrown with bushes and trees. It was as if the city had found a way to cordon off this ten-by-twenty-block district to further isolate it.

The streets were lined with parked cars in varying degrees of condition. Some were obviously abandoned, making driving feel quite claustrophobic. They were all haphazardly parked as if no one cared about them, and all the roads were one-way, making navigating even more complicated.

The houses were a combination of debris, decay, and dilapidation, with worn-out chain-link fences surrounding them all. Chris didn't see a single house without at least one section of fencing that was either broken, sagging, pushed over, or missing. Some residents had erected makeshift exterior walls using tin roof sections or cinder blocks so their back yards could be hidden from sight, allowing for clandestine activities. Above all the structures was a canopy of phone lines, electrical power lines, and illegally connected television cables.

The entire area was replete with tall grass, various overgrown vegetation, and stray dogs, thus adding to the air of lawlessness that abounded. No children could be seen playing in the streets or their yards, and the few people out walking glared at passersby. There was a plethora of abandoned buildings with boarded-up windows, and the few bars and corner stores that dotted the area were dark and gloomy, giving them a nefarious feel.

After canvassing the somber neighborhood, Michael and Chris agreed to try one of the corner grocery stores for information first. It seemed to be slightly less fraught with danger than the bars. Chris parked on one of the side streets about half a block from a corner store. They got out and walked toward the entrance.

"Look around for a few minutes while I try to talk to the cashier," Michael said.

"Okay," Chris replied.

As they entered, Chris saw there was only one other person shopping. They were standing in front of the refrigerator section where the beer was located. Michael walked toward a cashier who was partially hidden behind a plexiglass wall. The store was quite small and smelled of garlic and mildew. The aisles were so narrow Chris had to turn sideways at times. He looked around to see if there was something he would actually buy and decided that if he did, he would never eat anything. He lingered for a couple of minutes and then picked up a bag of potato chips and a Coke. He could hear Michael talking to the cashier as he approached.

"Okay, thanks," Michael said and left the store, leaving Chris to pay for his items.

As Chris exited, he saw Michael was standing on the sidewalk smoking. "What did you find out?" he asked.

"Nothing," Michael replied. "He said he's never heard of him."

"Do you believe him?"

"No. Let's go."

They walked back to the car, and after they got in, Michael continued, "We can't go around asking everyone about this guy.

Sooner or later, someone is going to get suspicious. Let's pick one of the bars and give it our best shot."

They drove for a few minutes, deciding which of the handful of bars would be their best opportunity.

At the end of one of the many one-way streets was something that struck Chris as completely incongruous. There sat a brand-new children's playground, complete with fresh mulch spread around the grounds. There were swings, two slides, a seesaw, monkey bars, spring riders, and a merry-go-round. And yet there was not a single child playing on the equipment, which looked pristine—it looked like no child ever had.

A couple of streets over, they found a bar in between two houses with the name "El Sol Poniente" on a hand-painted sign across the top of the door.

"Let's try this one," Michael said.

Chris found a parking spot right in front of the place. Before going inside, Chris asked, "You're not going to drink, are you?"

"When we get in, order two beers. I'll either pour some of mine out when the bartender is not looking, or we can switch after you drink some of yours," Michael replied.

"You think of everything," Chris said with a grin.

"I've done this with Garcia a few times since I stopped drinking. Follow my lead when I start talking."

The men went inside to what was a scrubbed-clean and tidy little place. The linoleum floor looked brand new, the walls displayed different hand-painted murals of a sun setting over the mountains or the ocean, and it didn't smell of beer. The bar stretched across the entire left side of the building; it had been slathered with at least a dozen coats of varnish. There was just enough room to enter it on the far end and a dozen red and chrome bar stools sitting in front. On the opposing wall were six blue and white vinyl-covered booths.

"Buenos tardes," came an enthusiastic voice from behind the bar. Chris and Michael walked over to discover a middle-aged Latino standing behind it, his head barely sticking above the top of the bar. Chris calculated he was not even as tall as Garcia.

"You are my first customers!" he said in an even more fervent tone.

"You mean for the day?" Chris asked.

"No! I just opened today! You are my first customers in my new business!" He held up his hands, proudly displaying his new decor.

Chris and Michael looked at each other, unsure what to make of this, then sat down at two adjoining bar stools.

"What may I get you?" the bartender asked.

Chris glanced at the sign displaying what beers were being served and replied, "Two Lone Stars, please."

He hurriedly grabbed two glasses and neatly poured the beer, then set them in front of his two new patrons.

"What's your name?" Michael asked.

"Diego," he replied. "And what are the names of my first two customers?"

"I'm Chris, and this is my father, Michael." They reached across the bar and shook hands.

"The old neighborhood isn't like it used to be," Michael started. Chris sensed he was casting his fishing line.

"I know, I used to come here as a little boy to visit my grandparents," Diego said. "It was so nice with families cooking out, and people would walk around visiting the neighbors. But a few of us, we are trying to bring it back."

"I lived here long ago before moving to Brownsville for work," Michael said. "I remember it just like you said. The yards seemed so clean and well-groomed." Chris sensed Michael felt he had hooked one.

"How long ago did you live here?" Diego asked.

"Oh, it's been about thirty-five years, over on Zaragoza Street."

"That is just a couple of blocks away! What are you gentlemen doing here?" Diego inquired.

"We were just riding through Laredo, and I wanted to visit my old neighborhood. I remember there was this one big house, people used to say that the whole neighborhood was named after it," Michael said.

"Yes, that's right! It is a house that is over a few blocks. It's next to the drainage ditch. I think someone told me the family who lived there had owned all the land around here many years ago. It has a large sign in front that says Azteca."

"Do you know who lives there now?" Chris interjected, helping Michael reel in their catch.

"I have heard of the man. He is very old, some say they are afraid of him. They even put up walls in their yards so he cannot see them. I have only seen the man a couple of times. I do not know him, but I can understand why people might be afraid."

"What do you mean?" Chris asked.

"I have only been back here for a couple of months, and I have spent all my time working on my business, so I only hear a few things. But..." Diego moved his head from side to side as if to temper his information. "He is a very strange-looking man."

"Really?" Michael said. "Strange how?"

Diego seemed reluctant but continued, "He is very tall and has an odd way of walking." He stopped to think for a second. "I do not want to speak badly of my neighbor." He paused but was urged to continue by the understanding nods Michael and Chris gave him. "He is an odd color."

Michael was quick to get him to elaborate. "Really?" he said.

"He does not look Latino or American Indian, he is the color of brick." Diego had his hands up and shrugged, searching for the most accurate description.

Michael and Chris again looked at each other, then Michael asked, "Where is this house again?"

"It is three streets up, and then turn left and go all the way to the giant culvert. It's the house right next to the drainage ditch."

Michael realized it was time to exit and said, "Diego, it was great talking to an old neighbor. I will be back for dinner real soon."

Michael got up to leave, and as Chris stood up, he reached into his pocket and gave Diego a hundred-dollar bill, saying, "This is for all the hard work you've done and to wish you good luck with your business."

Diego held up the hundred-dollar bill and was still staring at it as they left.

After they were back in the truck, Michael chuckled and said, "I've never ceased to be amazed by the chance of probabilities in the nature of life. Here we find a guy that has been here long enough to know some things but hasn't been here too long to be afraid to talk. And has literally just opened his bar the hour we walk inside."

"Sometimes people get lucky for a reason," Chris replied.

They drove up the street, turned where Diego had instructed, and came upon a dead-end cul-de-sac designed to appear as if it was separate from the rest of the neighborhood. They had not driven by it before because it was oddly placed, as the neighborhood was laid out in a block-by-block pattern except for this isolated section. Chris pulled over and parked diagonally about fifty feet from the front of the house, which looked out onto a poorly maintained and overgrown culvert that cleaved the area.

The dwelling was much larger and older than the other houses in the neighborhood and was surrounded by a more recently built cinder block wall that further isolated it. It was painted a pale yellow which accentuated the cracks that permeated the structure, showing dark gashes like open wounds on the building. The terracotta roofing was a darker shade of red than usual and was chipped and broken throughout, with small pieces lying on the

262

roof. A heavy black iron gate stood like an ominous sentinel in front and was slightly taller than the six-foot-high wall. On top of the gate were individual tridents threatening anyone who attempted to climb over it with certain impalement.

Towering above the gate was a wooden sign that arched over a dozen feet from side to side. It was set on two large wooden poles that had been poorly incorporated into the block wall. The sign was a dark brown color with brilliant gold lettering, which appeared to be the only well-kept structure on the property. The sign said "AZTECA" with smaller lettering beneath reading, "Live by the sun, die by the sun."

"What do you think the sign means?" Chris asked.

"He's obsessed with Aztec culture and believes he's descended from them. They were sun worshipers who frequently sacrificed people to the sun gods," Michael responded.

"Kind of gruesome, don't you think?" Chris said.

"Seems like this guy's M.O. You think we should check in with Speedy while we sit here?" Michael asked.

"Yes, good idea," Chris answered. "Let's see what kind of progress he's making."

Michael picked up the phone and dialed Speedy's number, and he answered immediately. Michael talked to him as Chris watched

263

the house, looking for any signs of movement. Michael said "Okay, great" and hung up.

"He said he's made terrific progress. There seem to be quite a few people willing to throw this guy under the bus. He has one more person to meet with and thinks he'll be done in a couple of hours," Michael reported. "He said he'll have to spend all of the thousand dollars you gave him."

"Did you give him the address?" Chris asked.

"He said he already knew it," Michael replied.

The two men sat in the truck for about an hour, the intense heat of the day making it miserable inside. Michael smoked and slept while Chris monitored the house. Just before two o'clock, as the sun was at its most intense, a black Mercedes pulled in front of the house. A stocky man who had been driving got out of the car and walked around to open the rear door. A thin, gangly man unfolded from the back seat. He was very tall, at least six-foot-four, and had short black hair that was thin and oily, reflecting the sun's rays. He wore black pants and a vibrant red long-sleeved shirt that looked like it was made from silk. As he walked, he had a slow and measured gait that reminded Chris of how a large stork would move. His arms were off kilter with his body, giving him an awkward appearance, and his prominent nose was almost beaklike. His skin color was a peculiar shade, similar to the terracotta roofing on the house. But the most haunting characteristic of the man was his eyes. When he glanced toward the truck for just a moment, Chris could see his large round eyes were all black, like giant pupils, and they were lifeless, like a doll's eyes. Even though he saw them only briefly and from a distance, Chris felt an irresistible wave of evil from those eyes.

The driver unlocked the gate and, making sure it latched behind them, went inside the house.

"That's the same face I saw forty-five years ago," Michael said, surprising Chris that he was awake. "You don't forget a face like that."

Chris started the truck and slowly drove away, eventually turning onto a one-way street that would lead him out of the neighborhood. Just as they were leaving the area, Chris's cell phone rang. Michael answered it, talked for just a few seconds, and hung up. "That was Speedy. He said to meet him at the place we met this morning in thirty minutes."

"Well, if nothing else," Chris said, "he has good timing."

Chris and Michael drove quietly for a while, both thinking about what they had learned that day and anticipating what their intrepid ex-cop investigator had discovered. As they got close to their destination, Chris asked, "What do you think Speedy found out today?"

"From what it sounded like, everything we need to know," Michael said with a certain amount of satisfaction.

When they pulled up to the abandoned cemetery, Speedy was already there looking over his notes. He had Michael's green box next to him on the ground.

As they walked over to Speedy, he began by saying, "You didn't tell me how much of a creep this Sacarras guy is." He handed the box to Michael.

"We knew some things, but they were vague. Tell us what you have," Michael said, taking the box.

"First, he is known to the locals as El Loco Diablo because he has been deranged for some time. That's why the police and people that know him are so afraid: He's capable of doing anything because he's so erratic. He doesn't seem to have much influence beyond his connections in Laredo. He used to be in the drug, prostitution, and intimidation business, but that has changed over the last ten years. He couldn't compete with the cartels, so now he just deals in small amounts of heroin for some select clients and his few minions who trade services for drugs. They are not

266

professionals. He is still in the prostitution business, some of it is now…more specialized."

Speedy looked up from his notebook to emphasize what he was about to say, not reading from his notes but looking at Michael and Chris as he spoke. "He deals in young boys and girls, ages eight to fifteen, and from what I'm told, he keeps some of the young boys for himself."

"You mean he's a pedophile?" Chris asked, not really surprised.

"Yes," Speedy said.

Michael was unmoved by the statement and simply said, "Tell us what else you have."

"He's seventy-one and not in good health. He's obsessed with Aztec antiquities, which I'll get back to in a minute. He wears a ring that is a duplicate of an Aztec god's ring. In it are two emerald stones that are the god's eyes, with a golden head. It's engraved on the inside with the phrase 'Live by the sun, die by the sun.'"

"We saw that on the sign in front of his house!" Chris said excitedly.

"That's the information I got from my first contact. He used to work for him, but he left because he despised Sacarras, which apparently lots of others do also. My second contact knows his bodyguard very well, and he tells me the bodyguard is willing to set him up, but he's concerned about being involved. Sacarras has too many associates in Laredo who could retaliate."

"Why would the bodyguard do that?" Michael prodded.

"He may want out, maybe Sacarras has something over him. He may want to take over part of his business, or perhaps it's about money. I've seen this a lot, it's very common."

"Can you trust your informant?" Chris asked.

"Absolutely," Speedy replied. "He's never steered me wrong. He also said he'd be the go-between if I want to plan something with the bodyguard. That could prove vital."

"Excellent, that's something we can use," Michael said, obviously very pleased.

"Now, do you want to know about the Aztec pieces?" Speedy seemed quite eager to share his information. Michael and Chris both nodded their heads.

"My contact called the bodyguard and said he knew someone selling some Aztec antiquities and wanted to know if Sacarras was interested. He called me within five minutes and asked me to meet with them so they could see what I had for sale. I told them I was a representative of the seller but had a genuine piece with me and pictures of the rest."

"So, you actually met Sacarras?" Chris asked.

"Yes, and a creepier person I cannot remember. He seemed to be very odd in so many ways. Never has a person given me the chills like he did when he looked at me."

Speedy appeared very disturbed as he was saying this.

"What happened when he saw the jade piece and the pictures?" Michael asked.

"He flipped out! He said he was very interested and wanted to know how soon he could meet the seller to negotiate."

"What did you tell him?" Michael asked.

"I told him I would call him back tonight to let him know when they were available."

"That's good, Speedy. You did a good job," Michael said. "Call them back and set something up."

"A couple of other things," Speedy said, putting away his notebook. "As I said, I usually get five hundred a day, plus expenses, and I get a bonus for any dangerous or additional information. Having said that, I was a cop for years, so I have always had a genuine interest in putting bad guys behind bars. This guy, Sacarras, is one of the most despicable humans I have ever met, and I want to help you get him."

"Thanks, Speedy, I appreciate that. We can use a guy like you," Chris said.

"We spent a thousand dollars on my contacts. Usually, I would ask for another two thousand dollars for the work I did today, but all I want is the five hundred and the opportunity to help you get this guy."

"We would love to have your help," Michael said.

"Here's your five hundred dollars," Chris said as he pulled the money out of his pocket and counted it out.

"Speedy, you said there were a couple of things. Was there something else you wanted to tell us?" Michael asked.

"Both of my informants did confirm that Sacarras had your friend killed in the desert, but one of them told me something quite disturbing."

"What was it?' Chris asked.

"When they killed him, they cut out his heart."

Chapter 12

"I'm going to kill that fucker with my bare hands!"

Chris screamed as he quickly drove off. "Just like Garcia did...I'm going to strangle him while looking into those black eyes as he takes his last breath."

"Take it easy, son," Michael said, trying to quell the rage in Chris. "I know that's a hell of a thing to hear, but you can't lose your head now. Stick to our plan, you'll get your revenge."

"I don't think that will be enough. Just putting him in prison for all the things he's done, not just to Chico but to everyone else," Chris said as the truck's engine screamed from his heavy foot.

"He's the most reprehensible man I've heard of in a long, long time," Michael said in a calm voice, "but I truly believe there's Karma in this world. Maybe there's even an accounting beyond this one."

"You've never expressed any belief in that before." Chris was surprised at Michael's comment.

"Well, we don't know, do we? That's one of life's great mysteries, isn't it?"

"Yes, I guess that's true." Chris was slightly less angry. "When do you think Speedy will call us?"

"Soon. Right after he talks to Sacarras or his bodyguard."

"Are you surprised he was so interested in the antiquities?" Chris asked, his anger starting to subside.

"No, not at all. He reacted just as I expected. When someone is obsessed with something, it can't be turned off. It's like a disease."

"Is that the weakness you were hoping for?" Chris asked.

"Yes," Michael responded. "Let's stop here and get something to eat," he said, pointing at an out-of-the-way restaurant they were just about to pass.

Chris pulled into the Mexican restaurant and went inside to order some food to go, since Michael said he had wanted to get home and go to bed; the day had taken a toll on him. While he was inside, Speedy called and talked to Michael regarding his conversation with Sacarras's bodyguard and about their plans for tomorrow. Chris returned with the food and set it on the seat, then they headed down highway 83.

"Speedy called," Michael started out. "He talked to Sacarras's bodyguard."

Chris, in the middle of wrestling with a giant burrito, said, "What did he say? Are they coming?" He was excited in his tone.

"He said they're going to meet him in Brownsville tomorrow evening, and he'll drive them to the house around six," Michael responded.

"Wow! So, this is going to happen that quickly. Can we get ready in time?" Chris was concerned it was too soon to lay their trap for them.

"I guess we'll have to. We're only going to get one pitch to swing at on this trip to the plate," Michael said in a resigned tone.

"What do we need to do to get ready?" Chris asked.

"I need to get Garcia to help, but I've already talked to him about my plan. I just need to let him know it's tomorrow. I'll call him in a minute."

"What about your F.B.I. contact?"

"I'll alert Agent Polk in the morning. They'll be happy to help. I've worked with them before. This will be an easy catch for them, and they'll look good in the eyes of the Mexican government returning such valuable museum pieces," Michael said.

"What are you going to tell them about the Aztec pieces? Won't Polk know you have them?"

"I'll tell him that Sacarras contacted me and Garcia about selling them to us, but I knew they were stolen, so I called them to report him. I am a good citizen, after all." Michael chuckled at his joke, then coughed. "As long as Sacarras buys them tomorrow, we'll be set. He'll have them in his possession when they arrest him."

"Isn't the bodyguard going to be in trouble also? He'll be in the car with Sacarras."

"I'll tell them he was just the driver. They'll believe me. I'll also say he helped in setting up the sting."

"What's the plan for Speedy?" Chris asked.

"He said the bodyguard was going to call him tonight after Sacarras goes to sleep to work out the details. He has to make sure they get there on time and give you all the information you need to call the F.B.I."

"Me? Why am I doing that?" Chris asked, surprised.

"Because you're going to be watching from Herman's office from across the street. He's going to help, too."

"Have you asked him?" Chris was getting a little anxious.

"Don't need to, he's too good a friend," Michael stated matter-of-factly.

274

Chris and Michael finished eating as they drove, then Michael called Garcia. After speaking with him for a few minutes, he said, "He's going to meet us at the house at nine. He said he'll bring the rest of the pieces, and we can get everything ready. I'll call Herman and Agent Polk then."

"You think this will work?" Chris asked.

"Probably, but there are no guarantees in life," Michael said. He then lit a cigarette, leaned back in the seat, and stared out the window.

Chris drove on for a while. It was five thirty—they would be home in two hours. Michael had now fallen asleep, and Chris spent the time thinking about all the moving parts that were planned for tomorrow. He thought about the irony of Sacarras doing such heinous acts against so many people for so long, including the death of his friend—and yet he was going to be put behind bars for having a few pieces of what many would consider old junk. The juxtaposition pleased him greatly. He just hoped it was satisfying enough.

After an hour or so, Michael awoke and sat quietly looking out the window. After a few minutes, Chris said, "Garcia said you were a hell of a pilot in the war."

"That was a long time ago," Michael responded.

275

"I know, but you've never told me any of those stories," Chris said, prodding him.

Michael, still looking out the window while lighting a cigarette in preparation for his story, started, "I was a terrific pilot when I came out of flight school, so good they sent me to command training, where I learned how to teach other pilots, but all I wanted to do was go kill Germans. After six months, I finally got to go overseas. They sent me to England and gave me a brand new, shiny P-51 Mustang. It was a beautiful plane, everything where you wanted it to be. You didn't get in it, you kind of wrapped it around you. My first mission, I was scared shitless. I had trained to fight and had practiced in dozens of dogfights, but here I was up against really good, battle-experienced German pilots that had live rounds in their machine guns. Nothing prepares you for that!

"I got the hang of it damn quick, though, to the point that I looked forward to the rush you would get from being in battle. I'll never forget the first time I shot down a plane. We were flying out over the English Channel and a Messerschmitt 110 was coming out of the sun, straight at me with both wings firing, but he was out of range. I remained cool even as I saw his tracer bullets whiz past my plane. I waited until he got closer to me, then I squeezed

276

the trigger and blew off his canopy, blood trailing out behind him. He spun into the water, and I watched him the whole way down. I loved it. I got six kills in my first tour and became an ace.

"I was sent home for six months to train more pilots but couldn't wait to get back to killing Germans. I was sent to France after that. They had changed the Mustangs by then and put in this new super-charged engine built by Packard. That son of a bitch would fly like a bat out of hell! I got five more kills in that tour, one of them was a German Ace who had shot down thirty-nine planes. I had stalked him for a while as he was flying in and out of the clouds trying to hide. When he came out of one, he gunned his plane and tried to outrun me, but he hadn't been up against this model of Mustang before. I surprised him as I closed on his ass and lit him up, peppering his fuselage until his plane caught on fire. I pulled alongside his plane as he tried to eject, but he couldn't get it to work. I remember seeing the fear in his eyes realizing he was a dead man.

"I went back for one more tour in January 1945. That's when I saw Garcia. I was flying fighter escorts for the bombers to Germany. Those Mustangs were the only plane that could fly there and back. February 15th, we were flying escort for the 8th Air Force bomber squad to Dresden, Germany. The Brits had bombed them the day before, and we could see the smoke from the fires over a hundred miles away. When we got over the city, the bombers were supposed to drop their bombs on the train yards, but most of them missed and hit office buildings, schools, and apartment buildings. After that, the bombers carrying incendiary bombs came in and set most of the city on fire. The fighter planes they sent up against us were flown by kids. They had little ability to fly or fight. It's one thing to kill someone that is trying to kill you, but it's a completely different thing when you're shooting children."

Michael took a break for a minute. Chris didn't know what to say, then he finished by recounting further.

"The bombs took out the train station and railroad tracks, but they also destroyed thirty thousand homes, over a hundred thousand apartments, churches, banks, hotels, and killed twenty-five thousand people. That's when I started drinking heavily."

Chris kept driving, not saying a word. He could sense the emotional drain the stories had taken on Michael.

Just outside of Brownsville, the sun was setting behind a bank of long, thin clouds that cast a pinkish hue onto the sand, making it look as if it had been spray painted. The sun's rays projected thin beams of reds and oranges in varying sizes and shapes from behind clouds that glowed purple from the backlighting. All the trees and bushes projected long dark shadows that contrasted with the pastel-tinted ground.

"God still makes the best fireworks," Michael said as he looked upon the last gasp of light. "I'm really going to miss this world."

Neither man spoke until they arrived back home.

Chris parked the truck in the old tool shed and helped Michael into the house. As they passed the tree, there was an unusual number of flowers and wreaths at its base. There were also several notes with prayers pinned just beneath the image of the Virgin Mary. As Chris helped Michael up the stairs, Chris saw another note on the front door. It read, "Call me when you get home, Sophia."

Chris put the note in his pocket and opened the door. Helping Michael down the hallway and into his bedroom, he seemed unusually tired. Chris retrieved their suitcases from the truck and set them down in the living room. He then went to the phone to call Sophia.

"Hello."

"Sophia, hi, it's Chris. We just got back home."

"Is everything okay?" she asked.

"Yes, fine. I just put Michael to bed. He's very tired."

"Good. What are you going to do now?" she asked.

"Nothing special. I may make a couple of calls. Why?"

"May I come over? I'd like to see you." Sophia's voice was warm and gentle in Chris's ear. She had a soft and feminine quality to her voice.

"Sure. Give me about half an hour," Chris said.

Chris called his supervisor to check in and then his daughter to speak with her for a few minutes. It was an hour later for her, and she was getting ready for bed. After hanging up, Chris sat in the old wooden chair for a minute thinking about how much he missed her.

He then went to take a shower, making sure to leave the door ajar once again, and changed clothes. A day in the Laredo heat and driving in a non-air-conditioned truck left an odor no female would find sexy.

Chris had just gotten dressed in jeans and a white linen shirt when there was a knock on the door. He opened it to see Sophia standing in the dark, only lit by the full moon that was just peeking above the buildings. She wore a sleeveless crimson dress that was pleated at the bottom, stopping just below her knees. She had on white sandals that accentuated the string of pearls draped along the neckline of the dress. Her black hair was down, and it caressed her shoulders, shimmering in the moonlight. Chris was taken by how she was so casual and elegant at the same time. She seemed to have an aura about her. There was a peculiar look on her face that Chris could not define.

"Well?" she said.

"Sorry, come in," Chris said, opening the door wider, not realizing he had been staring at her just a little too long.

Sophia entered and kissed him gently on his cheek. As she did, Chris became aware of the intoxicating fragrance she wore.

They sat in the same chairs as the night they had first met, and Chris turned on the lamp that bathed her in a soft yellow glow.

"How was the trip?" Sophia asked.

"It was interesting, to say the least."

"I was worried about you," she said softly.

"Thank you, Sophia, but there are some things going on that I can't talk about right now."

"I know," she said. "I'm fully aware you have something inside that is driving you to finish what you've started. Men like you are just like that."

"What are men like me?" Chris asked.

"Strong men, men with principles," Sophia stated matter-of-factly.

"Thank you, I've tried to be like that. I've made promises to Michael, your father, and, more importantly, to myself that you won't be involved in any of what we do until this is finished. I don't want you knowing anything at all."

"I respect that, Chris, and I appreciate you for thinking of me." She smiled as she spoke.

Sophia stood up and walked over to Chris, took his hand, and said, "Come, I want to show you something."

Chris stood up and walked across the moaning floor, still holding her hand. They walked down the hall, at the end turning right to see a hidden staircase that was behind the bathroom Chris had been using. The stairs wound up to the second floor and groaned loudly as they climbed. Sophia led him down another hallway that was illuminated only by the rays of the bright moon outside. As she entered a room at the end, she let go of Chris's hand and walked to a table in front of a window. There was a candle on the table, which she lit and set down. Chris could see the room was small, with a freshly made bed. The candle flickered as their shadows danced on the walls.

Sophia walked back to Chris and stood on her toes to playfully bite his lower lip. Chris lowered his head, giving her full access to his mouth, to which Sophia enthusiastically responded. He put his

282

arms around her lower back and pulled her against his athletic frame, knowing this would further arouse her. He lowered his hands and slowly lifted the back of her dress, exposing her voluptuous ass. He then placed his hands there and gently squeezed, something he had wanted to do since he had first met her. Her kisses grew more passionate as Chris found the zipper on the back of her dress and pulled it down in slow motion, taking time to unhook her bra on the way. He lifted her arms up in the air and slid her dress over her head, messing up her hair in the process, giving her an even more sexy look. Before Sophia could lower her arms, Chris placed them around his neck as he now returned her passionate kisses with equal fervor. After a few moments, she started to unbutton the front of his shirt, her hands moving down to his waist, then sliding inside, touching his taut stomach.

Chris returned his hands to her ass, holding it tightly. He lifted her up as Sophia wrapped her legs around his body. He carried her to the bed and lowered her down, placing her lengthwise onto the crisp, cool sheets. The light from the candle and the moon bathed her in a soft glow as he stood over her looking into her eyes. He removed his shirt and then slid down his pants and underwear, taking a moment to allow her to gaze at his muscular body.

Laying down beside her, he softly kissed her stomach and gently slid her panties down one leg, then the other. He was preparing to display his talents that he knew women so thoroughly enjoyed. He slowly kissed her inner thigh almost down to her knee, then up to the top of the other, pausing just for a moment to heighten the sensation. He could feel how wet she was and gently touched her with the tip of his tongue, causing her to arch her back, her moans of expectation encouraging him on. He lightly teased her, licking up and down, then in tiny circles, sensing which she enjoyed the most. As he increased the speed and pressure and her moans grew much louder, Chris passionately continued, now having found her spot. After just a few seconds, she raised her torso off the bed, pressing herself against his mouth, her body convulsing and legs trembling as she let out a deep moan of ecstasy, causing the entire bed to shake.

Chris was pleased her orgasm lasted so long. He waited there until she stopped quivering to see if she desired more. He tested her sensitivity by touching her with his tongue again, like a feather sliding over her. Her soft whimpers begged him to continue. He slid his strong hands under her, cupped her round ass, then slowly increased the strength of his touch until she came just as quickly and loudly as the first time. Her body now glistened in the afterglow.

Chris moved from between her legs to lay down beside her, knowing he loved having this power over women and how much they enjoyed his skills. Sophia quickly moved on top of Chris and straddled his torso. Her hands reached behind her and she grinned broadly, realizing he was ready for her. She positioned her body over him and lowered herself down, her ample wetness allowing him to enter her easily.

The candle now was backlighting her so her disheveled hair and tanned skin sparkled from the dripping perspiration. Chris looked into her dark brown eyes, her face full of desire. She began gyrating her body slowly, wanting Chris to enjoy himself as much as she had, her eyes locked on his. Chris reached up and took hold of her hands to help support her in her back-and-forth, up-and-down movements. Sophia took her time, loving the view from being on top, her movements gradually increasing until she was ready again. Chris sensed she was close and rose to her, whispering, "Kiss me when you cum."

His words brought her very near the edge, each thrust onto Chris becoming more intense and louder until she leaned down close to his face, her hot breath pulsating over him in preparation.

She exploded violently for the third time while slipping her tongue deep inside Chris's mouth. He had been holding out for as long as possible, her sexy body begging him to release, but with her tongue so passionately thrust inside of his mouth, he could no longer resist, and he let go inside of her, causing more soft moans from Sophia that went on for some time as she enjoyed the pleasure of feeling his strong body convulse beneath hers. Sophia collapsed and lay on Chris for a while, incapable of moving. Her hair was soaked, and the sweat from her tan body and black hair dripped onto his.

Neither lover spoke; they both knew words would detract from the pleasure of being in each other's arms. Chris remembered how he had sensed she was an amazingly sensual woman when he first met her. He now thought he had underestimated her abilities.

Finally, with what little energy Sophia had left, she rolled off Chris's strong body and lay next to him, her head on his chest.

The heat of the small room and their passion had drenched both them and the bed. Chris softly stroked Sophia's hair as she lay next to him, one arm and one leg sprawled across his body. She liked feeling small in his arms.

"Tell me about Virginia," she said in a soft and husky voice.

"It's very green," Chris said as he stared at the candlelight flicker across the ceiling. "It has rolling hills and large mountains, and beautiful meadows where we grow things and horses graze. The springs are full of life with warm and breezy days, the summers are hot and humid, the falls are a beautiful display of colors and cool temperatures, and the winters are not too cold, but we still get snow. It's a wonderful place to live."

"I've never touched snow," Sophia said. "All the places I've traveled to have had warm climates, or it was too early for snow. I've seen it on mountaintops, but I've never been able to touch it."

"When we were kids, we would have snowball fights and make snowmen while playing in the snow. We'd take our sleds to the top of Parham Road where you could slide down for a quarter of a mile. And when we were done, we would make snow cream." Chris smiled as he reminisced.

"I bet you had a lot of fun when you were young," Sophia said.

"Yes, I did. I guess one of the perks of growing up without a father was I got to do whatever I wanted. My mom didn't know what to do with me."

"Was it difficult growing up without a father?" she asked, now having rolled on her side to look at him.

"I have nothing to compare it to. It was what it was. I guess it's a double-edged sword. I had a great time, became a pro baseball player, and now I have my own business. Who knows what life would have handed me if things had been different?" Chris replied.

"I guess you turned out alright," Sophia said and laughed. Chris really liked the feminine lilt to her laugh.

Chris turned to look up at Sophia, his face and tone growing serious. "I want you to promise me something."

"Sure, Chris. What is it?" Sophia asked.

"Promise me you won't come over here or come anywhere near this house tomorrow." Chris was adamant, and she could hear it in his voice.

"Is it that important to you, Chris?"

"It is, Sophia."

"Then I promise."

Chapter 13

The game is afoot.

Ever since Sophia left last night, those words kept turning over and over in Chris's head like an ear worm. All the dominoes were in place. The question now was, would they fall in line, or would something happen to stop the sequence of events? Would Sacarras and his bodyguard show? Would Speedy do his part? And would Michael and Garcia close the sale and send him away into Agent Polk's arresting hands?

"The game really is afoot," he said out loud this time, as if to emphasize the reality of the situation. Chris had woken up several times last night in anticipation, each time catching a hint of Sophia's scent that was still on his body.

He arose and looked at his watch. It was now eight thirty, quite a bit later than he normally got up. He figured last night's activities and his waking up during the night were the culprits. Looking out the window, he noticed there was an inordinate number of people standing at the oak tree, perhaps a couple dozen, much more than a typical workday morning usually brought. He got dressed, forgoing a shower this morning, and went outside to see if there was anything unusual.

When he walked onto the front porch, Michael was sitting there smoking. Chris asked, "Why are there so many people here this morning?"

"Go look," Michael responded.

Chris walked down to the sidewalk and toward the tree, where he saw even more wreaths and flowers placed underneath and even more notes and photos pinned to the trunk than they had seen last night. As he approached, he looked up at the image of the Virgin Mary. He saw that somehow, over the last couple of days, the image had grown in size and prominence. It now protruded even farther from the bark of the tree, as if it were ready to burst from its confines. There were two men standing there discussing the image's physical characteristics while dozens more were praying on their way to work.

Chris walked back to the front porch and sat in his usual old metal chair that was three over from Michael's.

"Weird, isn't it?" Michael asked.

"Yes, very strange. What do you think it means?"

"I don't know," Michael said, putting out his cigarette. "Probably nothing. Garcia will be here in a few minutes."

"Is he bringing the rest of the Aztec pieces with him?" Chris asked.

"No, we'll get them later. We have plenty of time. We just need to set up a few things in the house first."

"Like what?"

"We'll need a table and a couple of chairs so we can display the pieces, and we have to make sure Sacarras buys them," Michael said.

"How are we to determine a price? You can't make it too expensive or he'll walk out, and if it's too cheap, he might smell a rat."

"I've thought of that. I'll have to play that by ear. I'll ask him to make an offer and take it from there. This is a real opportunity for him. I know that, so we have that on our side. He wouldn't be running here so quickly if he wasn't extremely interested."

"What about Agent Polk?" Chris asked. "If we don't have him lined up, none of this matters, does it?"

"Don't worry about that," Michael said.

Garcia pulled up in front of the house, dodging the numerous people occupying the streets. He jauntily walked up the sidewalk toward Chris and Michael. Chris was always impressed by how active and healthy Garcia was for being in his seventies and smoking as much as Michael.

"Good morning, everyone," he said, sitting down between the two men. "Am I late for the meeting?"

"Morning," Chris replied. "We just started."

"Michael," Garcia asked, "is the number of people at the tree going to be an issue with our plan this evening?"

"Probably. I have an idea about that," he replied. "We don't want to scare away our fish before we hook him."

Michael saw Herman enter the bank across the street and said, "Let me go call him before he gets too busy," then went inside the house.

"Garcia, have you talked through this plan with Michael?" Chris asked.

"Yes, I have," he responded.

"Do you think it's going to work?" Chris asked.

"You can never be sure of anything. Life is a mosaic of activities," Garcia said, waving his hands in a circle. "There are always percentages and possibilities."

"That doesn't sound like you're too confident," Chris stated.

"I'm realistic," he replied. "If we get everything in place and our guest arrives, we should be fine. But things happen." He made more gestures with his hands as he spoke. Chris always appreciated his honesty.

"What are the odds we will succeed?" Chris asked apprehensively.

Garcia thought for a moment, then said, "Fifty-fifty."

Just then, Michael walked back onto the porch. "Herman said to come over now."

The three men walked across the street and entered the bank. The employees were busy preparing for their day, and the tellers were opening their windows. There was only one customer waiting. Chris walked by Graciella's desk. She smiled and said, "Good morning." Chris returned the greeting. She was an attractive woman, always dressed well with a professional demeanor and a nice figure, too. However, she seemed ordinary and plain when compared to Sophia. Chris knew all too well what that meant.

Michael struggled with climbing the stairs to the second floor, so Garcia and Chris held on to one arm to assist him. They walked to the end of the hall and entered Herman's office.

"Gentlemen, gentlemen, welcome." Herman walked to Garcia first and said, "Garcia, my old friend, how are you?"

"Fine. Good to see you, Herman," Garcia responded.

"Michael, Chris, good morning," Herman said.

Chris admired people that could appear upbeat all the time. He found it too difficult for him on a daily basis.

All four men sat down, with Herman sitting behind his desk. Addressing Michael, Herman asked, "What can I do for you, my friend?"

"Herman," Michael started out, "we have a business deal occurring at six o'clock this evening at my house, and I would like you and Chris to monitor it from your office."

"What kind of business deal are we speaking of, Michael?"

"We're selling some pieces of art to a buyer from Laredo," Michael answered.

"Are you worried about this buyer?" Herman asked.

"Let's just say he doesn't have the best reputation. I don't think there are going to be any issues, I just want to play it safe," Michael said.

"Michael," Herman paused for a moment. "You know I would do anything for you, but I cannot get involved in any illegal activities."

Chris started to wonder if the plan was going awry before it even began. Perhaps Garcia was right.

"What we are doing is not illegal, Herman, and there won't be any guns or anything like that. I just want to make sure I don't get ripped off."

Herman thought for a second, then turned his chair to face out the window, looking at Michael's house. "No, I don't like it. It sounds too convoluted. I don't like the fact that we will not be able to see inside the house." Turning back around, he said, "What if something goes wrong inside? How will we know? Am I supposed to wait until they exit the house to figure that out?"

"Do you have any suggestions?" Michael asked.

"I do," Garcia interjected. "I can get a remote camera put inside the house, just like the ones I have in my store. You can watch us on a monitor."

Herman smiled at this suggestion and said, "Excellent, my friend. Garcia, you would have made a terrific private eye!" Herman then busted into his typical robust laughter.

"I will get someone to set up the equipment in the house. We'll bring you the monitor this afternoon," Garcia said.

"Fine, I'll see you then." Herman stood to shake hands, then asked, "When will you be here, Chris?"

"I'll be here just before closing," he answered.

The three men exited Herman's office and walked down the stairs, Chris and Garcia again steadying Michael as they went. Chris noticed Graciella was on the phone, but she still smiled and waved as he left the bank.

As they walked across the street to the house, Michael looked toward the tree. There were still several people standing underneath. "We're going to have to do something about these crowds. They're going to scare away our pigeon."

After climbing the porch steps, they sat in their usual chairs and started discussing the next steps of their plan.

"I'll need to go get the cameras soon. They could take a couple of hours to get set up," Garcia said.

"Where are you getting them?" Chris asked.

"Do you remember a man at the Thieves Market selling electronics? He also has a legitimate business doing surveillance work and installs home security. I'll get him to set them up."

"I need to go see Agent Polk right now," Michael said, then turned to Garcia. "We should pick up the rest of the Aztec pieces while we're out."

"What would you like me to do?" Chris asked.

"Two things," Michael responded. "Eat something, and then find some way to keep people away from that tree today."

"Didn't you say you had an idea?" Chris asked.

"Yes," Michael said, "having you take care of it was my idea." He laughed heavily at his joke, which led to a lengthy coughing spell.

Garcia helped him to his car, and they left to put the last pieces of the puzzle in place. Chris meanwhile looked at the tree, thinking how he could keep people away. After watching the crowd gathered under the tree for a few minutes, he left, taking Michael's truck, and drove to a sign shop he found in the yellow pages. He asked them to make a sign two feet by three feet, wrote down what he wanted it to say, and told them he needed it within the next two hours. He agreed to their additional charge for the same-day service, then asked where the nearest hardware store was. Conveniently, there was a Lowe's only about ten blocks from Michael's house.

As he walked into the store, Chris had the feeling he was back in Virginia, where he had frequented these stores for years, rushing from one job to the next. He soon found the section he was looking for and bought several tall traffic cones and two rolls of caution tape. He drove back to Michael's house and distributed the cones along the outside of the sidewalk. Next, he ran the yellow caution tape around the tree, fencing, traffic cones, and the few parking meters that were nearby, marking off a section that was a quarter of a block in each direction and would not allow anyone on the sidewalk near the tree.

He then returned to the sign shop to pick up the other part of his plan. A pimply-faced, twenty-something young man brought the sign out to him from the back of the store, proudly presenting his work. Chris paid him and went home to get a ladder, a hammer, and some nails. There were no people standing at the tree when he returned, the caution tape performing its desired duties. Chris climbed the ladder and neatly nailed the sign to the tree, hiding the image of the Virgin Mary. He then climbed down, looked up at the sign, and nodded, signaling he was pleased with the results. The sign looked professional and official. It read: "Temporarily closed for scientific research."

Chris returned to his post on the porch and waited anxiously for Michael and Garcia to return. While he waited, he watched as the occasional tree visitor was rebuffed by the newly installed deterrent. He took this time to mentally review the plan for today, looking for anything they might have overlooked, any trivial item that would assist in its success, or any flaw he could see in the

298

overall plan. Something did occur to him, and he planned to discuss it with Michael and Garcia after they got back.

It was now almost lunch time, and Chris had forgotten the other thing Michael had suggested he do while he was gone—eat something. He went into the kitchen and opened the refrigerator to see there was little that appealed to him. Sitting at the table for a moment, he looked around at the hodge-podge items in the room: mismatched cabinets, three separate brands of appliances, different colored chairs with a miss-matched table, and a long-ago patched-up fireplace that had probably been used to cook food before the war. He could sense his anxiety building and said out loud to himself, "I hate the waiting."

Chris then heard someone coming in the door and rushed to the front room to find Michael entering, with Garcia closely behind him carrying a small wooden box.

"I saw the sign you put up," Michael said, laughing as he spoke. "Very clever, seems to work nicely."

"Thanks!" Chris said. "What's happening with our plans? Any word from Speedy?"

"I spoke to him, and he's all set. He's confirmed everything with the bodyguard, and they are meeting him this evening. He'll be here at six," Michael explained.

"Okay, great. What about the surveillance cameras?"

"I have someone who will be here shortly to install them for us," Garcia answered. "He said it will take about two hours because we also have to disguise them."

"That's something I wanted to talk to you about," Chris said.

"I thought you were in agreement with Herman about the cameras," Garcia said.

"I am," Chris replied, "but we can only see you with the cameras, right? I want to be able to hear you, too."

"It's a little late to set that up," Garcia said.

"No, I have an idea," Chris responded. "Take my cell phone and tape it under the table. I'll call the number before he gets here, and you just have to leave the line open. Herman and I will be able to hear everything that's said."

"He might see it," Garcia said.

"No, he's right," Michael said. "We'll put a tablecloth over the table. Besides, he'll be so focused on the pieces, he'll never notice it, but you'll have to be careful not to make any noise."

"Herman's phone system has a mute button on it. I have the same kind in my office back home," Chris said.

"Okay, that should work," Michael said. "There are a couple of other things we need to go over with you, Chris."

"Alright, what are they?"

"When I spoke to Speedy, we set up a signal for if he smells a rat," Michael said.

"What do you mean by that?" Chris asked.

Garcia interjected, "It's just a precaution in case they bring another person, or if Speedy feels Sacarras is wise to the plan."

Chris was uncomfortable with the idea but decided they knew best. "Okay, what's the signal?" Chris asked.

"Speedy said when he pulls up, if he locks the car doors after they get out, and you see the car's lights flash, they are on to us."

"What do we do then?"

"I'll lock the door, grab the box, and sneak out the back," Michael answered, "where Garcia will be waiting for me."

"Wait, I thought Garcia was going to be here with you." Chris could feel his anxiety level elevating.

"I can't be, Chris," Garcia said. "They'll know something is up if there is anybody but Michael in the house. Sacarras may be a despicable man, but he's no fool."

"What happens to the plan then?" Chris asked.

"It will be off. We just can't take the risk," Michael answered. "Which leads me to the other thing we need to tell you." Michael was suddenly very serious. "You need to leave the house now."

"What do you mean?" Chris asked.

"I spoke with Agent Polk. Here's his phone number." Michael handed Chris a neatly folded piece of paper with a number written inside. "He's coming here at four, and he wants to talk to me regarding the sting we're setting up. You can't be here when he arrives."

"Why not?" Chris was beginning to think the plan was not going to work; something seemed amiss.

"Because I don't want the F.B.I., or Sacarras, to know you're involved. You cannot be a part of what we have planned here. I would never forgive myself if something happened to you," Michael said in a somber tone. "You and Herman will be safe watching us from across the street."

"But this whole thing was my idea. I'm the one that wanted justice. Why am I being left out at the end?"

"You're not!" Michael said, slightly raising his voice. "You were the one that showed honor when you wanted to find your friend's killer, you showed bravery even when you knew you were in danger, and you showed perseverance to get the plan this far. Those are qualities Garcia and I greatly respect, but we have to be the ones to finish it." Michael took a few deep breaths, finding it a little hard to breathe, then continued, "You have to trust us, son."

Chris stood in the room looking at Michael, then Garcia. He realized it was the smart thing to do, and they were right in wanting to protect him at this stage, but it was difficult to relinquish control after coming so far.

"Alright," Chris said reluctantly. "Any suggestions where I should go until five?"

"We have made a reservation for you at The Hyatt," Garcia answered. "It is four blocks behind the bank." He pointed across the street.

"Why a hotel? I'll only be there for a few hours," Chris asked.

"Because you have to take your clothing and other items with you. There can be no evidence in the house that you have been here," Michael said.

"Besides, there's no sense wandering the streets when you can take a shower and eat, perhaps take a nap," Garcia said. "We still have a long way to go with this, Chris."

Accepting the well-thought-out logic, Chris said, "Okay, I'll go pack."

He went to his bedroom to gather his things as the men moved a few pieces of furniture around. Chris returned and handed Michael his cell phone while asking, "Anything I can do to help?"

"No, we're just making it a little more conducive to displaying the merchandise," Michael said. "I'll walk you out."

They walked out the door and onto the front porch. Chris felt odd standing there with his suitcase.

Michael spoke first. "Look, I know I didn't have anything to do with raising you, but I just want to let you know how proud I am of you."

Chris was taken aback by such a heartfelt show of emotion. He turned to Michael and did two things he had never done before. He said, "Thanks, Dad," then shook his hand.

Michael quickly turned to go back inside, and Chris walked down the broken and heaved sidewalk, through the tilted gate, and across the street. He could not escape the ominous feeling he had in his gut.

As Chris walked to the hotel, he began to think that the idea of him leaving for a while was a good one. He would probably grow increasingly anxious as the day progressed, and there was really nothing for him to do back at the house. Michael and Garcia's reasoning was empirical; he knew they were right.

The hotel was on the corner just four blocks behind the bank, like Garcia had said. It looked ubiquitous, as so many downtown hotels did. *Just change the name*, Chris thought. He entered the lobby, observing that he could be in almost any city in the country and have the same view. After walking to the counter, he was told there indeed was a room reserved in his name. They gave him his key after he registered, and he was relieved to see it was only on the third floor; he hated elevators.

He took the stairs to his floor and located his room halfway down the hall. He ordered some room service food, ate, showered, and looked at his watch. It was now two forty-five. He called the front desk, asked for a wakeup call at four fifteen, and laid on the bed, wondering why he still had such an ominous feeling and if he would be able to fall asleep.

The phone rang like a jackhammer inside his head. Chris reached to answer it, realizing it was only a foot away.

"Your four fifteen call, sir."

"Thanks," Chris said and hung up. He had forty minutes for a five-minute walk. He decided to take another shower, debating whether it was the heat from his walk to the hotel, the grogginess he felt from his nap, or the unclean feeling he was getting from the impending presence of Sacarras that should be blamed. He left his suitcase and clothing in the room, deciding it would certainly be easier to retrieve them after the evening's festivities than suspiciously carry them to the bank.

Chris walked in front of the bank at four fifty. He took a moment to discreetly look at the house across the street. There was no movement inside or out, and his barrier he had placed around the tree earlier that day was working well.

He entered the bank and saw the majority of the employees scurrying to leave for the day, a couple of tellers still diligently handling transactions. Graciella was on the phone, looking bored with her call, but perked up noticeably when she saw Chris. She waved subtly while flashing him a bright smile. He thought to himself she would make some lucky man a good wife someday.

Chris climbed the stairs and walked down the hall to Herman's office. He could not shake his feelings of imminent danger but dismissed it as just being his anxiety. Herman had his door closed and the drapes that faced the hallway drawn, an unusual procedure. Chris knocked on the door and heard Herman scramble out of his chair and open his door.

"Come in, Chris," Herman said, a little more serious than normal. "It's good to see that you are always on time. That is very important to bankers."

Chris entered Herman's office and saw two small monitors on his desk. One was Herman's computer, and the one next to it showed the inside of the old rundown house across the street. On that screen there were two images, one showing the left side of the room, and the other showing the right side. He could see all the way down the hall, past his bedroom to the bathroom door. Chris thought how he was glad no one had been watching last night when he walked down that very hall and went upstairs with Sophia. He was not sure if he could embrace all of this new technology. It seemed to be too invasive, and he didn't like the loss of anonymity.

On the monitor's screen showing the right side of the room, he could see the kitchen table had been placed there with a large white tablecloth draped over it, covering it halfway to the floor. There was a chair on opposite sides, facing each other. A small brown wooden box was set in the middle of the table. Chris could not see Michael in either monitor image.

"Herman, have you seen Michael?" he asked.

"Come here," he responded, motioning Chris toward the drapes that had been drawn shut over the large window that faced the house. Herman opened them slightly, and Chris could see Michael on the front porch smoking a cigarette.

"He seems quite relaxed," Herman said.

"Yes, he does," Chris responded. "Not a care in the world."

"I have to make sure everyone has left and everything is locked up securely. Please wait here, I shall return shortly," Herman said and moved toward the door.

Chris sat back down at the desk looking at the empty room on the monitor's screen, wondering what would transpire there over the next hour. He took out the neatly folded piece of paper he had in his pocket and set it on the desk next to the phone. He noticed there was a switch on the monitor, which allowed the viewer to see just one side of the room or both on a split screen. He assumed the installer had set up two cameras to allow them to be viewed individually or together. He pushed it a few times before leaving it to show both sides of the room.

Herman returned to the office and closed the door, taking the time to lock it behind him. He saw that Chris had noticed this and said, "The cleaning crew comes in between six and seven. I want to make sure we are not disturbed if they get here early."

Chris felt his claustrophobia rear its head but tried to distract himself with the more important matters at hand. Realizing he was sitting in Herman's chair, he got up quickly and said, "Sorry."

Herman laughed as he moved around the desk to occupy the seat. "How have you enjoyed your stay here?" he asked.

"Well, Herman, some of the places I've seen have been quite lovely—South Padre Island, for example. But I've been mostly working with Michael on this deal he's making tonight."

"Yes, I understand. Michael seems to be very interested in this sale. He must hope to make a lot of money," Herman said.

Chris sensed Herman was more aware than he was letting on. "Herman, I must say, I was a little surprised you agreed to help us."

"Michael and I are friends, why wouldn't I?" he asked, shrugging his shoulders.

Chris glanced at his watch: 5:30, half an hour. "Yes, of course, but this is not just an ordinary favor. You're sticking your neck out a little, aren't you?"

Herman shrugged again as he tilted his head. "Perhaps. I owe Michael a lot. Even if I had to stick my neck out more, I would." He seemed quite emotional with his last statement. "Has he told you about our friendship?"

"No, not really. Just that you've known each other a long time," Chris responded.

Herman watched the monitor as he spoke. "We go way back. We were always friends... No, we were drinking buddies. A few years ago, when I was vice president of this bank, my drinking got worse. I spent many evenings with Michael on his front porch drinking, and several bank customers saw me there after hours. Michael had decided to stop drinking, but I kept going. It got bad. I was about to lose my job, my wife, and probably my kids.

"Michael helped me. He helped me when no one else believed in me. I would not have stopped drinking if it wasn't for him." He paused for just a moment, then continued, "Then two years ago, one of my sons was on drugs. We thought he was going to die. Michael saved him. Somehow, he saved him." Turning to look at Chris now, he asked, "How much is that worth?"

"I understand. I guess you can't put a price on that kind of friendship," Chris stated. He looked at his watch again: 5:40. Then he said, "I'll need to call Michael in a few minutes. Can you put the speaker phone on and mute it so they can't hear us?"

"Of course. Garcia told me you were going to do that when he was here this afternoon," Herman said.

"Did he say anything else to you?" Chris inquired.

Herman thought for a moment. "He said, if we do not see him, not to worry, he would be nearby. I didn't want to ask him, but what does that mean?"

"He doesn't want to be in the house when they arrive, it might scare off the buyer. He's just hanging around as a safety net in case there's a problem," Chris said in an off-handed manner.

"Is there going to be a problem?" Herman asked.

Chris took a deep breath and responded by saying, "I sure hope not, Herman."

Chris walked over to the window and pulled back the curtains so he could peek out. Michael was still sitting on the porch smoking. Most of the after-work traffic had gone, and there were only a few that were heading home late to dinner or to pick up the kids from soccer practice. The street was mostly quiet, eerily quiet. Chris walked over to Herman's phone and dialed his cell number. Michael answered on the second ring.

"Everything ready?" Chris asked.

"Yes," Michael spoke in a calm voice. "You guys ready over there?"

"Yes, we are. Go ahead and tape the phone under the table. We'll be listening and watching. Good luck."

Michael walked into the house and picked up a roll of duct tape he had on his desk. He pulled off a couple of feet and went to the table, bent down, and taped the phone to the underside of the table. Standing, Michael asked, "Can you hear me?"

"Yes," Chris responded. "I'm now going to mute the speaker phone." He pressed the mute button, and Michael looked toward the camera and gave him a thumbs up.

Chris saw it was now 5:52.

"You're worried, aren't you, Chris?" Herman said in a kind voice.

Chris had now walked back to the window and was peering out at the house, watching for Speedy's black car. "Yes, I've had a bad feeling about this all day. Perhaps it's just anxiety," he said, not looking at Herman.

"Michael used to talk about you when we would drink sometimes," Herman said.

Chris, not taking his eyes off the house, said, "What is there to say? He never knew me."

"No, he never did, not until a few years ago, but he knew about you," Herman said with an uptick to his voice.

Chris glanced over at him briefly. "What do you mean?"

"For many years, your mother would send newspaper clippings of you playing baseball," Herman said.

"She did?" Chris responded indifferently while looking at his watch. It was 5:59.

"Oh, yes. He was always telling his friends his son was a professional baseball player. That is a very big deal around here." Herman was watching the monitor.

"What's Michael doing?" Chris asked.

312

"He is just sitting at the table smoking," Herman said.

There was silence for a minute or two. Chris looked at his watch again: 6:02. "Where the fuck are they?" Chris asked. "Herman, do you know Michael's friend Speedy?"

"Speedy? Yes, I have known him since he was a detective on the police force."

"Detective?" Chris exclaimed. "No one ever said he was a detective."

"Yes, and a very good one. He just got caught with his hand in the cookie jar one too many times." Herman laughed at his comment.

Chris didn't want to talk anymore, he just wanted to see Speedy turn the corner so they could get on with this. Had something already gone wrong? Had they not shown up? Has his one chance at getting justice gone awry?

At exactly 6:06, Speedy's little black car turned the corner and pulled up in front of the house.

"They're here!" Chris said excitedly.

"Watch them until they go in the house, then come over here," Herman said.

Speedy exited first from the driver's seat, then the bodyguard got out from behind him and walked around to open the back passenger door for Sacarras. He slowly unfurled from the back seat with a good deal of help from both men. They closed the doors and walked toward the house. There was no locking of the doors or flashing lights. Chris was relieved that the plan was still on.

Sacarras gingerly stepped across the pavement and was assisted up the stairs by the bodyguard. Speedy knocked on the front door and waited for it to open.

"Yes?" Michael said after opening the door.

"These are people who are interested in the Aztec pieces," Speedy said.

"Come in," Michael said and left the door open as he walked back to his chair on the far side of the table and sat down.

As the men entered the house, Chris walked over to Herman's desk and stood next to him, watching them now on the monitor. Speedy and the bodyguard stood just inside the door as Sacarras walked over to the table.

"He is a strange-looking man," Herman said quietly, almost to himself.

"You have no idea," Chris responded, his voice just as quiet, not taking his eyes off the screen.

"I am Villatoro Sacarras," the man said to Michael.

Chris had not heard him speak before. His voice was very guttural sounding, almost other-worldly, and he elongated the last "s" on his name, as if he was hissing.

"I understand you have some interesting pieces to sell?" he said to Michael. "May I see them?"

Michael did not speak. He opened the brown wooden box and slowly removed the Aztec pieces one by one, and just as slowly laid them on the table, as if taunting Sacarras. When the twelve pieces were set out on the white tablecloth, Sacarras lowered his frame down into the chair. The bodyguard and Speedy stood motionless behind him.

Sacarras examined each piece, carefully picking them up and turning them around. No one spoke; the room was ghostly silent.

Michael stared at Sacarras while smoking a cigarette. He noticed Sacarras had long fingernails that were dark and broken.

After what seemed like an eternity, Sacarras spoke, saying, "How much are you asking for these pieces?"

Michael did not blink. "I'm interested in what you will offer me."

"Yes, I'm sure you are. But why should I buy something that I paid to be delivered to me over forty years ago?"

"Oh, shit!" Chris exclaimed under his breath, his eyes still glued to the monitor.

"What are you talking about? I own these pieces," Michael said emphatically, gesturing with his hand that held the cigarette.

"I may be old, but I have a long memory," Sacarras said, looking at Michael with his coal black eyes. "I remember a man telling me that he had broken his leg when his plane crashed, and someone had looted my cargo. I believe that man's name was Michael Hamilton."

"We've got to stop this!" Chris said. "He's going to kill them!"

"Be still," Herman said, placing a hand on Chris's shoulder. "We can't do anything now."

Michael returned Sacarras's stare as he dragged on his cigarette, and then said, "You knew the whole time, didn't you?" Michael had a smirk on his face.

"Of course, Mr. Michael Hamilton. I recognized the jade piece immediately. I have thought about these pieces every day for over forty years." Sacarras placed his dark red hands on the table, slightly leaning back in his chair, and said, "I have just one question for you—you might say it will be your life saving question."

"Ask your question," Michael said, still staring at his eyes.

"Where is the rest?"

"What do you mean?" Michael asked, still smirking as if he was continuing to taunt him.

"I have had people watching for the items taken from the plane since the day it crashed. I even killed a man because he claimed half of the cargo was his, but I wanted it all." The two men glared at each other, neither looking away. "If you had sold any of it, even to your thief friends, I would have known." Sacarras leaned forward. "So you must still have it."

Michael continued to look at Sacarras while he smoked, then said, "I had hoped you would have died long ago. Then I would have been free to sell everything. Instead, I have had to live in this shit hole all these years."

"How appropriate," Sacarras said, grinning slightly, showing his yellow teeth. "Where is it hidden?" He stared into Michael's eyes, a gesture that scared most people into compliance. "If you do not tell me now, I will kill you and your friend and then tear this house apart looking for it."

Michael hesitated for a moment, then broke his stare to glance at Speedy.

"Your friend cannot help you. We made sure he didn't have a gun before we came here," Sacarras said.

Showing resignation, Michael said, "It's hidden under the floorboards in a room upstairs.

Sacarras forced his lanky frame to rise from his chair and said, "Show me."

Across the street in the bank, Chris was yelling at Herman, "We have to do something!"

"Do what?" Herman asked. "Do you have a gun?"

"No, of course not! Maybe I should call the F.B.I.?" Chris reached for the folded paper on the desk.

"They'll never get here in time. Look!" Herman screamed.

Chris turned back to the monitor to see the four men walking down the hall toward the bathroom. He clicked the switch to have it on full screen.

Michael was leading the way, followed by Sacarras, then Speedy, then the bodyguard.

As Michael reached up to open the bathroom door, Chris wondered what he was doing. The stairs to the second floor were around the corner. It was difficult to see clearly on the screen with all four men in the hallway.

Michael partially opened the door and held it for Sacarras, who started up the brown stairs. After crossing the second step, he stopped when he realized it was not a full set of stairs but the

318

entrance to a darkened bathroom. At that moment, Speedy and the bodyguard rushed forward and pushed Sacarras into the bathroom and tried to close the door. Sacarras managed to keep his left hand in the door jamb, making it impossible to close all the way.

Garcia suddenly appeared from an adjacent bedroom and grabbed the door handle, drawing it back and slamming it shut with all his weight and strength. Sacarras's hand was still on the jamb, and the sharp edges of the heavy door severed all four fingers from his left hand. Chris could hear him scream through the phone; not like a human scream, more like the howl of a wolf. The door closed completely, and Garcia reached up and pulled out the worn door handle, locking Sacarras inside.

Chris could see Garcia turn to Speedy and the bodyguard and heard him yell at them, "Get out, go!" They ran down the hallway and out the front door as Garcia reached down to pick something up off the floor. Michael had been shoved into a corner in the melee. Garcia grabbed him and guided him down the hall. Michael walked to the table and hurriedly put all the Aztec pieces in the box, reached under the table to grab the phone, and staggered toward the door. Chris could still hear the screams from Sacarras through the phone.

319

Speedy and the bodyguard ran to the car and quickly drove away. Garcia ran back inside the bedroom he had heroically emerged from as Michael stumbled and fell out onto the front porch. Garcia came running down the hall as a ball of fire exploded in the bedroom, blowing out the bedroom's windows and swiftly engulfing the bathroom and hallway in flames. Garcia was now out on the front porch and helping Michael up, as he was having difficulty walking and breathing.

"Come on, let's go!" Chris yelled to Herman, who quickly moved to unlock the door, then ran down the bank's stairs. Herman hurriedly opened the bank's front door, and Chris ran across the street to help Michael, yelling over his shoulder, "Call 911!" Herman went to the nearest desk phone and called for an ambulance and the fire department.

By the time Chris reached Garcia and Michael, they were at the gate, and most of the first floor of the house was now on fire.

"He's having trouble breathing!" Garcia screamed over the noise of the wooden house being consumed. Chris lifted Michael into his arms, feeling the heat from the fire as Garcia picked up the box and cell phone, and together they ran back across the street to the bank. Herman was holding open the door as Chris entered and laid Michael on a sofa in the waiting area. His breathing was labored and weak.

The flames had now engulfed the entire bottom floor of the old house, and the screams and banging from Sacarras had stopped. The house seemed to burn extremely fast, the hundred-year-old wood acting like so much kindling, cracking and popping loudly. Smoke billowed out of the broken windows to encapsulate the entire structure. The second floor soon succumbed to the intense heat and appeared to detonate as a giant rush of air was sucked in from below, causing the entire house to become a giant raging inferno.

Firetruck sirens could be heard nearby as Michael's breathing worsened. Chris ran outside to see if the ambulance was there. He could feel the extreme heat radiating from the house fire from over a hundred feet away; it was as loud as a freight train. He looked around the corner and saw there was an ambulance just pulling up on the side of the bank. Chris ran to meet them. "He's inside the bank!" Chris yelled.

Two men jumped out of the ambulance, retrieved a gurney, and followed him. Herman held open the door as Garcia knelt beside his friend. The EMTs opened the gurney as Chris and Garcia helped lift Michael.

As they exited the bank, firetrucks were just pulling up to the now towering fire. The flames were so powerful that they had set the old oak tree ablaze and all of its branches were burning, making it harder for the firemen to get near the house.

The ambulance left with Michael, and Garcia turned to Chris as they watched it leave. "Let's go get my jeep and meet them at the hospital." Chris was not surprised at how cool Garcia was under stress.

"Where is it?" Chris yelled in response.

"It's three blocks on the other side of the fire. We may have trouble getting there," Garcia said loud enough to be heard over the blaze across the street.

They circumvented the fire trucks while also trying to avoid hoses, firemen, and the burning tree. People had started to gather along the peripheries to gawk at the fire. Thousands of gallons of water were being poured onto the house to help quell the fire, but it was obvious the firemen were only trying to keep it from damaging any other structures. There was no saving Michael's home.

Garcia saw the fire captain standing in the street next to a firetruck, watching his men battle the blaze. He walked up and grabbed his arm.

"Garcia! Isn't this Michael's house?" he asked, yelling above the noise of the fire and the water being sprayed.

"Yes…it was," Garcia shouted in reply.

"What happened?" the captain screamed against the background of deafening noise.

"I don't know. I got here just in time to get him out."

"Was there anybody else in there?"

"No," Garcia said and walked away.

Chapter 14

"I've killed my own father,"

Chris said remorsefully as they got in Garcia's jeep.

"Don't be so hard on yourself. Michael knew the risks," Garcia said as he backed the car out and headed toward the hospital.

"Why didn't he tell me what he was doing?" Chris asked, his voice full of frustration.

"Because he knew you wouldn't agree to our plan, and we had to keep you out of it. Michael did not want you involved in a murder," Garcia emphatically stated.

Chris knew he was right, but he still felt responsible. "There never was any Agent Polk, was there?" he asked, knowing the answer before asking the question.

"No, of course not. We had to make him up to give you something you could believe and to get you out of the house." Garcia was driving very swiftly through the streets. "Besides, you never would have been happy with just having him arrested, would you?"

Chris thought for a few seconds whether Sacarras's arrest really would have satisfied his quest for retribution. "No, probably not. I just…never thought killing him was an option."

Garcia laughed ironically and said, "Be realistic, Chris, it was the only option."

"Do you think they'll find his remains?" Chris cautiously asked, thinking now of the aftermath.

"No way," Garcia replied. "They are not looking for anyone, and he's buried under two stories of charred debris by now. And besides, I know what I'm doing."

"What do you mean?" Chris asked.

"That fire burned too fast and hot to leave any remains. There won't be any evidence left behind."

Garcia pulled up to the ER, and they both jumped out and walked quickly to the entrance. After inquiring at the front desk, they were directed to where Michael had been taken.

Chris asked the duty nurse if he could see Michael. "He's in the ICU right now," she told him. "I'll have the doctor come talk to you in a few minutes." She then asked, "Are you a relative, sir?"

"Yes," Chris said, "I'm his son." He thought how odd that still sounded.

Chris walked over to Garcia, who was waiting just outside the ER's doors.

"The nurse said a doctor will be out soon to talk to us."

"Okay," Garcia replied. "Look, Chris, you cannot hold yourself responsible for any of this. Michael wanted to do this. He knew the risks."

"I don't understand why he did it. This was not his fight, it was mine."

"Perhaps. Maybe Michael thought this was what fathers are supposed to do for their sons. It's possible he took it a little more personally after he realized that Sacarras was involved. But I think..." Garcia took a deep breath as if he was divulging a secret. "I think he thought one last heroic gesture might help balance out a lot of the bad he's done in his life."

Before Garcia could say more, the doctor walked out and introduced himself. "Good evening. I'm Doctor Turner. Are you the son?"

"I am," Chris replied, then thoughtfully said, "This is my father's oldest friend, Garcia. You can talk to both of us."

326

"Fine," the doctor said. He spoke in a matter-of-fact tone. "Your father has had a severe heart attack, but that's not all. You're aware he has lung cancer, aren't you?"

"Yes, he has told me that."

"He is very weak. I've reviewed his records, and the cancer has affected his lungs and other organs. Quite frankly, I'm surprised he's lived as long as he has."

"What are his chances of recovery?" Garcia asked.

"None," the doctor said. "To be honest, I doubt he'll make it through the night."

"May we see him?" Chris asked.

"We're only supposed to allow in family members in these situations," Doctor Turner said apologetically.

Garcia interjected before Chris could protest, "It's alright, Chris. Your father and I have already said our goodbyes."

Doctor Turner led Chris to Michael's room. Michael was hooked up to a heart monitor and had on an oxygen mask.

"He's been given some morphine for the pain, but he's not very responsive. You can stay in here with him, and we have some forms you need to sign."

The doctor left the room, and Chris walked over to the bed. Michael slowly turned his head toward Chris, and his eyes opened a little when he recognized him. He motioned to remove the oxygen mask, and Chris reached down and pulled it away. As he did, Michael took Chris's other hand. His grip was very weak.

Michael spoke in a very hushed voice, almost a whisper, taking several breaths between words.

"We...got...him...didn't...we?" He started to cough, and Chris put the mask back on Michael's face. After a few seconds, Michael motioned for it to be removed again. He spoke, straining for every word.

"...bank...fireplace...forgive...me."

Michael's hand went limp in Chris's. The heart machine beeped in a single continuous tone. Chris looked up at the monitor, which showed no sign of a heartbeat. A nurse came rushing in and moved Chris aside. "You have to leave now," she said. The doctor returned just as Chris walked out of the room. He didn't need to be told. Chris knew Michael was gone.

He walked out and into the waiting room and did not see Garcia. He exited the doors that led outside to see him sitting on one of the benches smoking a cigarette. Chris slowly walked over to him and said, "He's gone, Garcia."

Garcia reached down to put out his cigarette and said, "I know. Let's go home."

As they walked to the jeep, Chris asked Garcia, "How far is it to my hotel?"

"About twenty blocks. Why?"

"Do you mind if I walk there?"

"Of course not," Garcia said, handing him his cell phone. "I'll see you tomorrow." Garcia walked over to his jeep and drove away.

Chris started his walk back to the hotel, not entirely sure which way he should head, but quickly got his bearings when he saw a tower of smoke in the distance. He wondered how much of the house would be left when the firemen finally brought the blaze under control. He knew Garcia was right about not being so hard on himself about Michael's death, but he couldn't shake the feeling of guilt that had come over him.

He had not asked Garcia specifically, but he was sure part of the reason for them insisting he get a hotel room was they knew he would need a place to sleep tonight. Michael had not only put his life at risk, Chris told himself, but he had sacrificed his house also. It was the place where Michael had lived for so many years, and now they were both gone in the same night.

As he walked, his feelings of somberness began to diminish, and he reflected on how grateful he was for the effort and risk both Michael and Garcia had taken on his behalf. Garcia had done it mostly because of his lifelong friendship with Michael, to be sure. However, Michael never wavered in his commitment once he was satisfied Chris was determined to finish the hunt for Chico's killer. Chris thought that even though Michael was gone, maybe destiny had a hand in the myriad of events that had aligned for Michael to have such an exciting journey at life's end.

Chris also acknowledged that this had been a fortuitous opportunity for him to get to know the man who had disappeared so many years ago. He had been able to see some of the pieces of the puzzle about which his family had only heard rumors and third-hand stories. He had never held any animosity toward the man he didn't know, but there were always questions, and Chris now understood that even though everyone has flaws, some run so deep it makes all the good things about a person irrelevant.

As he neared the hotel, he could smell the still lingering smoke from the fire that had raged just a few blocks away. He resisted the urge to keep walking and go look at what carnage had been left behind. He would save that for the light of the next day.

Chris had worked many long hours in his life and hiked hundreds of miles of trails, but he could not remember when he had been more exhausted than he was this night. He climbed the three flights of stairs to his room, peeled off his clothes, and crawled into bed. He had no schedule for the next day. He slept for nine hours.

When he awoke the next morning, Chris felt surprisingly rested. Perhaps it was because the building anxiety of the last few days' events was gone and he had achieved what he, seemingly long ago, promised to Chico and himself. It also might have been the walk he took last night—at the beginning he had felt guilt and remorse, but by the end, he had developed a more positive perspective and some acceptance.

He knew there were still some things that he needed to do before he left town. The first thing was to contact Garcia about arranging and attending Michael's funeral. Did Michael have any business that needed to be taken care of? What about the property? Did he have a will? Chris couldn't imagine there were any assets left behind, and he was sure he would have to pay for any kind of funeral that would take place. Hopefully, Herman and Garcia would have some answers.

Chris's thoughts wandered to what Michael had hoarsely whispered to him last night. *Was it "bank's fireplace, forgive me?" What did that mean?*

"Was Michael hallucinating from the drugs before he died? Was it a secret only Michael and Herman knew? Was it a riddle?"

Chris's mind then landed on the problem that was Sophia. Of all the inopportune, geographically inconvenient, and bad times to meet someone, this one took the cake. However, he knew full well she was not just "someone." She was kindhearted, funny, intelligent, and confident, gifted with the beauty of her mother and the common sense and pragmatism of her father. She was a rare find, and he knew he would have to do something about her before he left.

After taking a long shower and getting dressed, Chris called the front desk to make sure he could have the room for the next couple of days. He left the hotel, taking his cell phone, a habit he was grudgingly developing.

He walked down the street toward the house. Remnants of smoke still wafted through the early morning air, drawing him to it like a moth to a flame. The whole evening was a blur; it seemed so surreal, he had to make sure that it really did happen. Chris wanted the reality of physical proof.

He stopped across the street from the house. The entire block, from the bank to the old fence, was cordoned off with police tape. Two fire trucks were parked on the side street, still pouring water on the smoldering hulk that had once been a house. The second floor had collapsed onto the first floor, leaving a giant mound of charred wooden rubble, and there was just one section of a wall, next to the chimney in the kitchen, that was still standing. The old tool shed that had housed Michael's ugly workhorse of a car had also burned and unceremoniously collapsed onto the old girl.

All the leaves on the massive oak tree were gone, and most of the branches were turned into cinder, exposing its frame, naked to the world. What remained was a tree trunk that was burned severely on the side facing the house and completely untouched on the side facing the street; the one that had the impression of the Virgin Mary. The sign Chris had placed over her had been melted away to reveal the image had completely disappeared. There was no evidence the image had ever been there, just the ordinary bark of the tree. "Garcia was right," Chris said, remembering what Sophia had told him the day they first met: "My father says it will go away when Michael dies."

"I'm sorry about your father," an ethereal voice said from behind him, startling Chris.

Chris turned to find Herman standing there, his eyes red behind his gold-rimmed glasses.

"Thank you, Herman," Chris said. "How did you find out?"

"Garcia called me last night," Herman said in a soft-spoken tone. "Michael may not have had many friends, but we were very close."

"Yes, I can see that. I'm sorry you lost such a good friend, Herman. You certainly knew him better than me," Chris said respectfully.

"I will have to keep the drapes in my office closed for some time. I don't want to see that view every day.'"

"I understand," Chris said. Then, remembering what Michael had cryptically said to him last night, asked, "Herman, in the hospital, Michael said something about the bank. Do you have any idea what that means?"

Herman looked at him knowingly, then said, "Follow me."

Chris followed Herman into the bank and up the stairs to his second-floor office. He did not notice if Graciella was there.

Entering Herman's office, Chris could see the drapes were indeed closed, and the monitor was still on his desk. Pointing to it, Herman said, "Garcia said he would get that later today."

Herman walked over to a tall, well-built cabinet on one of the walls of his office. He unlocked it to reveal several individual doors inside, each with its own lock. Herman unlocked one of the larger ones near the bottom and removed a large metal filing box. He set it down on a table in the corner.

"I knew this day would come. I just never knew who I was going to give the box to. Michael never told me," Herman said, staring at it sitting on the table. He turned to Chris and said, "I'll give you a few minutes to look through the contents." Herman then left the room, closing the door quietly behind him.

Chris sat down at the table with a sense of curiosity. "What could Michael possibly have saved?"

When he opened the box, he first found dozens of rolled-up newspaper articles wrapped in a rubber band. Unrolling them, he discovered they were all from his baseball career; from his high school days to being drafted and playing professionally. There had to be at least a hundred of them. There was also a small box with his medals from WWII. Chris didn't recognize any of them except the one that had a purple heart attached to it.

Inside was also a picture of Chris with his two sisters, taken when they were ages one, three, and four. Chris had the exact same picture in his home on the kitchen wall. There was also a black and white picture of a pretty woman in a 50s-style bathing suit. He turned it over and saw that someone had written "Daytona Beach, 1952" on the back. Chris turned it back over and, after looking at it for a few seconds, realized it was his mother before she and Michael had married. There was nothing else in the box: no important papers, no deeds, no letters from attorneys, no stocks, no will.

Herman came back in the room and asked, "Have you had enough time, Chris?"

"Yes, Herman, thank you. Is the box all that Michael has here at the bank?"

"Yes, it is. I know you and your father were not close, so you probably were not aware of his financial situation," Herman said.

"I knew nothing at all about it, Herman, but I'm not asking if he has any money. I'm not interested in that. I was just wondering if this was all he left behind?"

"I'm afraid so. Even the house he lived in was sold to the bank a few years ago. He was given lifetime rights to stay in the house. He needed the money to live on and pay his hospital bills." Herman seemed apologetic with the information.

After a moment, Chris asked, "Herman, is there a fireplace here in the bank?"

"A fireplace? No. Why do you ask?" Herman was quite curious.

"Michael said something about a bank and a fireplace last night. Perhaps I misunderstood what he said. He was having a great deal of difficulty speaking." Chris rose and then asked, "May I keep the box, Herman?"'

"Yes, of course, Chris." He then continued by saying, "It may not seem like much of a legacy to leave behind, but some things are more valuable to one person than another," Herman said.

"Quite true, Herman. Thank you for all that you have done," Chris said.

Chris shook Herman's hand and slowly walked back to his hotel while trying to decide what do next. Once in his room, he inquired about renting a car, since Michael's "reliable" truck was not so reliable anymore. It turned out there was an Avis office just a few blocks away from the hotel. Leaving Michael's box in his room, Chris walked over to the Avis office and soon left in a yellow 1995 Jeep Wrangler, similar to the one he had driven the day he spent with Sophia at the beach. He headed over to Garcia's store, hoping he might have some idea about what Michael had said last night and to talk about the funeral. It was already after eleven, and Chris was getting hungry, having skipped breakfast again. He lamented that one of the things that had suffered the most on this journey was eating on a schedule. After parking his jeep next to an identical green one, Chris went into the store to find Garcia sitting in his little café area. He was talking to a very

337

serious-looking, heavily bespectacled man who was just getting up to leave as Chris approached them.

"Thank you," Garcia said to the man and shook his hand. He didn't seem at all surprised to see Chris.

"Please sit down," Garcia said, motioning to the seat that had just been vacated. "How are you this morning?" he asked. While not in his usual jovial disposition, he was still relatively upbeat, considering the events of the last twenty-four hours.

"I'm doing okay, Garcia. Thanks for asking."

"I was just making final arrangements for the service for Michael," said Garcia.

"What, just now? That was fast." Chris was becoming accustomed to how quickly Garcia got things done.

"No, not really. We have known this was coming for months now. Michael and I had discussed it many times. We already had everything in place. I just needed to make a few phone calls."

"When is the service?" Chris asked.

"Ten o'clock Saturday morning. There will just be a graveside service, and only a few close friends will be attending. There will also be a short military presentation, but that's all."

"Thank you for taking care of all this, Garcia. That was one thing I was going to talk to you about today. Is there anything I need to help you do?"

"No, thank you, we are all set. I hope you are staying for the service," Garcia said with raised eyebrows.

"Of course, Garcia. Michael and I were not close, obviously, but my respect for him had certainly grown in the last few days. I couldn't look myself in the mirror if I didn't go. I owe him that much, at the very least."

"Good, I'm happy to hear that. What else would you like to discuss?" he said, sitting back in the booth.

Chris ran through his mental Rolodex to see where he wanted to start. "Are you sure we're not going to be in any trouble for last night's fire, among other things?"

"Yes, I'm sure. You are in the clear. Not only were you registered at a hotel blocks away, but you were also in the presence of the bank president during the whole incident. Certainly, Speedy and the bodyguard are not going to tell anyone because they both got what they wanted."

"What about you? I'm mostly concerned about you," Chris said in a very serious tone.

"As I told the fire chief, I was not there until the fire started. They will never look for a body because only Michael was known to be there, and no one will be reported missing. Besides, even if they did, they would never find anything."

"So, they'll just attribute it to Michael falling asleep with a cigarette?" Chris asked, looking for final reassurance.

"Exactly. The only person that they think is responsible is gone, so do not worry," Garcia said, waving his hands about as usual.

Changing the topic, Chris said, "Last night, when I was in Michael's hospital room, he whispered something to me before he passed."

"What did he say?" Garcia sat forward again.

"First he said, 'we got him,' then, 'bank fireplace, forgive me.' What does that mean?"

Garcia looked down at the table, thinking, then said, "I'm not sure. I suppose he was glad we got Sacarras, and I would guess he wanted to be forgiven by you at the end. I'm not sure about the bank fireplace. Have you gone to the bank and asked Herman?"

"Yes," Chris replied. "He gave me a box containing some newspaper clippings and a couple of pictures, and Michael's war medals."

"Perhaps that is how he wanted to be remembered. Sometimes an entire life can be summed up in a few simple things. I think he was trying to tell someone what was valuable to him." Garcia appeared to be touched by the simplicity of the contents.

"Yes, I thought the same thing, Garcia, but I think he was trying to tell me something else, something more. Do you think Michael thought he might die during the events of last night?"

"If he did, he didn't tell me. I do know he had grown weary of being sick, to be honest. I'm surprised he made it as long as he did. Sometimes life itself drains the life out of you." Garcia showed sadness for the first time, as if he had contemplated this statement recently. He then looked up with a happier expression on his face. "I have something for you. It is from last night."

Garcia struggled in the confined space of the booth to get his hand in his pocket. Finally, his hand re-emerged with a handkerchief that appeared to have some blood stains on it. Garcia opened it up to display a solid gold ring with the head of an Aztec god and two emeralds for the eyes. It was the ring Sacarras had worn!

"I don't think he will be needing this anymore," Garcia said with a smile. "I thought you might want it as a small memento of your trip here."

341

"You son of a bitch!" Chris exclaimed with a smile. "You're the only man who would stop to pick up something while burning down a house!" He took the ring to look at it more closely and noticed there was an inscription that read, "He who lives by the sun, dies by the sun."

Chris knew instantly what he had to do with the ring. He would have to make a phone call later.

"I should tell you that I have told Sophia of Michael's passing," Garcia said.

"Thank you. Herman said you told him also." Chris was genuine in his appreciation. "Are you sure there is nothing about a fireplace that you can think Michael would refer to on his death bed?" Chris was mystified.

"We do not have many fireplaces in such a temperate climate as we have here. It seldom gets cold enough to warrant one. The only one I can think of is the chimney Michael had in the kitchen. They used to cook with that fireplace before the 1930s, but it has been bricked up for years."

Chris thought about what Garcia said for a few seconds, then asked, "Do you know when it was bricked up?"

"I think it was in the early fifties. I'm really not sure," Garcia said, shrugging.

"Really? That's interesting," Chris said, looking at the ring in his hand.

"Why?" Garcia asked.

"Because you just gave me an idea."

Chapter 15

What the hell am I doing?

Chris thought as he stared at the charred building with a brick chimney protruding from one corner. *What do you think you are going to find?* he asked himself. "After all you've been through, and now you're going to get hurt—or worse—doing something stupid."

He walked down the street to see how he could even get access, since the entire block was wrapped in police tape. When he reached the corner where the oak tree was, he saw city trucks blocking off the streets and tree trimming trucks with buckets and woodchippers standing by. Apparently, the partially burnt tree was considered a danger to traffic and pedestrians, so public utilities were preparing to cut it down. He recognized this would at least be a distraction, and the noise from the chainsaws and woodchippers would cover up any banging he may make.

He saw a couple of police standing near the trucks, but there was no one monitoring access from the empty field where he had seen kids playing soccer the day he arrived, which also happened to be the same side where the chimney was located. That was his best chance.

Hurrying back to the jeep, he drove to the Lowe's that was only a couple of miles away and purchased what he thought he would need for this crazy endeavor—a twenty-pound sledgehammer, leather gloves, a brown canvas tarp, a brick chisel, a five-pound hammer, a hard hat, and some duct tape. As he was leaving, he noticed a food truck parked outside and decided to eat lunch before he got started. After devouring two tacos and a beef burrito, he made an observation. Mexican food here in Brownsville and Laredo—even from a food truck—was far better than what restaurants served in Richmond.

Arriving back at the house, the tree-cutting operation had begun, and traffic had been cordoned off in all areas, keeping onlookers and previous worshipers at bay. Chris parked the jeep a couple of blocks away, opposite from all the activity, and casually carried a load of tools down the street and through a section of fallen chain-link fencing.

He wore his hard hat to give the impression that he was a city employee, just in case anyone spotted his stealthy undertaking.

As he walked up to the chimney, he could see the line of sight from the policemen near the tree was blocked by the partial wall that was still standing and the remaining mound of burned wood and ashes that had once comprised the second floor and roof. On his second trip, he stood near the chimney and looked around to determine who would be able to see him during his clandestine work.

The only place he would be visible from was the bank and the adjacent office building. He figured by draping his brown tarp over the still-standing wall, he could create a lean-to type of cover that would keep him hidden from sight. He doubted if anyone would notice the brown tarp, and if they did, they probably wouldn't give it too much thought. Hopefully, they would assume it was some safety precaution.

He wondered if he got caught and was asked what the hell he was doing, whether he might somehow get tied to the fire once they discovered he was Michael's son. He was aware no one knew of the death of a person whose bones may lie just a few feet away, and Garcia was probably right; they would never find any evidence, but he reasoned that being as discreet as possible was wise.

After getting all his tools in place and hiding behind the wall, he checked to see how compromised the area was where he would be working. The floor was charred but only seemed to be burned halfway through. The wall was supported more or less by the brick chimney but appeared to be stable. There was nothing directly overhead that could possibly fall on him. He quickly jumped up onto the floor and threw one side of the tarp over the wall, then took his brick chisel and mallet and set them on the part that draped onto the floor, securing it in place. It was haphazardly done, but it was sufficient cover for him to begin his work. He figured if he needed to switch tools, he would alternate them to hold down the tarp.

The woodchippers were going full blast, and the noise was more than enough to muffle the impact of his hammers. His swing would be limited by the confined quarters, but he'd have to make it work. He looked at his watch; it was 2:30. He had no idea how long the tree trimmers would be here today, so he had to work fast. The old hearth opening was about five feet wide and four feet tall. That was the section that needed to come down.

Tink. The first blow bounced off the old brick like it had hit pre-stressed concrete. *Tink, tink, tink.* He had barely made a dent. "Damn! This shit is hard," Chris said to himself. He hit it several more times with very little result. Someone had used very hard brick and mortar. He kept at it for a few minutes with little success.

It was getting very hot under the tarp in the afternoon sun, and his water was back in the jeep, but he didn't want to stop. He decided to try the brick chisel and five-pound mallet. After a few blows at the other end, he found he could loosen one brick, then another. After about fifteen minutes, he had a dozen of the bricks removed, just enough to see inside the hearth.

Chris peered inside. "SHIT!" he said. There was another wall built just behind this one. He set his tools down and wiped the sweat from his face. He needed a break. "I'd pay a thousand dollars for an air chisel right now," he said.

He looked out from behind the tarp, then jumped down to the ground and casually walked to the jeep to drink his water, which was now hot. Fortunately, there was a 7-11 store only a few blocks away, so he walked there to get several bottles of cold water.

"Am I wasting my time?" he kept asking himself. After downing two bottles of the six he had bought, he felt revitalized, so he sneaked back under his cover and began again. He discovered once he had a few more bricks chiseled out, he could pry them with the sledgehammer from the inside, making them much easier to remove. A little more than half of the first wall was now gone, and Chris took a break to throw out what he had accumulated inside the tented area. He stopped for a minute to listen for noise. The tree trimmers were still going, and he looked at his watch. It was 3:45. He'd been at it for over an hour.

He finally removed most of the first wall and started on the second, where the mortar didn't seem quite as hard. He had to remove the first dozen or so bricks before he could see inside. The light was limited because of the tarp, and the small opening that Chris had just made did not allow any of it to pass through. He decided to put his hand inside and feel around for something other than brick and mortar.

"HOLY SHIT!" Chris screamed. "It feels like metal. There is something here." He felt a surge of adrenaline and quickly removed another couple dozen bricks, creating a large enough opening for him to put his head inside the dark space. Once his eyes adjusted to the darkness, he could make out the silhouette of what appeared to be metal boxes inside the fireplace.

His heart was now racing, crazy ideas filling his head. "What could this possibly be?" he kept asking himself. The heat, sweat, and thirst forgotten, he eagerly pried and pulled at the brick, his curiosity running wild. Within twenty minutes, the front wall was completely gone and most of the second wall was torn down.

349

He sat on his debris pile of bricks, and with the small amount of light that was beaming in over his shoulder, he could clearly see that someone had neatly stacked dozens of metal boxes on top of each other inside the fireplace hearth. They had been entombed behind a double wall to keep them safe from theft or fire.

Chris reached over to remove one and it felt as if it was stuck. Perhaps they were rusted together. He tried again, and this time the box moved slightly. He then realized it wasn't stuck but very heavy for its size. It was only about eighteen inches long by twelve inches wide and no more than three inches thick, but it must have weighed over a hundred pounds.

There were about six of the small boxes on top and others of varying shapes and sizes below them. Each was locked with a keyed padlock. Chris was ecstatic with his discovery and yet bewildered at the same time. *What's in them? How did they get there? How long had they been here? This had to be what Michael was talking about, didn't it?*

He sat for a minute looking at what he had discovered, sweat pouring from him in his makeshift sauna. Even if the boxes were valuable, and even if he could get them out, he would never be able to carry them all in his jeep. *They probably weigh close to a ton!* he thought. He was going to need help moving them, or all his work and discovery would be for nothing. "Damn!"

He quickly walked back to the jeep, making sure he was not seen by the authorities, and all the while not taking his eyes off the brown tarp. He laughed at himself for needing his cell phone again, surrendering to the idea that it was probably going to be an everyday tool in the future. He called the only person that could help him, and he prayed he would be there. It was now 5:00.

"Garcia's, may I help you?" some young girl said for probably the hundredth time that day.

"Hi, I need to speak to Garcia. My name is Chris. It's very important," Chris said, restraining his urgency.

"Let me see if he's here," she said, setting the phone down and not waiting for a response.

Chris could hear people talking and girls giggling while he waited, thinking of what his other options were if Garcia was not there.

"Hola, Garcia!"

"Garcia, it's Chris. Can you talk?" Chris asked cautiously.

Garcia instantly recognized Chris's tone and knew this was not a social call. "Give me a minute." Chris could hear him tell the girl who had answered the phone to hang up after he picked it up in his office. He heard the girl put the phone to her ear. After a few seconds, he heard, "Okay, I have it." The girl hung up.

"What is it, Chris?" Garcia asked with concern in his voice.

"I've found something," Chris said. "I need help."

"Found what? Where are you?"

"I'm at Michael's house. I opened up the old fireplace that was in the kitchen, and Garcia, there are boxes in there!" Chris tried to contain himself.

"What kind of boxes?" Garcia asked

"They're made of metal, and different sizes, and one was very heavy."

"How many are there, Chris?"

"Probably about twenty, and another thing: the city is cutting the branches off the oak tree today, so there are workers and police around."

"Is there a way to get a truck near where you are?" Garcia asked, sounding undaunted.

"Yes, there's a section of the fence that is down, but there are too many eyes around right now. What time does it get dark?" Chris asked.

"About seven-thirty," Garcia said. "Can you wait until then?"

"I'll have to. Can you get a truck?"

"Yes. I'll be there at seven-thirty."

"Okay. And bring a couple of flashlights," Chris said.

"Call me if anything changes," Garcia said and hung up.

Chris was still buzzing about his find, but he knew to stay calm. Besides, it could just be bricks or old worthless Mexican pesos in the boxes, or anything.

He could keep an eye on the brown tarp clearly from his jeep but thought it would be wise to take a look at what was happening at the other side of the property.

He took his phone and walked around the back of the house, staying clear of the street with the bank. He didn't want a run-in with Herman or Graciella right now. The tree guys looked like they were wrapping up for the day, which probably meant the police would leave soon also.

Chris decided to go back and remove the remaining bricks from his work area while there was still traffic noise for cover.

He picked up the remaining bricks lying on the floor and tossed them from under the tarp onto the ground, occasionally peeking around to see if there was anyone around. Ditching the bricks gave them a clear path to drag out the boxes and hopefully be able to load them directly onto the truck.

It was now six o'clock. Garcia would not be there for another hour and a half. Chris casually strode back to the jeep for another water bottle, trying to cool down from the dirty, sweaty work while simultaneously keeping an eye on the tarp and checking to see if anyone had seen him coming and going.

He looked at his phone and saw there was a missed call...it was from Sophia. He thought that now would be a better time to talk to her than later, hoping he and Garcia would be busy with his discovery that evening.

"Hello." Her voice was warm and pleasant.

"Hi, Sophia, it's Chris."

"Chris! I've been so worried. Are you okay?" She sounded sincere and relieved.

"I'm fine. I apologize for not calling you sooner."

"It's alright. I know you've had a lot going on. Chris, I'm so sorry about Michael."

"Thank you. I should say the same to you. You knew him better than I did."

"You know about the funeral arrangements, don't you?" she asked.

"Yes, your father told me about it this morning."

"I hope we can see each other before then?" Her voice was soft and inviting.

"Yes, that was my hope also, but something has come up for this evening."

"Chris," she said, her voice changing to sarcasm, "another woman, so soon?"

"No, it's another man." They both laughed at this. "I have some business with your father tonight, and I'm not sure how long it will take."

"You're not in danger again, are you?" Her tone changed again to one of concern.

"No, I think all of that is over. This is something different. Are you available tomorrow?"

"Yes, I had taken the day off to help Garcia with the funeral arrangements, but he says it's all taken care of."

"How about I pick you up for breakfast then?"

"That would be lovely. Dad can give you my address. Is nine o'clock good?" She seemed happy and excited.

"Okay, I'll see you then."

After hanging up, Chris noted he would have to add one more quality to her growing list of personality traits: being understanding.

To kill time until Garcia arrived with the truck, Chris walked around the block a little, carefully avoiding any police and a possible run-in with Herman; he just wanted to be incognito right now.

The tree cutters were gone, as were the police and all the equipment. There was the usual traffic, except on the street between the bank and the house that was still blocked off. The tree was a heartbreaking sight. Its charred trunk supporting only the amputated arms of the once-glorious live oak that had provided shade, beauty, and, most recently, religious fervor to so many. Chris calculated the tree was even older than the house, probably dating back to the Civil War. He walked back toward the opening in the chain-link fence and stepped it off to see if a truck could drive through it and back up to the section of the house where his mysterious discovery lay, still hidden, waiting to be transported.

Chris spent the rest of the time keeping watch from his jeep and debating what to do with the other unexpected treasure he had fortuitously discovered while he had been in Brownsville...Sophia. Even though they had just met and only been together three times, he realized he could not just leave her without a conversation about their unique connection.

Chris had been accused of being distant and non-committal in the past. When he and his ex-wife had split, he was surprised how quickly he got over her. It wasn't that he didn't love her, he just never felt a deep connection; something he had only felt once, when he was much younger and not ready to settle down. He had often regretted that youthful decision, and he knew that was part of the reason he eventually married many years later. He wanted to have children. Chris also knew he had been given one of the rarest gifts people get: a second chance at a once-in-a-lifetime opportunity.

Headlights flashed in his eyes as a truck with a stake side bed approached; the sun was now setting behind the urban behemoths. Garcia found a parking spot across the street and casually got out of the vehicle. Chris liked how he always knew what attitude to have. He walked over to Chris, who was now leaning against his jeep, and took out his cigarettes.

"Tell me what we have," Garcia started out saying, leaning against the jeep while lighting his cigarette.

"There are no police or workers left. There is a section of fence down behind the house we can back the truck through. I've cleared out the brick from the hearth so we can drag the boxes across the floor and into the truck. The top ones are small but heavy. I don't know about the rest yet."

Garcia looked toward the house and said, "Good work, Chris. You would have made an excellent criminal."

"Perhaps it's more genetic than I knew." Chris and Garcia gave each other a knowing look.

"When it gets completely dark in about fifteen minutes, I'll back the truck through the fence and up to the house. How long do you think it will take to load everything?" Garcia asked.

"If I can slide everything out to you and you can load the truck, probably ten minutes."

"Okay. Go get ready, but walk back through the fence opening so I can see where it is. Move the boxes as best you can. I'll be there soon," he said as he handed Chris one of the flashlights and then went back to his truck. Chris walked down the sidewalk and through the downed section of fencing.

Returning to his hideaway, it was almost dark now, and Chris wasn't concerned about being seen. When he reached the tarp-covered section of the house, he turned on the flashlight, making sure it was pointed at the boxes and could not be seen from outside. He pulled at one of the top boxes and slid it forward until he could grasp it with both hands after it was free from the others and had clunked loudly onto the floor. "Damn, these things are heavy!" Chris said to himself.

He positioned his body to better support the boxes as he removed them. He had stacked four boxes on top of each other when he heard Garcia's truck approaching. He looked out to see Garcia backing the truck toward him without his lights on. Chris jumped down to help guide him and get the truck positioned within a few feet of the house. Garcia got out, walked around to the back, and dropped the tailgate down.

"Okay, let's go," Garcia whispered.

Chris handed Garcia the first box, who slid it onto the truck as Chris worked the next one toward him. After removing the heaviest boxes from the top of the stack, he could stand up and reach down to get the rest. The larger boxes were not quite as heavy, but they all were cumbersome to move in such a tight space. Garcia never slowed down as he loaded the boxes onto the truck. Chris's respect for him, being so strong for his age, grew even more.

After loading the last box, Garcia stuck his head into the area where Chris had been working. "Hand me all your tools and take down this tarp before you leave. I'm going to the store. Meet me there. Just pull around the back," Garcia said. He was sweating and breathing heavily.

Chris handed him his tools, and Garcia quietly placed them in the back of the truck. He then slowly drove away, not turning on his headlights until he was half a block away. Chris looked around to make sure nothing was left behind, turned off the flashlight, and removed the tarp from the top of the wall.

He could barely see, with just a few streetlights assisting him. He folded the tarp, grabbed the flashlight, and walked to the jeep, then threw it in the back. He then took one last look behind him before he raced off to Garcia's.

Turning in behind the store, he saw Garcia standing at a concrete ramp entrance to the basement, the truck poised at the top. He motioned where he wanted Chris to park.

As Chris walked over to the idling truck, Garcia said, "I'm going to go open the door. When I do, pull the truck inside."

Garcia walked down the ramp that was illuminated by the truck's headlights, pulled out a set of keys, and used one to unlock the heavy-duty roll-up door. Chris noticed the door was thick and corrugated and he doubted even the truck would make a dent in it.

When the door was fully open, Chris slowly drove the truck into the darkened basement, the truck's headlights lighting up the interior to reveal a giant uninterrupted space that was a combination of a garage, workshop, and storage for the store's wares. When the truck was fully inside the space, he turned off the motor as Garcia turned on the overhead lights and closed the roll-up door securely behind them.

Garcia walked up to Chris while removing a pack of cigarettes from his pocket. "That was quite a workout."

"You alright?" Chris asked, noticing his shirt was soaked with sweat.

"Oh, yes, I'm fine," he said as he lit his cigarette. He looked at Chris for a moment, each wondering who was going to address the elephant in the room first. "Well, what do you say we see what we have?" Garcia said, beating Chris to the punch. Chris was always impressed how Garcia remained in control of his emotions, as they were both bursting to see what treasures they possibly held.

The men walked around to the back of the truck and let the tailgate down. Chris could now see all the boxes in the light for the first time. They were all a flat, dark-green color, like military surplus, but with no markings on them. Identical padlocks secured each box.

"Pick one," Garcia said, pointing at the stack of boxes.

Chris grabbed one of the small, heavy ones that had been sitting on top. He could now hold it by the small handles on each side, but it was still very cumbersome for its size, even for a strong man like Chris. He followed Garcia to a large wooden workbench and set it down. Garcia tried some bolt cutters, but they would not sever the lock's shackle. They found a grinder on another workbench and after sending showers of sparks shooting through the air, the lock fell off the box.

Garcia turned the box and slowly lifted the top. Inside was a piece of brown wax paper covering up the contents beneath. From the fluorescent lighting above, they could make out there was something shiny beneath the opaque paper. Garcia slid the wax paper aside almost in the way a magician would dramatically move a silk scarf to reveal their trick.

The paper was covering up four bars of gold, each stamped on top with "400 troy ounces," and under that, another stamp that read ".999 pure." Each bar was about ten inches long, three inches wide, and an inch-and-a-half thick.

"Oh my God!" Chris said softly. "Are they real?"

Garcia did not immediately answer but instead stared at the bars, calculating their beauty and significance. "How many of these boxes are there?" Garcia said, finally breaking his stare.

"Six, I think," Chris said.

"That's twenty-four bars just in those boxes," Garcia said. He looked off in the distance, running numbers through his head, then said, "Let's open another one."

Chris quickly retrieved another of the small boxes. Garcia ground off the padlock and slid away the wax paper to find four identical bars of gold. Garcia picked two of the bars up and tapped them together. They made a distinctive ping sound.

"It sounds right. I think they are real, Chris," Garcia said, showing the first signs of emotion. He was stunned.

"I've handled some gold in my life, but nothing like this," Garcia said, looking down at the two opened boxes.

"Let's try a different box," Chris suggested.

Chris brought a larger, much lighter box over to Garcia, who promptly cut off the lock and opened it. Inside, wrapped in old newspaper, were about a dozen Aztec antiquities similar to the ones they had used to lure Sacarras into their trap. Chris then had an epiphany.

"I'll...be...damned!" Chris said slowly. "It's from the plane!"

Garcia looked up at him. "What plane?"

"The one Michael crashed, the one he got the other Aztec pieces from!" Chris said excitedly.

"No, that's impossible!" Garcia was adamant. "He had broken his leg...I went to pick him up, the plane was empty." Garcia was trying to convince himself that the evidence in front of him was not enough.

"No, think about it," Chris said. "It's the same kind of Aztec pieces he gave you after the crash. The plane was overweight because of the gold and other boxes. He couldn't sell any of it because Sacarras would have found out, so he hid it all in the one place no one would ever think to look—an old, never used fireplace. That's why it had two layers of brick, in case there was a fire."

Garcia stood up and walked around the room, then said, "But how could he have transported it? He had a broken leg. I saw it." Then, turning back to Chris, he asked, "Why wouldn't he have told me?"

"To protect you, Garcia. He knew they would come looking for him, broken leg or not. He probably did not want to get you involved."

"I just think it would have been impossible for him to crash in the middle of nowhere then come back later and haul all this away, especially with a broken leg." Garcia was quite animated in his dismissal of this explanation, gesturing many times.

364

Chris then laughed, thinking of another possibility. "What if the plane was already empty when Michael crashed?"

"What do you mean?" Garcia said, sitting back down on his stool.

"What if Michael emptied the plane before he crashed it? Maybe it was too heavily loaded and he landed somewhere else first, hid the cargo, or buried it, and then crashed a plane that was already empty? He might have faked the broken leg and paid a doctor to put a cast on a good leg, or he may have actually broken his leg when he crashed."

"If he hid the cargo or buried it, he could have gone back weeks or months later to get it, couldn't he?" Garcia now seemed to believe it was a possible explanation.

"Do you remember taking him to the plane after you picked him up at the hospital?" Chris inquired.

"Yes, just like it was last week. He was very upset that the plane was empty."

"Do you remember if there were any tire tracks around the plane from a car or a truck?" Chris thought he was now making a believer of Garcia.

Garcia got off his stool and walked around again, thinking of that day, then said, "I don't remember seeing any...but they could

365

have been there..." Then he finally admitted, "I just don't remember."

"Sometimes you only see what you're looking for," Chris said with resignation. "The only person that knows for sure what happened took all the answers with him."

"Well, sort of. He did remember to tell you the most important part of his secret," Garcia said, looking at the gold bars in front of him.

"Yes," Chris said. "And we still have to find out what else he left behind." He walked away to get another box.

Garcia and Chris worked for the next two hours opening boxes, with childlike anticipation, to discover the wondrous contents. Every box was filled with beautiful and amazing things: gold bars, Aztec antiquities, jewelry, gold coins, even a portfolio of several coin collections. The two men were living out every man's fantasy—finding a real lost treasure.

After opening all the boxes, they decided it would be wise to catalog all the items and make a copy for each of them.

- 24 gold bars .999 pure at 400 troy oz. each
- 500 gold 50-peso Centenarios, ungraded and uncirculated

- 9 portfolios of coin collections containing 176 individual coins, all ungraded
  - 240 modern jewelry pieces
    - 45 watches
    - 92 rings
    - 41 bracelets
    - 35 necklaces
    - 27 other various pieces
  - 85 Aztec pieces
    - 26 rings
    - 20 bracelets
    - 12 necklaces
    - 7 pendants
    - 9 ear plugs
    - 11 various other pieces

It was almost midnight when they finished, but neither man had looked at their watch the entire time. They both knew this was the discovery of a lifetime. When they finished cataloging all the pieces and they were laid out before them on two huge work benches, Chris asked Garcia, "Where do you think it all came from?"

"That will be impossible to know or find out. Some from theft, some from safety deposit boxes, drug cartels, and some of it from one man robbing another who was himself robbing yet another. Some of this might even be from Nazi looting. Mexico has a very sordid history of such things." Garcia almost seemed apologetic with his explanation.

"Do you have any idea what it's all worth?" Chris asked, almost as an afterthought.

"It will take weeks, perhaps months, to find out. Some of it may still be considered stolen. The gold bars and gold coins alone are probably worth several million dollars." Chris sensed that Garcia was overwhelmed, perhaps for the first time in his life.

"What do you want to do with your treasure?" Garcia asked, looking at Chris.

"What do you mean mine? Don't you mean ours?" Chris was surprised by his question.

"You found it, it was in your father's house, and you are his son. That makes it yours," Garcia stated strongly.

Chris took a minute to understand the magnitude of the situation, then asked, "Does the bank that bought the property from Michael have any legal claim to it?"

"Probably not. The contents in the house were his, this would be included in that, but they could challenge it...if they knew about it."

Chris then said, "Some of these questions we'll have to answer another day. What do we do with it now?" he said, looking to Garcia for a suggestion.

"Follow me," Garcia said and walked to a large cage-like section of the basement that housed tools and valuable store products. He unlocked a gate, turned on some overhead lights, and then walked over to the back wall. Buried in the concrete wall was a large commercial safe door. "This building was a Federal Reserve until the 1960s," Garcia said as he spun the rotary dial to unlock the safe. "My safe is bigger than Herman's, but don't tell him." He laughed at his own joke. He opened the vault and turned on the lights. It was an impressive safe, with shelves and drawers on each side. Chris was amazed how Garcia always seemed to have something up his sleeve.

Garcia retrieved several rolling carts from within the safe, and the two men transferred their newfound treasure onto the floor in the middle of the safe. After turning off the lights inside and closing the safe's door, Garcia walked Chris out of the basement and to his jeep.

"Thanks for all your help, Garcia."

"It's been an interesting evening. You are definitely the son of my old friend," Garcia said, shaking his hand.

Chris left and headed to the hotel, which was ten minutes away. He was excited, almost overwhelmed from all the discoveries they had made that night, but he was very tired and needed to get some sleep.

As wonderful as all the treasures he saw tonight were, he had one more treasure to deal with tomorrow.

Sophia.

Chapter 16

"I need a secretary,"

Chris said to himself as he sat at the desk in his hotel room making a list of things to do today; calls to make and arrangements needed for leaving tomorrow.

Today would not be one of finding treasure or retaliation, but it was still a very important day. There were plans to make that would affect his future.

Looking in the mirror hanging over the desk, Chris said, "I need a vacation from my vacation."

Turning back to his list, he had several stops to make that morning—the front desk, concierge, Sophia's, Garcia's, and then his very important trip that afternoon. He checked the number of phone calls he had to make, then looked at his watch. It was almost eight. He had to shower and dress, go to the front desk, and be at Sophia's by nine.

"Damn it! I'll have to make some of these calls on the road." He admitted defeat to his new appendage that was the cell phone.

There was one he had to make now to confirm his meeting for this afternoon. After the call, he wrote down that the meeting was scheduled for five that afternoon, then went to shower and get dressed.

He was thankful he'd thought to send out his laundry to be cleaned yesterday; his limited wardrobe with the sweat and grime from his demolition yesterday would have left him little to choose from if he had not. He then made another note that he would need to purchase something more appropriate than his casual clothing for Michael's funeral tomorrow. "UGH!" he said. Perhaps he could go shopping with Sophia after breakfast.

He showered and put on the same jeans and shirt he'd worn the night he had made love to Sophia. He swore the shirt still had her fragrance on it.

He went to the front desk and confirmed he would be checking out tomorrow, picked up an envelope that was waiting at the concierge, and walked out to the hotel garage. It was a little cooler this morning, a pleasant relief from the endless heat. He decided to put the top down on the jeep.

As Chris had written the directions that Garcia had given him last night, he thought he sensed a smile from him when he said he was meeting Sophia for breakfast. The drive to her house was about fifteen minutes, and the cool morning air felt good in his hair.

Driving through her neighborhood, he saw several streets of cottage-style houses with stucco exteriors and terracotta roofs. Each house was unique, a nice change from the perpetual cookie-cutter houses in Suburbia, USA that Chris was so used to working in. Every house here seemed to be well-maintained and individually accented with landscaping, different colors, and details. He liked them.

Chris pulled in front of Sophia's house, noticing hers was one of the few with a front porch, designed in the craftsman style he so enjoyed. The house was painted a butter yellow and had lots of colorful flowers growing in the boxes underneath the front windows.

The house had a distinctive hip roof that appeared to house a single room on the second floor. The front door looked original to the house and was stained a dark wood tone contrasting with the lighter paint. Chris thought for a moment how often houses emulate their owners. This one was unique, inviting, well maintained, and beautiful...just like Sophia.

After parking the jeep, he jumped out and walked to the front door. As he knocked on the door, he felt like a teenager picking up a girl for their first date. Sophia opened the door.

"Good morning," she greeted in her usual cheerful fashion with an inviting smile. She wore an ankle-length skirt that was white with red roses, and her short-sleeved blouse was a medium shade of green, matching the stems of the roses. She had on leather sandals and a gold necklace that had a heart-shaped pendant around her neck. Her hair was combed back just like the first day he met her, and she was not wearing any lipstick.

Chris stepped inside and closed the door. Sophia moved closer and put her arms around him, melting into his much larger frame. They held each other for a moment, Sophia whispering "I missed you" into his ear with her soft, mellifluous voice before lifting her face up to his. They kissed like new lovers do when they have been apart for a while. Chris loved the sweet, passionate way she kissed, the way she held him while caressing his back. He thought how wonderful it would be to pick her up and take her into the bedroom right now. He knew how receptive she would be, but he had promised himself he would be respectful of what they were developing and save the intense passion and chemistry they shared for another day.

"Let's go eat before we get carried away," Chris said, looking down at her and seeing that dreamy look in her eyes that women get when they desire a man.

"Yes," she said. "I suppose you should at least feed me first." Sophia laughed at herself. Chris enjoyed her innocent yet naughty sense of humor.

They drove to a café that was just a few blocks away, a local breakfast place called Buenos Dias! that had been converted from a gas station. After ordering coffee, they asked the waiter to give them a few minutes before eating breakfast.

Sophia started by saying, "How are you feeling?"

"I'm fine, Sophia. It's a little strange when your father passes away, even one you didn't really know, and yet you've spent the last week with him unraveling mysteries, listening to stories, and finally getting to know him, at least a little. So, yeah, it's odd. How are you doing? You knew him a long time."

"I guess I'm like my dad. We knew this was coming for a while, so we were prepared, but it's still sad. He was Garcia's best friend for over fifty years, and I've known him since I was a child. That's a lot of memories."

"Did your father tell you what happened?" Chris asked, not knowing what details Garcia may have shared with her.

"He said when he went to the house, Michael was apparently having a heart attack and had dropped a cigarette on the newspaper, causing the fire. It's a good thing my father got there when he did."

Chris mentally thanked Garcia for sparing him from having to lie to Sophia, then said, "Your father was a good friend. He was always there for Michael. Did he tell you what happened to the oak tree?"

"No. I've decided I don't want to know about or see the house or the tree. It would be too sad right now. I want to keep my memories of Michael and the house as I remember them...for a while at least."

Chris decided to change the subject and save the sad and astonishing news about the tree for another day. It did not go unnoticed that she did not ask any more questions about the goings-on at the house or why he had asked her not to come around.

"Let's order," Chris said to lighten up the mood. "I'm hungry."

They ordered and spent the rest of breakfast discussing their work and things they enjoyed; the more mundane topics that people who had met under normal circumstances would talk about. Chris really enjoyed her company. She was easy to be with, listened well, and she always looked into his eyes when he spoke, conveying a sense of genuineness.

After they finished eating, Chris told her, "I have to take a trip this afternoon, but I'll be back this evening."

"Chris, please, this isn't anything dangerous again, is it?" Sophia always had a way of showing sincere concern.

"No, it's nothing like that, I promise. But before that, I also need to go shopping to get something to wear for Michael's funeral tomorrow."

"Okay, I can show you a couple of places." She seemed happy to be able to spend more time with him.

After walking back to the jeep, Sophia asked Chris to leave the top down. She loved the wind blowing her hair; somehow, she seemed even sexier to Chris with tousled hair. He knew they had only been together a few times, yet it seemed like they had been friends and lovers for years. She was so much fun to be with, always understanding and perpetually beautiful.

After shopping at a few stores, Chris capitulated to Sophia's request and purchased a gray suit with a black tie and black shoes. It was apparent that she thoroughly enjoyed helping dress him up.

Chris loved the look in her eye when he tried on the suit; the sexual tension was palpable.

Chris, Sophia, and the suit went to the jeep. On the way, Chris asked, "Can we go back to your house and talk for a bit?"

"Sure, that would be great," Sophia said with a slight look of concern on her face.

Chris took his new suit and an envelope from the glove box into the house with him, then hung his clothes on a coat rack Sophia had by the door. Her home was decorated in a very comfortable and casual style with a warm cloth-covered sofa and overstuffed chairs. It was all in earth tone colors which accented the brick-red tile floor. There was an air of elegance in how it felt, empty from all the knick-knacks that filled her father's store. Chris felt utterly at home in her home—and her presence—as they both sat on her dark green sofa.

"I didn't want to wait until tomorrow to have this conversation. It just didn't seem appropriate," Chris started out saying. "I'm not sure how to discuss this, and I know we just met, but I didn't want to leave Brownsville giving you the feeling I don't care about you." Sophia sensed his awkwardness and reached out to hold his hand.

"I know better, Chris," Sophia said, trying to help. "I can see it in your eyes when you look at me. You're too honest of a man to have eyes that would lie."

Chris never took compliments well. All he could muster was a "Thank you."

"Tell me what you are thinking, Chris. What do you want to do?" Sophia's eyes started to well up.

"It would have been so wonderful to come over here this morning and make love with you. I'm sure you sensed that?" Chris said as Sophia nodded in agreement. "But that's not what I want this to be about. I think we have a special connection."

"No, Chris," Sophia said, interrupting him. "I don't see it as just special." Chris was mystified by her comment.

"Do you know what 'duende' means?" she asked.

Baffled by this question, Chris said, "It means unique, doesn't it?"

"Yes, but it's more than that. It also means magical, passionate. When I first met you on Michael's front porch, I knew you had that quality. When we made love, I felt it throughout my body. Being with you that night was…amazing. I have thought about it many times since then."

Chris saw Sophia's eyes fill up even more, and he didn't know what to say.

"I want to be with you like that again," she said, looking down.

Chris lifted her face with his hand. "Okay, but the next time I want it to be on my terms," he said, kissing her gently in an attempt to assuage her apprehension. He stood up from the couch and walked over to get the envelope he had brought with him, then came back and sat next to her again. Handing her the envelope, he simply said, "Here."

Sophia wiped away a tear and asked "What is it?" while opening the envelope.

"It's a plane ticket for you to come visit me next Friday. It doesn't have a return date."

Sophia, overwhelmed with emotion, began kissing Chris passionately. When she stopped, she gathered herself to ask, "So, what are your terms, sir?" She gave him a knowing, naughty smile.

"My terms are very simple. The next time we make love, it will be at my twenty-acre farm, in my rustic lodge, on my king-sized bed."

Sophia laughed while wiping away the last of her tears, then put out her hand to shake his. "Okay, I will agree to those terms."

They shook hands, then Chris kissed her while holding her beautiful face. She loved the feel of his hands and could not wait to feel them again on the rest of her body in a week.

"Will there be snow there soon?" Sophia asked.

"Probably not. It's too early in the year. You'll have to come several times if you want to see snow," Chris said to her, smiling at his offer.

"Then I will come several times," she said in her serious voice. "I want to be with you when I touch snow for the first time."

Her brown eyes were so full of passion and desire that it took every ounce of restraint Chris had to not take her on the couch right then.

"I have to go see your father for a few minutes before my trip this afternoon, but I'll see you tomorrow."

"Yes, and in your new suit!" she said, smiling and pointing to it hanging near the entrance.

Standing by the door, she asked, "I guess you're leaving after the funeral tomorrow?"

"I have to. I'm already a week overdue," he said, looking down at her.

"Then this will have to be our goodbye kiss. It would not be right to kiss you like this tomorrow at the funeral." Sophia then gave Chris a deep, passionate kiss, standing on her toes as she did, wrapping her arms around his strong back. Chris wondered how her kisses could be so gentle, sweet, and passionate all at the same time. Kissing her was electric.

Sophia pulled away slowly and said, "That will have to last you until next week."

Chris left with his suit and set it in the passenger seat of the jeep, then he looked back at the house where she was still standing in the doorway, leaning against the door jamb, her arms folded. At that moment, he wished he could have had a picture—no, a painting of her—as she was right now. He thought of the painting of her mother he had seen in the store. It seemed so long ago.

A few minutes later, Chris walked into Garcia's and passed the very painting he had just been thinking about. The store was not especially busy that day. He asked about Garcia, saying he was expected, and was directed to a door that was hidden behind some drapes. Chris opened it and walked down a long set of very steep stairs, announcing himself as he went.

"Hello?"

"Chris, Hola! I'm in the cage."

Chris passed the workbench that had held a fortune just hours earlier and found Garcia exiting the cage that led to the safe.

"Come! Let's sit down over here," Garcia said, guiding him to a couple of chairs set off to one side of the basement. There were also end tables and a coffee table, creating a makeshift living room.

"I have done some checking on some of our items we cataloged last night," Garcia said, leaning back in his chair. "There don't seem to be any issues with the gold bars or gold coins. They are not traceable and have no Nazi connections that I can find."

"What about the jewelry?" Chris asked.

"They would be nearly impossible to trace or uncover their previous ownership unless there is something extremely valuable there that already has a previous claim."

"Okay, I guess we'll have to address that if it comes up. One thing I want us to agree on is to return all the Aztec antiquities to the museum they came from. I don't think it's right to keep them. They belong in a museum or to Mexico."

"I'm glad to hear you say that. I told Michael the same thing many years ago. Besides, I think they have bad karma."

"You can have the credit for returning them, if you want, or you can return the artifacts anonymously, but either way, leave me out of that part if you don't mind." Chris was in his business mode.

"Yes, absolutely. I have a few connections that I think can get the government to look the other way. A no-questions-asked kind of policy, you could say. I think they should be returned anonymously, just so it's not tied in any way to the rest of the treasure. I may not send them back immediately. I'd like to see most of the items sold first, if you don't mind."

"Fine, I'll leave that up to you. However, speaking of money," Chris said, "we need to discuss payment for you."

Chris saw Garcia begin to object but kept speaking. "I know you say what I found is mine. Okay, fine, but I don't want you to spend all your time selling the hundreds of items without being fairly compensated. This is a business deal we're discussing, and I need your help, so please, don't tell me this is something you're doing in Michael's memory."

Garcia laughed at what Chris said. "I bet your father would be very happy knowing that you ended up with his stolen treasure after all these years he managed to keep it hidden away." He then lit a cigarette and said, "You know we are talking about a lot of money here, Chris."

"How much, if you would venture a guess? Say we sold everything, without the Aztec pieces?"

Garcia leaned over to the ashtray while he was thinking. "The gold bars and gold coins are easy to figure. The jewelry is a bit tricky. It will have to be determined piece by piece. But I would say…four to five million, maybe more."

"Okay. Let's agree that you get fifteen percent of everything we sell."

"No, Chris. That's too much. You're talking about almost a million dollars." Garcia was quite genuine in his refusal. His honesty never ceased to impress Chris.

"No, I don't think so. I'm giving a man I know I can trust the responsibility of making me three to four million dollars. Can you put a value on that?" Chris asked rhetorically.

"You have the same kind of character your father had. He would be proud of you," Garcia said sentimentally. "Do you want me to have a document drawn up regarding our arrangement?" Garcia asked.

"Garcia, you are the only man I have ever known whose handshake is more valuable than a signed piece of paper."

Chris stood up and walked over to shake his hand. Garcia stood up also, shook his hand warmly, and said, "It's done then."

"Now I have to get on the road. There is one more thing I must take care of before I leave tomorrow," Chris said, looking at his watch.

"I will see you tomorrow morning, then," Garcia said, waving goodbye.

On his way out of the store, Chris noticed a small handmade wooden box that he thought would be ideal for his trip. He purchased it and hurried to the jeep, aware he would now have to hurry to be on time.

As he pulled into the familiar circular driveway, Chris glanced at his watch. It was 5:01.

Looking up, he could see Eduardo standing at the top of the stairs. Next to him were the two señoras, all three were dressed in black.

Chris greeted them by shaking Eduardo's hand and politely nodding to the señoras. Eduardo then led the procession through the courtyard and the house, across the patio, and down the paths lined by the tall hedges before emerging at the large iron gates that Eduardo opened so they could enter the family cemetery. They gathered around Armando's grave site, where they all stood in silence for a moment, the señoras in prayer before crossing themselves. When Chris looked at the headstone, he noticed someone had recently chiseled out a small square alcove near the bottom, about two inches square. Chris handed the wooden box to Eduardo, who opened it and handed the box's contents to the señoras. Isabella kneeled down and placed it in the small alcove made specifically for this occasion. It was a gold ring with the head of an Aztec god and two emeralds for eyes. An inscription inside the ring read: "He who lives by the sun, dies by the sun."

Rising, Isabella said, "May you rest in peace now, my beloved brother."

Rosa turned to Chris, saying, "Thank you for what you have done for our family. You are welcome here anytime." Isabella and Rosa then walked together back to the main house.

Eduardo was still looking at the grave, caught in the emotion of the moment. After the señoras were out of sight, he said, "You have done a wonderful thing, Chris. I am proud to call you my brother."

Chris was touched by this show of genuine emotion and responded, "Eduardo, I have never had a brother, but I can't imagine having a finer one than you."

"Come," Eduardo said, gesturing toward the gate. "I have something to show you."

As they walked, Eduardo surprised Chris by saying, "I've heard you have lost your father. I am very sorry. He was a good man, and I have said a prayer for him. I know you must return home for his funeral tomorrow but promise me that one day you will tell me about this great adventure of yours."

"I promise, Eduardo, and that day you must tell me how you discover all your information so quickly."

They both laughed at Chris's comment, then Eduardo said, "Yes, those will be better days, not filled with such sadness as these."

They arrived at the old stables where one of the workers who was waiting for them proceeded to open one of the doors.

Inside, freshly washed, was Chico's Pajero.

"You got it back!" Chris exclaimed.

"The señoras called one of their friends and it was returned the next day," Eduardo said proudly. "We would like for you to take it home with you."

"What? You want me to have Chico's car?"

"The señoras would consider it a great honor. It is their way of saying thank you for all that you have done for the family."

Chris knew there was no arguing after hearing this. It meant he would have to figure out a way to return the rental car, and he would have to spend an extra day driving home, but he knew he couldn't leave Chico's Pajero behind.

"Tell them Thank you and that I will take good care of it, Eduardo," Chris said.

Chris called the Laredo Avis office, and they assured him he could return the jeep there. There would be a one-hundred-dollar additional fee, but their office was only ten minutes away. Eduardo followed Chris to the dealership in the Pajero, then drove him back to the house.

On the trip back, Eduardo asked many questions about Chris's father, either out of genuine interest or politeness. Chris was sure it was some of each. Either way, he was honored to have such a friend he could call "Brother."

It was getting dark by the time the men returned to Casa de la Guerra. Eduardo and Chris got out, and Eduardo handed him the keys, saying, "I hope to see you again soon."

"You will, Eduardo. I will be back, I promise." The two men hugged as brothers do.

As Chris began the trip back to Brownsville, he wondered how long it would be before he would be back. He had grown fond of Eduardo and Casa de la Guerra.

As Chris approached Brownsville, it had been dark for some time now, and he was driving through a particularly barren section of the highway. There were no cars and no streetlights.

The stars appeared in the sky as if they were fabricated, too perfectly proportioned and clear to be randomly formed. It was as if you were inside an art exhibit where a painter's giant black canvas was stretched overhead, and the painter had poked varying sizes of tiny holes, allowing the luminescence to shine through. There was one section where you could see deep into the Milky Way, like a small section of the canvas had some of the black paint rubbed away. The stars were so bright in the desert, surely you were able to reach out and touch them, instead of the unimaginable distance away they truly were.

Chris contemplated how some of the stars could be so far away that they could have died out millions of years ago, and yet we were still able to see the light that had escaped them and traveled so far. The desert seemed to have so many facets to it, so many varying forms. It was ever-changing, unlike any other place Chris had ever seen.

Epilogue

"Time to go home,"

Chris said, staring at his reflection in the bathroom mirror. He had just finished shaving and had stood there for just a moment before admitting he was now officially homesick. All the traveling, running around, detective work, sacred trees, romance, treasure, and death were over. Just one more duty to perform before he could be on his way.

Packing everything into his bag, he was avoiding putting on his new suit for as long as possible. Wearing the suit today while carrying a cell phone was as uncomfortable a feeling for him as anything he had done on this trip. It would only be for a while, he assured himself while placing more casual clothing on top for when he would stop and change somewhere after the funeral.

Chris ordered room service that morning, wanting to get on the road as quickly as possible after the funeral. Even though he would not get home until late Sunday night, with two twelve-hour stints

391

of driving, he would forever have the Pajero to remind him of Chico and his adventure. He took two small items from the box that Michael had left with Herman and put them in his suit pocket before grabbing his bag and closing the door behind him.

He checked out and walked to where the Pajero was parked, happy he had agreed to accept the señoras' gift. When he opened the back door to put his suitcase inside, there, lying on the floor, was his old leather duffle bag with all his clothing and his wallet. He had not thought to ask Eduardo or check to see if they had been returned along with the vehicle.

The morning was cloudy. It felt like it would rain soon, and it was much cooler than the previous days. The downtown area felt barren that Saturday morning, and there was almost no traffic and no pedestrians. Chris avoided driving past what was left of Michael's house and the oak tree, thinking how wise Sophia was to keep only the good memories for a while. The cemetery was about fifteen minutes away, and Chris was thankful he had learned the city streets well enough over the last few days to navigate them. He had become fond of Brownsville and, strangely, thought how much he was going to miss this place, since he'd called it a "shithole" when he first arrived.

Arriving at the cemetery about twenty minutes before the funeral was to begin, no guests were there; just the minister and the funeral home's director. Chris introduced himself and spoke with them for a few minutes, asking if there was anything he could help them do, or if he could answer any questions they might have regarding Michael. The minister said he had already prepared his eulogy from information given to him by Garcia. Chris then handed him an envelope to pay for his services that morning, at the same time making an unusual request. He asked if they could open the coffin briefly, just long enough to put something inside. The minister agreed, saying people often did this, and they walked to where the coffin was already sitting on the casket lowering device. It was opened just a few inches, and Chris removed from his pocket a picture of three small children, ages 1, 3, and 4, and a black and white photograph that had been taken at Daytona Beach in 1952, then slid them inside.

The first of the invited guests arrived. It was the always-punctual Herman. Chris greeted him like they were old friends, the brief time they had known each other being intensified by the bizarre circumstances that had thrown them together. A military vehicle pulled up, and two army personnel got out wearing their dress uniforms and carrying a flag. Garcia and Sophia arrived

393

next—Garcia looking very serious and Sophia looking stunning in a black, knee-length dress. Chris wondered for just a moment if there was a color that did not look good on her.

Chris greeted everyone as they arrived, taking a few extra moments to thank the military representatives for their time and their service. They said it was an honor to perform the ceremony at the funeral of a WWII veteran and purple heart recipient, obviously having done their homework on Michael.

Chris had ceremoniously shaken Garcia's hand and hugged Sophia, who showed her graciousness by also greeting and thanking everyone individually. Chris noticed there were two women he did not know that had arrived at the last minute who stood near the grave site with the rest of the guests. He did not inquire who they were; he was sure Garcia had invited them for a reason.

At ten o'clock precisely, the guests took their places; Sophia standing next to Chris, holding his hand. The two soldiers placed an American flag on the coffin, took three steps back, and saluted as Taps was played on a small sound system. After the song, the soldiers folded the flag in a triangle, respectfully handed it to Chris, turned to salute the coffin once more, then marched quietly to their vehicle.

As the eulogy started, Chris spotted a lone figure dressed all in black about a dozen grave sites away. His head was bowed in prayer. He was not surprised when he realized that the man he recognized was Speedy. *He just loves cemeteries*, Chris thought.

The minister spoke about the love of Michael's friends who had gathered here today, his longtime presence in the community, and his service to his country long ago. While Chris thought the speech was well done, he understood the minister did not know Michael and accepted the eulogy being rather generic. It did not begin to describe the complex, interesting, and flawed man they had buried today.

It's just ceremonial, Chris thought. *What does it matter what you say about a man? The people who knew him will write their own eulogy.* Chris thanked the minister for his work just as a light rain began to fall.

He talked to Herman for a moment, promising to visit him when he came to town again. "I will not open my drapes again until the whole mess is gone," Herman swore, referencing the burned house and the remnants of the once glorious tree. Chris was moved when he noticed Herman had shed a few tears during the ceremony.

Chris looked around to thank the anonymous women he had seen in attendance, but they had already gone. He knew they were another piece of Michael's very complex puzzle, and perhaps Garcia would share that story someday.

Speedy had scurried off before the eulogy had finished, disappearing into the mist and amongst the headstones like some mysterious crime fighter. Chris wondered if he would ever see him again. Chris made sure to keep his phone number. *You never know*, he thought.

As he walked them back to their car, Garcia was courteous enough to say his goodbyes and leave Chris and Sophia alone for a minute.

"I'll be talking to you soon, my friend," he had said, shaking Chris's hand.

"I don't know how to thank you for everything you've done, Garcia," Chris replied.

"You already have," he said as he got in the car.

Chris was curious if Garcia was referencing the treasure and the money they would make together, or Sophia, or something else. It really didn't matter; he was just glad he had a man like Garcia as a friend, business partner, and..."

"What does he mean by 'I'll be talking to you'?" Sophia asked, looking up with an innocent look emanating from her brown eyes.

"Your dad and I are going to be in business together…for a while anyway," Chris said, trying to explain.

She gave him a look of confusion. "Sophia," Chris continued, "I promise when you come visit, I will explain everything to you. I don't want secrets between us."

Sophia raised an eyebrow, sending a message without speaking.

"What?" Chris asked.

"Another long story, I guess," she answered. She kissed him on his cheek while whispering in her most soft and feminine voice, "I'll see you next week." Then she got in the car.

All the guests had now gone, and there were just two men left that were slowly lowering Michael's casket into the ground. Chris stood for a few minutes as he watched, taking the time to say his own goodbyes and a message of thanks. He then said softly, "To whoever is listening, please forgive him."

Chris walked to the Pajero with a growing sense of melancholy he could not understand as the rain grew in intensity. *We finished just in time*, he thought. The entire process took only about an hour.

He drove away from the cemetery thinking about how he couldn't wait to get back home. He missed his daughter, missed his home, missed his dog. He also wondered if this sadness he was feeling was from saying goodbye to a man he had finally got to know, or to his new group of friends. After all, he would see Sophia again, and very soon, and there would be business conversations with Garcia and probably a trip now and then when he could see Herman. When visiting Brownsville, he could drive up to Laredo to see his charismatic and newly found brother, Eduardo, and even the señoras, who he now thought of more fondly, having been given a tremendous compliment by inviting him to visit "anytime."

Chris thought of some of the others, ones like Mando and Juan who had saved him and risked danger to find out who had killed Chico. Then there was Speedy, who had proved to be an amazing detective with or without a badge; he was as brave and clever as any of them. And there were others—Lisa, Antonio, and Graciella, who were so pivotal in his success. So many faces and so many memories in such a short adventure.

Chris was on the outskirts of town and looked over at the terrain to see the rain was now pouring down onto the trees, plants, and sand that lined the highway, stretching into what seemed like infinity. He had seen beautiful sunrises, color-filled sunsets, and awe-inspiring night skies during his time in Laredo and Brownsville.

He wondered how long it would be before it snowed in Virginia.

Made in United States
Orlando, FL
05 February 2023

29528811R00222